TANGLED

INTERNATIONAL BESTSELLING AUTHOR
SIMONE E LISE

Copyright © 2021 by Simone Elise

All rights reserved.

Edited by Ryder Editing and Formatting

No part of this book may be reproduced in any form or by any electronic or mechanical means, including information storage and retrieval systems, without written permission from the author, except for the use of brief quotations in a book review.

ONE

Soph

It's fair to state, I did not get my fairy tale ending. If a fairy tale ending involved him breaking my heart, then yeah—I got the perfect fairy tale ending. He also slept with my best friend, which he kept from me for three solid months. How do I know it was for three months? Well, he told me.

His relationship with Kayla just "happened." How the hell do you just stop loving one person who you spent three solid years with, and suddenly, out of nowhere, start to fall in love with my best friend? Of all the girls in our year, and years below, he picked Kayla! Why? Just to hurt me more? Because not only did he break my heart, he also took the one person I could turn to away from me.

I should have known something was wrong when Kayla was cagy about who she was seeing. It was normal for Kayla to go through men. So I thought that was what was wrong with her. I assumed she had fallen for an older guy and was going to be heartbroken again when he used her for sex and broke it off when she got clingy.

I was so wrong.

Well, she had fallen for a guy—my guy, who is really good at lying. Really good. They got away with it for three months. I should have picked up on the small things. Like the way he started to carry her books as well as mine. The way he always made a point to sit in between me and Kayla. Those little things should have led me to discover their secret. Instead, I was a dumb blonde for three months. I didn't see that my guy—a guy I loved for three years, the guy who chased me down, falling in love with someone else... I didn't even see it.

I thought it was normal for the guy you are with to care for your best friend because you want the guy you love to love them like you do. I never saw him falling in love with her, nor did I notice her red lipstick on his school uniform.

That is, until last month, when he thought it was a brilliant idea to break up with me and tell me the truth on my birthday—at my birthday party, publicly. Kayla stood beside him, with this evil little smirk on her face as he told me. Then linked hands with him! In front of our family and our friends! Everyone.

I swear I have never been so humiliated.

How did I react?

Well, then the tears started falling—from shock, and from my heart being squeezed tight. He always said he loved me. It had been hard to believe that a guy like him would ever take an interest in me. I was an outcast. Publicly. At school. In life. I was the girl you didn't notice. And I wish it had stayed that way. I wish he never took an interest in me. Curse that art partnership that put us together. He was charming. I mean, he was that good looking any girl would fall for his charm. I put up a fight. I didn't just drool over his every word when he took an interest in me. I didn't give him my number when he asked because somewhere, deep down, I knew he was trouble. But in the end, I was stupid and followed my heart, and my brain was left behind. The fact he was bad news meant nothing to me. If anything, it lured me in more.

I loved the fact he had an edge to him. I loved that there was more than just charm in his voice. It was like chocolate—sweet and very seductive. That was the power his voice had over me.

My own personal chocolate. As soon as I got a taste, I was addicted. I had to get more—needed more. I couldn't get enough. Before I knew it, we were having sex, and I suddenly had a claim over a guy that shouldn't have even noticed the invisible girl.

I was brought into the spotlight being his girlfriend. His friends took me in, and they quickly became my friends.

His kisses were always sweet. His smirk always wiped away any of my concerns. His touch… I melted at his touch. I Loved when his large hand took mine, loved it even more when those hands were exploring my body.

Like I said, I was addicted. Completely and utterly addicted. That's how it was.

I was his.

I stopped fighting the need to keep distance between him and I. I fell in love with the golden boy at school and the devil in the bedroom.

You know what hurts the most? I think what hurts the most is I don't think he ever truly loved me. Cause if he did, he wouldn't have done this to me. He wouldn't have slept with my best friend and then had a relationship with her! He wouldn't do that if he loved me.

He didn't love me. That fact ran through my head again.

All those kisses, all those memories, all the time he wasted chasing me, well, it was all for nothing. Not one of those memories was real. Not one of those memories meant enough to him to not do what he did.

And what do I have to face now?

School. It's my first day back.

I saw his car park, and I immediately became a mute, acting like a social outcast again.

Our "friends" were really his friends. And my one best friend, well, I was watching her get out of his car. Of course, they would be facing the new year together as a couple. I was an idiot to think they would keep it a secret, or at least not shove it in my face.

But in order for that to happen, that meant one of them had to care about me.

They didn't.

So, I shouldn't be surprised or hurt as I watched them link hands and walk across the lot to the school. They were facing a new year together, while I face a new year without my best friend and without my boyfriend. Two facts that broke what was left of my heart.

I got out of the car. Darn my parents for being back from their cruise early. Otherwise, I would be skipping the first day. At least they leave again tomorrow. I was going to take the opportunity to avoid school altogether.

That was my plan. I picked up my bag and noticed a dozen miss calls from my mum and dad. How odd? They knew it was my first day back. I hadn't seen them yet; they got back late this morning. They were asleep when I left, so I dialled mum's number.

* * *

This just can't be happening. Nope. It wasn't happening. I couldn't accept it. I won't accept it. It'd be over my dead body. I was eighteen, for god's sake!

I opened my locker. Today couldn't get any worse after the news Mum just told me. At first, I wanted to kill her, and that feeling hadn't gone away.

I glanced to my left, and just when I thought my day couldn't get any worse, it did. Kyle was heading directly towards me.

Please don't stop. Please don't stop.

"Hey, Sophia."

Fuck my luck!

I turned with regret to face him. "Kyle."

"Guess you've heard then?" He leaned against the locker, standing way too close to me.

I pushed back against my locker door. He was in my personal space and he didn't have the right to be there anymore. I kept my lips clamped shut. I was not talking to him. The last time I saw him, I threw my glass of wine at him and told him and my so-called best friend to get the hell of my house.

"Look, it doesn't have to awkward. It will only be awkward if you make it awkward, Soph." His words were gentle, and like always, melted me. For a second I thought he cared about me again, but that was quickly wiped away when I saw the mark on his neck. Kayla always liked to mark her men.

"It's Sophia," I corrected him. Only friends called me Soph. He sure as hell wasn't a friend.

He rolled his eyes. "So, you want to be childish?"

I gritted my teeth. I wasn't biting back at him. I wasn't giving him the pleasure of a fight with me in this crowded hallway. My "friends" already had a show starring me and him when he dumped me and admitted to being in a relationship with Kayla.

"Look, it's only for a couple of months. I'll stay out of your way. You stay out of mine?" He was suggesting a plan that was impossible.

"So, that's your plan? Me coming to live with you for two months?" I crossed my arms. "I hate you, Kyle. Hear me when I say this. I hate you!"

My parents had cut their cruise short because doctors were needed in Africa. And Mum and Dad always went when needed. Though this time, because they had watched me withdraw from my life and stop caring about anything or everything, well, they didn't want me home alone.

Their solution? Dump me at Kyle's.

Our parents had gotten close over the three years Kyle and I had been together. Close enough that Mum and Dad didn't see the problem in my moving in with them for two months. My parents didn't even consult me on it! They just did it. They decided that the best thing for me was to dump me at Kyle's because they "trusted" his parents to look after me.

I don't know what was worse, Kyle getting a real look at the mess I was, or the fact that I wouldn't be able to stop him from seeing it.

"Like I said, it's only awkward if you let it be. Come on, Soph." He was calling me by my nickname again, like he had a right to.

"Sophia," I corrected him. "I want nothing to do with you."

He sighed. "I knew you would act like this. I told Mum and Dad you wouldn't agree to it."

"Well, you were right, because I'm planning on never entering your house again."

"Why aren't your parents letting you stay home by yourself?"

Because of you. I clamped my mouth shut. I was never telling him how much he hurt me — To the point I didn't see a reason to keep living. I couldn't get up in the morning to face, yet another day, with a broken heart. I couldn't get up in the morning to face yet another day, with a broken heart. He betrayed my trust. Look where trusting people got me. Sick, depressed, and lonely.

Kyle was still looking at me, expecting an answer. I turned back to look in my locker. Now I just had to get my books and leave him behind. Hopefully we didn't have any of the same classes.

"If it makes you feel better, I won't let Kayla come over." He was being nice. I didn't want him to be nice. I'd rather he was rude because then I could have another reason to hate him. Hating him now was becoming easier, but I realized there was nothing he could say that would ever stop me from hating him.

"Do what you want. I'm not planning on being there much." I grabbed my books. I intended to spend a hell of a lot of time at cafes or in libraries—somewhere—anywhere but his place.

"I should warn you, Joshua is home, too."

My head snapped to look back at him. He had to be joking? Joshua had been in prison for two years. His sentence was for four. "How?"

"Made an appeal, and he won. He's on parole." Kyle took a step closer to me. "Just come and stay with us. I promise to behave."

He was saying that like he still cared about me. I had wasted two weeks crying over him. One week smashing everything in sight, and then the next realizing he didn't love me. Now I was back to crying. It was like I had done a full circle and we were back at the start.

"So, I'll see you tomorrow?" Kyle said, arching his eyebrows.

I didn't want to go there. But Mum and Dad weren't giving me a choice. "Yeah," I finally said with reluctance. "But just because I'm agreeing to come, doesn't mean I don't hate you."

A sad smiled crept across his face. "I really fucked up, Soph."

"I wouldn't say that. You just didn't love me anymore." I closed my locker door, ready to walk away from him.

An expression captured his face. I knew the look. It was regret. Well, there was nothing for him to regret.

"How I ended us wasn't acceptable," he said as he started to walk beside me.

I shrugged my shoulders. It hadn't been acceptable. He did it in front of everyone. It was like he waited until it was my birthday to tell me. Like he wanted to make it hurt more because every birthday from now on I will remember what he did.

I picked up my pace, hoping he would just stop following me. The second I reached my classroom door, his hand wrapped around my upper arm, dragging me back and forcing me to not enter.

I was about to yell at him for touching me.

"Why do you think I did it?" he asked, gripping my arm.

What do I think? Well, this time I was going to tell the truth. "Because you wanted her over me. Simple, really."

His lips clamped shut. It looked like he didn't like my answer. Wasn't that why he did it, though? He loved her. Hell, he had been sneaking around with her for three months and I hadn't noticed.

"Can you let go of me now?" I asked as his grip got tighter.

A depressing smile crept across his face. "One day you'll know the truth, and I hope that is one day soon."

"Kyle, I don't want anything to do with you. I can promise you; I'm not waiting on 'one day' for your actions to make sense." I pulled my arm from his grasp.

"Soph, I'm really sorry." It sounded like he meant it, too.

I scoffed. "No, you aren't, Kyle. Now go find that girlfriend of yours that you love so much." With that said, I turned and walked into the classroom just as the bell rang.

I had seen the anger on his face, but his anger hadn't been directed at me.

***

"Why can't I stay with Nana?" I asked Mum as we pulled up at Kyle's.

"Because your nana will let you do anything you want." Mum put the car in park. "Now, Soph, we talked about this. I talked to his parents, and they said he is rarely home at the moment."

Yeah, probably cause him and Kayla are on a sex bender.

I reluctantly got out of the car and moved the duffle bag on my shoulder. How awkward could this be? Living with him, his parents, and his criminal brother—surely, I could get through a couple of months. That was the reasonable side of me coming out. The other side was screaming for me to run far, far away from him and this house.

"Just behave, Soph," Mum said as we reached the front door and rang the bell.

This can't be happening. This was like every girl's worst nightmare, being forced to move in with your ex-boyfriend!

The door opened, and just my luck, Kyle answered. He greeted Mum like they were long-lost friends. Chit chat turned into ten minutes, and then he finally acknowledged me with the biggest smile on his face. Was he bipolar? Why the hell was he smiling at me like that? Like I was his favourite person, and he was seeing them for the first time in years. It didn't make sense, so I just ignored it.

We walked in and his mum, Louise, showed me the guestroom. It was right across from Joshua's room and next door to Kyle's. How many hours, days, weeks and months had I spent in that room with him?

Again, it had all been a waste of time.

Kyle's dad was running for Mayor, and like my parents, they earned good money, so the house looked similar to mine. Big rooms decorated expensively—yep, our parents were the same. Apart from Louise, she was an artist. How a hippy artist ended up with Jed, Kyle's dad, I don't know. But Jed loved Louise's quirky ways. Like how she always had at least ten bracelets on and always had paint or clay on her.

I never saw my mum becoming friends with her. They were opposites. But they did. They went for morning walks; Louise was always getting Mum on some herbal tablets. Louise was lovely. I was happy she was here. Just because I had wiped Kyle out of my life, didn't mean I had no time for his parents. They had always been kind to me.

My side was aching because Mum had been rushing me and I slipped on the stairs and hit my side on the rail.

Kyle, for some reason, was hanging around while Louise and Mum talked in my new room.

I said goodbye to Mum, and she gave me a final hug before leaving. Louise showed her out, which left me and Kyle in my new room. He leaned against the doorframe and looked fucking delighted that I was here.

"Why the hell are you looking at me like that?" I snapped at him as he kept grinning at me. Did he forget the part where we broke up and he broke my heart? Had that skipped his mind? Because he was looking at me like I was his favourite person. Hell, he was giving me that look he used to give me before he told me how much he loved me.

"My luck is turning around," he said, still grinning at me.

What the hell was he going on about? His luck was turning around? How was me moving in, making his luck better?

TWO

Soph

I needed to get tougher skin if I was going to survive being here. I had to sit through dinner with Kyle, who for some unknown reason—and I was questioning his sanity—took every opportunity he got to make conversation with me.

He was acting like he had forgotten all about the part where he broke my heart. He even asked if I wanted to watch football with him, like we used to. I couldn't understand how he had been so cold and blunt when we broke up, but now... now he was being the friendly and caring guy I had fallen in love with.

The thought even crossed my mind for a second... okay, maybe a max ten seconds, that he was trying to get back together with me. Then the doorbell rang and his new girlfriend, my ex-best friend, showed up.

Immediately Kyle changed. He went from friendly to defensive. I lasted ten minutes in the same room as them. Kayla was all over him, and it made my skin crawl. I couldn't cope seeing them together. The way he kissed her back. The way he didn't stop her from being all over him. I did notice that she was the one touching and kissing him. He didn't start it, but he also didn't stop it.

I had escaped from the lounge room right before I lost my shit. Now I was in the shower. This was the first time I had a shower in this bathroom. I always showered in Kyle's ensuite.

I was so lost in thought, basically plotting the death of Kayla, when the door swung open just as I turned the taps off.

"Fucking hell, Kyle, why are you using my bathroom?"

I spun around and saw Joshua.

His eyes were scorching with anger until he looked up and spotted me standing naked in the shower. The annoyed and angry expression on his face disappeared, replaced by shock.

I was just as shocked to see him. He wasn't wearing a top. He was bigger, more toned, and his body was covered in tattoos. Some of them I'd seen before, others I hadn't. His black hair was short. His sharp blue eyes were the same, but he looked older. And he didn't seem as carefree as he used to.

I think the only thing he did in prison was workout. My mouth fell open. As I gawked at him, and his eyes ran up and down my body. I think a few minutes passed of us just looking at each other.

He didn't do the gentleman thing to do and look away or turn around and leave. Instead, he was the Joshua I always knew—a man that didn't shy away from an awkward situation.

His eyes snapped off me and he picked up and towel and threw it in my direction.

It was an automatic reaction to catch it, even being in shock. The embarrassment slowly ticked in and I went bright red.

He crossed his arms. "Well, you've certainly grown up, Soph." A smirk was on his face.

I knew what he meant by that, too. When he last saw me; I didn't have breasts. I actually had plastic surgery to get the breasts I have now. Before that, I was flat chested. I was skinner too. In fact, I had changed a lot since he last saw me.

I wrapped the towel around me, still with flushed cheeks. I hoped he thought it was from the shower and not him seeing me naked. Only one person had seen me naked, and that was Kyle.

"Kyle didn't mention you were staying over. Why aren't you in his shower?" Joshua didn't leave, instead he stepped in and closed the door behind him.

I'm not going to lie. I'd always been attracted to Joshua. He was older, and he had this rough exterior I was drawn to. In short, he was a bad boy. While Kyle was the golden boy, Joshua didn't follow the rules. He didn't give a fuck what others thought of him. He lived to piss them off.

So right now, instead of doing the right thing, which was leaving, he leaned against the wall, his eyes trained on me.

Hadn't Kyle mentioned that he wasn't with me anymore? That I was being forced to be here? How had Joshua not seen his brother making out with another girl downstairs?

"Why aren't you talking?" he asked, frowning. "Don't tell me after all this time you're finally scared of me."

I rolled my eyes. The reason I hadn't answered was because I was trying to come up with a way to tell him Kyle and I weren't together.

"We broke up," I finally said and held the towel tighter around me.

He frowned. "No, you haven't. He's downstairs with your best friend." He clicked his fingers, trying to remember something. "Kylie?"

"Kayla," I corrected him. "That's his new girlfriend. So, she's not my friend."

His expression hardened. "He's dating your best friend?"

"Yeah, pretty much." That did sum it up. "I'm being forced to stay here while my parents are in Africa."

22

"He always was a dickhead," he muttered. "Guess that means we're sharing a bathroom." A grin appeared on his face. "I thought Kyle was in here just to piss me off."

"Nope, just me." I ran a hand over the fogged mirror. God, I looked drained. My flushed cheeks were the only thing giving me colour.

"You still cheering?"

I scoffed. "I'm the least cheerful person I know. So, the answer to me being on the squad is no."

"But you were captain."

Yeah, I had been. The youngest captain in history. I had always gone to gymnastics, so I excelled in cheerleading. I only joined the squad because Kyle pushed me to. I actually ran up the ranks and before I knew it, I was captain. But I wasn't this year.

"Like I said, I'm not a cheerful person. The thought of cheering depresses me."

I saw his eyes narrow at me in the reflection of the mirror. "Does my brother have something to do with your sudden change?"

"Nope." Yes.

"So how long you here for?"

"I'm hoping just two months." I turned around. "Are you going to let me get dressed?"

His serious expression changed, and he gave me the biggest smirk. "I've already seen everything, sweetheart."

I kept control over my reaction. I would not get embarrassed. He was challenging me, and the old Soph would have bolted from the room, taking my clothes, and changing in the bedroom.

But the new Soph didn't give a fuck anymore. So, I dropped the towel and his eyes went wide.

"Fuck, I was kidding, Soph!"

I shrugged and threaded my underwear on. I never thought the day would come that I would be naked in front of Joshua. But the new me just didn't care what people thought. When you have nothing to risk, you find yourself doing things you never thought you were capable of.

Like getting changed in front of your ex-boyfriend's hot brother.

"I guess I missed the memo where you were joking, Joshua."

His eyes ran up and down me and then finally locked with mine just as I was clipping my bra on.

"Call me Josh. I hate Joshua."

I smiled just a little. "But all your family calls you Joshua?"

"Kyle does it because he knows I hate it, and the parents do it to try to take the higher ground."

I nodded my head. "I only get Sophia from the parents when I've pissed them off. I hate it."

He grinned and nodded his head. "I'll make sure to always call you Soph then."

"And I'll make sure to call you Josh." I slipped on my dress and was going to close the zipper when I felt his hand move over mine and do it for me.

Our eyes lock in the mirror—his sharp blue eyes slicing through my hazel ones. I noticed something in them, something I hadn't seen before, but I couldn't explain what it was.

He gave me a small smile and his fingers hovered on the zip.

"I… um, won't barge in next time," he said, still with a small smile on his face. "I didn't realise it was you."

"No big deal." I think I had handled the situation well. I wasn't nervous or freaking out. Even though I had just shown him my naked body.

I turned around and noticed how close he was to me. I couldn't step away from him; I was already up against the basin.

My hands clamped down onto it and I tried my very best not to let my breathing become sharp. He towered over me and I just stared up at him.

"I always thought Kyle didn't deserve you." His words were gentle. "Glad you ended it."

I frowned. "I didn't. He broke up with me on my birthday in front of everyone and then told me he had been sleeping with my best friend for three months."

Josh looked down at me. "You're joking, right? He wouldn't have done that."

"If you don't believe me, ask him. His new girlfriend is mighty proud of how it ended." I knew that for a fact because of how she acted when he told me. She loved seeing him break my heart. Some best friend she was.

"He's a dick. You didn't deserve that."

I shrugged my shoulders. "Doesn't really matter now."

"Guess you're hating it here?"

"You could say that." Watching Kayla all over Kyle was hard—really hard. Especially when he had been nice to me all night and morning. And then she shows up and he immediately turns cold towards me, treating me like I'm invisible.

"Well, if you ever want to escape, I'm in the shed." He took a step back. "Kyle is allergic to anything involving a car."

I grinned. "You're right. He isn't really hands on, like you."

"You saying I'm more skilled?" I couldn't believe it, but Josh was actually flirting with me.

"When it comes to cars, yes."

"Well, my mission now is to show you I'm more skilled at everything."

I still had a grin on my face. For the first time in days of being here, I felt relaxed. "Don't get a big head now. I said you were skilled with cars, isn't that enough?"

He shook his head with a carefree grin. "I'll prove to you, when it comes to everything, you are better off without Kyle."

My grin fell. "I realized I was better off without him when he showed me his true colours." And that was the truth. I may have been heart broken, but I knew he didn't really love me. Because when you love someone, you do everything humanly possible for them not to get hurt, and never be the one to cause them pain.

Josh stepped back away from me. "I hope he hasn't ruined your faith in all guys."

I scoffed. "I'll never trust another guy, not after him. Anyway, it doesn't matter. I won't be giving anyone power like that over me again." The power to cause me to become an emotionless zombie. To be a tearful mess. To squeeze my heart so tight that I feel physically sick. Kyle had damaged me, and I still wasn't healing. So, the last thing I was going to do was fall for another male who would just do what Kyle did. I trusted Kyle and look where that got me.

"Um, I'll see you around, Josh." I stepped away from him and picked up my towel. "And next time knock." I gave him a smile before he could say anything else. The last thing I needed was his pity. I wasn't some helpless case. I was putting myself together. It was just going to take time.

So, I left Josh standing there before he could say anything.

THREE

Kyle

"Fucking stop it," I snapped at Kayla. "She's not even here." I hoped that would get Kayla off me. Instead, she kept to my side and her hand locked with mine. When she didn't pull away, I got up, fucking sick of the show. "You've made your point now piss off."

"I thought we could watch a movie," Kayla said, pretending to be innocent. "Come on, Kyle, calm down."

"You've come. You've made your point, now fuck off, Kayla."

"You know what? I don't think I have made my point because you are still clinging to the chance that she's going to take you back!" Kayla got up abruptly. "She still looks at you like you are hers."

"I am hers!" I would always be Sophia's. She was my other half. I never wanted to hurt her. I never wanted to be away from her. Right now, I was suffering.

"No. You're mine," Kayla put down a fake claim on me again. She could say it over and over. She could lay claim on me any way she wanted. It didn't change the fact that my heart, every single piece of me, belonged to Sophia.

"You better start living up to the expectations, Kyle, because I'm not getting the thrill out of blacking mailing you as I was at the beginning."

"How is it my fault that you're getting sick of your own game?"

One night—I had screwed up one night, and she just happened to be there. I regretted having that line of ice, more now than when Kayla first approached me. She had a picture of me doing that line., and if you looked at the environment around me, you would think I was a regular user. But I wasn't. It was my first time. I should have taken everyone's warning when it came to drugs. I shouldn't have done it. My one night of letting go had cost me everything. My dad was running for Mayor, and if that photo of me got out, he wouldn't have a chance in winning. Kayla knew.

Fuck, she was counting on me taking her offer, knowing I wouldn't want my dad's career to suffer because of my mistake. My one night of letting go—of forgetting the pressures that surrounded my life. One night, that was it, and it cost me the woman I love.

At first, I didn't think Kayla was serious when she approached me, but she meant it when she said she wanted me to end it with Soph.

I delayed it three months, but when Soph's birthday came around, Kayla said it was now or the picture was going to the press.

I never wanted to hurt Soph. I had promised her I would never hurt her. Instead of just hurting her, I betrayed her trust, broke her heart, and shattered our future together.

I knew that one of these days, the pain in Soph's eyes when she looked at me would turn to hate, and as soon as it did, I would never get her back. I would never be able to get that hate out of her eyes or heart.

I knew it was coming. I shouldn't feel joy when I saw the pain in her eyes, but I was thankful to see it because it meant she still felt something towards me. I didn't want her to suffer, but I didn't want her to let go of me completely.

Kayla was right when she said I was clinging to the chance of getting Soph back. I was. I was clinging to every chance. I was hoping when the election ended that I could tell Soph the truth and hope to God, she takes me back.

Soph

I rolled over. Another sleepless night. I couldn't get comfortable. I couldn't stop the racing thoughts. I couldn't turn the volume down. Always going over the same thing... how did I not notice Kyle was in love with someone else? How could he do that to me? How could he go from loving me to breaking my heart?

I sighed in frustration. It didn't matter how many hours I wasted thinking about him, trying to come up with a reason he did what he did.

It didn't matter because, at the end of the day, what he did was beyond me.

I still couldn't explain why he wanted to hurt me so badly by picking Kayla.

I guess you don't pick who you fall in love with. I sure as hell didn't mean to fall in love with Kyle. I didn't pick him. My heart did.

And now… now I was suffering because of it.

I lit up my phone. Just after two in the morning. It was now Saturday, and I had dinner with one of Dad's friends tonight. It was meant to be a whole family dinner with him —Jeff always gave me the creeps—so I wasn't looking forward to a one-on-one dinner with him.

I picked up on the fact that he would always make an effort to sit next to me. He would always touch me, just slightly, so it didn't come across like he was, and enough for me to explain it as an accident.

But those "accidents" happen every time he sees me.

JOSH

I lit up a cigarette while staring at the motor. Whose idea was it to replace the motor? Mine. Seemed like a good idea at the time taking this heap of shit and turning it into a fine muscle car. I had more time on my hands than anything else. Now I was questioning my sanity.

My phone buzzed in my pocket. I got it out automatically, not taking my eyes off the motor. I inhaled on the cigarette sharply and glanced at my phone. Then did a double take.

Soph's name was on my screen. How did she know I still had this number? More importantly, why would she be messaging me?

I hadn't seen her since I walked in on her in the bathroom. I smirked at the memory. She really had grown up. Fuck. It wasn't just her body that made me see that she had grown up. She was way more confident now. I had only been with her for a few minutes and when she didn't bolt from the awkward situation, I knew she had really matured.

I unlocked my phone and her message opened.

Help

I frowned. What did she mean by that?

Was that message for someone else? Something told me it was meant for me. Well, if she wanted help, she would have to tell me what, with, and where.

Where r u? I sent back and took the cigarette from my lips.

Diamond Carat.

Why would she be at that restaurant? It was for the rich. I guess she was rich. Well, her family was. Still, Soph never flashed money around. When it came down to it, Soph never rubbed it in other people's face that her parents earned more than someone's yearly wage in a month.

I dropped the cigarette on the ground and put it out. I looked down at my jeans and white T-shirt, both covered in grease and oil stains. I would have to change if they were going to let me in.

Something was telling me to hurry the fuck up. I flicked off the shed lights and headed inside. I'd change my clothes and then head for her. It wasn't like Soph to ask for help. In fact, I couldn't think of one occasion where she had asked for my help.

Knowing that made me move quicker.

FOUR

Josh

Prison. My time in there has defined me now. It reshaped my future, and it crafted my life. Before prison, I was empty, soulless, and reckless. I was still soulless, but I had found a purpose. That purpose being the Devil's Cut.

I never thought the most feared, and dangerous motorcycle club would give me a purpose. I didn't see my life heading anywhere. I didn't have a fucking direction or plan for the future. So, when they approached me in prison and drafted me, I didn't fight it.

It didn't scare me that I was going to join one of the world's most notorious motorcycle clubs. I lived my life by two qualities: loyalty and I don't give a fuck what others think. I didn't waste a second on what people's opinion of me would be. I didn't care if people thought I was reckless, soulless, or heartless. I didn't give a fuck what anyone thought.

I have no fear. Some would say, I was fearless. Hell, that's what other blokes called me until Wolf, the Mother Charter President of the Devil's Cut, gave me the Vice President patch. I went from being called fearless to Vice quickly.

I was the acting Vice President in prison. I was the enforcer there, making sure everyone was safe, protected, and that Wolf noticed my active role in making sure his members were safe in there. I did one year of being a prospect and I was given the vice president patch, six months after my prospect year ended. It was unheard of. A member had to serve the club for years, and even then, that didn't mean they would be given a title or become VP.

Wolf lasted six months with me behind bars acting as vice president, then he needed me out in the world—he needed his VP at his side. So, they organised an appeal. I sure as hell didn't see it being successful, but the club pulled strings, and before I knew it, I was out nearly two years early.

I got a four-year sentence for beating a man that deserved it. Still to this day I could never say I loved Christine. She was my girlfriend at the time. I was only with her because it was expected, and I was having regular sex with her. It made sense to be her boyfriend. I needed sex, and she was good at it. It wasn't like I was in love with her. I didn't feel love for anyone. Not even my family. Sure, I respected them and cared for them. But love? I don't think I could call it that.

I didn't really know what love was. My parents never showed it to each other. I got four years for hitting Christine's dad when he dared to hit her in front of me. It was an automatic response. I punched him, and like always, when the lid came off my temper it came right off.

How did Christine thank me? She broke up with me as soon as I was charged and out of her life. So, I didn't feel or do love.

Loyalty however I do feel. I felt loyalty for the club. I think if I had to pick what love was, I would say I felt it for the club. The first thing I did when I got out of prison was get the permeant patch which was a tattoo of the club logo and shield on my back.

It was my first tattoo and not my last. The tattooist was now working on my arm. When I'm finished, I doubt there'll be any bare skin left.

I pulled up at the restaurant. I wasn't in colours. It wasn't heard of for a member not to be in colours, especially when they are a vice president, but my dad wouldn't let me wear colours near the house. He publicly disowned me when I got let out. When he was questioned my early release, he confirmed what the media thought... he wanted nothing to do with me. The only reason I was at their house was because it was a condition of my parole. That, and for some reason, Mum wanted it. She thought she could change me; wouldn't accept the fact that I had made my decision, and I wasn't ashamed of being known as a criminal.

I had spent so many months keeping the order in prison it didn't really throw me when the same was expected of me in the club now outside of prison.

I locked the car and got out. I wouldn't normally stop what I was doing for anyone. Maybe if Wolf really needed me, but I wouldn't stop what I was doing for a woman.

Soph was a different story. She was an expectation to the rule. I still don't know how that happened, but it did. Maybe because before I went away, I watched her grow up. Though, when I left, she was still an immature teenager who was hanging on every word my brother said.

Now… well, now she was a woman that didn't give a fuck if I saw her naked. I still couldn't believe she just got dressed in front of me like that! She should know better. I was a man after all—a dangerous one.

I had wondered at the time whether she had done it because she felt comfortable or because she was hell bent on breaking rules that used to cage her in.

As I entered the restaurant I walked straight past the greeter and ignored his complaint that I didn't have a booking. He was the one causing a scene by following me and demanding me to leave. I continued to ignore him and scanned the restaurant, looking for Soph.

She always stood out. One glance at her slim figure and blonde hair from behind and I knew it was her. She was in the sunken area of the restaurant that looked like it was for intimate couples.

I scrolled through the restaurant, my eyes on her. I could see from where I was that she was tense. She looked stiff. I saw him move closer to her, and I think I could hear her panic.

She turned just slightly, I think to get away from him, and her eyes locked with mine. I saw panic along with relief in her hazel eyes. Never had anyone looked at me in relief before. Usually it was fear, and I encouraged that fear because it kept the unwanted away and the ones that needed to fear me, well, they got the message.

I was within earshot now and I could pick up on their conversation. It was a one-sided conversation because Soph's attention was on me.

She got up. "Babe, I'm so sorry. Our dinner just took a little longer." Her eyes were pleading with me to go along with whatever she was saying. I wasn't boyfriend material.

So how she planned on explaining us being together, I don't know.

I was the guy that everyone didn't want to associate with. I was the guy your parents warn you about. I would happily say I didn't just scare men off, I scared off the female population as well. I think it had to do with the fact I was double the size of the normal guy. I intimidated everyone. I didn't need the club doing that for me. My image sent the message.

"Your parents never mentioned you were dating anyone, Sophia." The man she called Jeff, turned around and stood up. I saw the judgment in his eyes. "They didn't mention you were dating Joshua Hawkins either."

Yeah, my mugshot had been plastered all over the newspaper about my early release. The media had been having a field day with it. Then my open connections to the Devil's Cut were highlighted, but the fact I was Vice President stayed out of the paper. So, it surprised me that Soph would want to even pretend that she was in a relationship with me.

I was bad news, everyone knew that. Didn't need a reporter to tell you about my case, just one glance at me was enough for people to stay out of my way.

"Funny, Mom and Dad didn't mention your marriage breakup either," Soph said and picked up her clutch. "I should really get going, Josh and I have plans."

"I don't think your parents would approve, Sophia." He said that like he had some control over whether she would be leaving with me or not. How wrong he was. Soph was leaving with me. I could tell from one glance at her that she was scared, nervous, and she felt unsafe. This prick seemed to be the cause of it all.

"I'm sure her parents would also be wondering why you would be taking their daughter, who could be your daughter, to a place like the Diamond Carat." I stepped to Soph's side. She looked like she was a second away from having a full-on panic attack.

I couldn't remember the last time I touched someone, but I found myself touching Soph as I took her clenched shut hand. Jeff didn't seem to have an answer to my comment. I was used to men like him thinking they had power because they earned a good wage. Most people are scared of people with power and money. I, however, couldn't give a fuck if they had money or a position of power, because when it came down to it, men like him didn't have a spine to begin with.

I eased Soph's clenched hand free and linked her fingers with mine. She would have to know I wasn't about to let this guy hurt her.

Jeff's eyes were on Soph. "Sophia, are you sure you want to leave with this man? Remember my offer?"

It was like someone had poured freezing ice-cold water on Soph. She was that stunned and shocked.

I didn't need Soph to tell me what she was feeling. I could see the panic in her eyes. She looked like a cornered animal.

I watched her gulp as she came up with a reason to deny his request again. He moved closer to her, and it was my automatic response to block his path to her. I stepped in between them.

"Sophia is too polite to tell you to piss off, but I'm not. So, back the fuck down and consider the answer to your offer a no." I stepped back and pulled on Soph's hand. She followed me out.

People pulled chairs in or stepped out of our way. I was used to that. People always stayed away from me. Soph was following in my shadow and I don't think she took a deep breath until we stepped outside.

I stopped pulling on her hand and turned to face her. "You alright?"

Her eyes were wide, and she still looked like she was in shock. I saw her gulp.

"Sophia, are you okay?" I repeated myself when she remained silent, with this look on her face that told me she was anything but okay.

She took another deep breath in. "Thank you, Josh." She pulled her hand from mine and looked like she was calming down. "I'm so sorry to get you involved like that. I just didn't know anyone else who would come." She ran a hand through her hair, looking upset. "I'm so sorry to bring you into my mess."

"Soph, don't stress about it." I didn't know what else to say to get her to calm down.

"Still, it's not acceptable." She shook her head. "I'm so sorry."

"Stop saying sorry. I said it was fine." I didn't know whether to add to that or not but then I found myself knowing I had to by the look on her face. "It's what friends are for, right?" I said awkwardly. I didn't do friends. I didn't bond with anyone. Unless it was made of steel, metal, or a club brother.

Her eyes went bigger, and I didn't think that was possible. "We aren't friends." She was saying that like it was the worst thing to happen to her. "I really didn't mean to use you like that, Josh. I don't expect you to like put up with me or anything. Seriously, we aren't friends because of that."

"We were friends before tonight, Soph, otherwise you wouldn't have called me." I felt, for some reason, that I needed to reassure her. "Now do you want to head home or are you hungry?"

She looked at me stunned. "You don't do friends," she repeated a fact about me everyone knew.

I didn't know how to be one, but I guess I was going to learn. Soph was worth it. She was sweet, she was drop dead gorgeous — beautiful—the sort of beauty that would stop you in your tracks. She had every man's attention. It was curves to her body, the shape of her perfect breasts, and her beautiful creamed colour skin. One glance at her perfectly shaped face and you were hooked.

Like I said, she was gorgeous, but it wasn't just her beauty or body that had me doing something I never did. It was her personality. And even though I hadn't seen or had a good conversation with her in years, I knew her personality hadn't changed.

She was the type of girl that put everyone before her, break a rule if it meant the benefit outweighed risk, and she was the only woman I knew that wasn't selfish.

I scratched the back of my neck, watching her eyes debate. She was weighing up the facts; she had always been good at that. Even when I left and she was only sixteen, she knew how to weigh up the odds.

I guess I just had to be honest with her. "You're right, I don't do friendships. This is a onetime thing." I forced myself to smile at her, while I felt a hell of a lot of nerves. I never got fucking nervous, but right now that was the only thing that explained how I was feeling.

Her serious expression broke, and she smiled. "I better not stuff it up then." Her hair blew across her face and I should have stopped myself but didn't when I tucked it behind her ear. For some reason it bothered me that it was in the way of her flawless face. "You want to head home?" I asked, my hand hovering at the side of her face. I wanted to cup her cheek, but I wasn't sure if friends did that. I knew for a fact that if she was my girlfriend, I would have my hands all over her. I didn't do boundaries when it came to girlfriends.

"Um, yeah." She smiled and stepped in closer to me, getting out of the way of a couple walking past. "Sorry to make you come and get me."

"How did you get here?"

"He picked me up."

I frowned. "That jerk was at my house?"

"He's meant to be a family friend." She glanced back at the restaurant and sighed. "I don't know why I attract men like that. It's like I have a sign around my neck telling useless men to approach me." She rolled her eyes and looked back at me. "Thanks for saving me from him."

We started to walk to my car, and I knew I shouldn't, but I took her hand. "Don't worry about it. You can always call me." I didn't say that to many people. Yeah, if they were my club brothers, I was always reachable, but for a female to call me in case she needed me—that I didn't do.

"You know I read something about you today." Soph didn't pull her small hand from mine and I had to say it fitted perfectly.

"If it's from Jill Mason, I'm telling you now it's all lies," I said. Jill Mason was a reporter who had it out for me. She was making it her mission to make sure my life was harder than it needed to be. She even had an investigator on me, which I paid off to feed her back useless information.

"Actually, it was on the Age." Soph came to a stop next to my car and turned to look up at me. "You're involved with a motorcycle club, aren't you?"

That I wasn't expecting. There had been rumours, but no one had ever confirmed it. I swallowed sharply. Guess I was about to see her reaction on what she thought of her new friend being a known criminal.

I stayed silent, watching her expression as she sighed. "I didn't expect you to confirm it. I read all about how you keep it quiet because of your dad." She kept staring up at me. She didn't look one bit scared or frightened.

Dad was the one keeping it quiet. Not me. I didn't give a fuck if it was plastered all over the headlines. Dad, however, did care and had control over the headlines and articles—at the moment.

If he didn't win this mayor election, he wouldn't have control anymore. The fact I was a criminal and a biker would get out.

"I know for a fact you weren't in one before you left. You know, no one has ever told me why you went to prison." She linked her fingers with mine, looking down at our linked hands. "You don't have to tell me though."

I remained quiet.

I didn't want to confirm her nightmare. At the same time, I wanted to tell her the truth.

For some reason, what she thought mattered to me.

Soph pulled up her strapless black dress and sighed. "Well, if you aren't going to talk, at least take me home."

I nodded my head. I could do that. I couldn't answer or confirm her thoughts, even if they were true. But I could take her home.

I let go of her hand and she walked to the passenger side of my car.

I knew I was going to remain silent, but even when I was silent around Soph, it was never awkward.

It just felt, right, I guess.

Not uncomfortable or forcing me to make conversation. I never experienced that with anyone. Didn't know what to call it. I got in the car, and like I expected, the silence continued. I turned on the radio and pulled out.

FIVE

Soph

I dreaded school. I suffered through every hour—every minute—of every day, which was a big change for me because I used to love it. I loved learning. I loved spending time with my friends, and I really loved the sense of accomplishment I got when I finished a day.

Now… now I hated every second of it—the teachers, the lessons, the sitting still. You know what I hated the most? That I was tortured by seeing my best friend and ex-boyfriend acting like they are sickly in love!

Art was the only class I had on my own. I wanted to go back in time and kick myself. The three of us teed it up last year. I made sure that I was in all of Kyle's and Kayla's classes. Now, when I wasn't over hearing Kayla gush about how sweet Kyle is to her, or what he had just purchased for her or how much she loved him, I was being forced to watch them as a couple.

Like I said, I hate school.

My grades were already dropping from my lack of interest, which scored me extra credit work to do. That is exactly how I wanted to spend my weekend—working on fractions and a report on endangered animals.

It was the middle of the day and I was at my locker, putting my books away. The first thing I did at the start of term was rip down every picture of me and Kyle or of me and Kayla plastered inside my locker.

I was getting out my sunglasses and shutting my locker door when I jumped.

"Hey, Soph." Adam grinned at me. I hadn't seen him standing there. Adam's locker had been next to my locker for years, but he had left to go overseas last year.

I ran a hand through my hair and nervously smiled. I was still slightly surprised to see him.

"Hey, Adam, how are you?" I had to be nice. He had been a good friend, but he had been more of a friend to Kyle than me. Like all my other "friends", they were more Kyle's than mine. So, it wasn't a huge surprise when they sided with him.

"Really good. I've missed you and it's already showing in my math and it's my first day back." He kept grinning at me like he really was that happy to see me. "How's Kyle? I haven't seen him yet."

And there was the question I was hoping wouldn't come up. For some stupid reason I thought I would escape before he asked that question.

Laughter filled the hall, and I thought this moment couldn't get any worse. But that laugh... well, that laugh now was the cause of most of my nightmares.

"Oh, here's Kyle and Kayla now. Should have guessed they wouldn't be far from you." Adam waved over my shoulder and then he frowned.

I took a stab in the dark and guessed that Kayla was probably clinging to Kyle's side, or they were doing what they always did—

kissing. I swear that was all they never did around me. Their lips were always locked. Disgust is what I felt when I saw it.

Adam looked back at me. "Am I missing something?" Well, that was a very good question. Yes, he was. He glanced back at the happy couple that were by the sound of it coming closer.

"Kyle and I broke up," I said.

Adam's eyes snapped back to me, wide and alarmed. "You're joking, right?" He looked at me like I was lying.

I glanced over my shoulder and saw Kayla back Kyle against the hallway wall, looking like they were about to make out. I looked back at Adam.

"Does it look like I'm lying? Kayla would be his new girlfriend," I clarified the details.

"Who broke up with who?" Adam did something I didn't expect, he leaned against his locker and seemed more interested in that question than the show behind me. Actually, I was surprised he wasn't bolting to go say hi to Kyle and blowing me off. It wasn't like he had to put up with me anymore…

"He broke up with me." I didn't give the details.

He gestured his head towards the happy couple. "How long until he started dating her?"

And that was a question I hated answering. Thankfully, I didn't have to tell many people because they had been there when Kyle broke up with me and had heard his blunt, rude, and direct explanation. He wasn't shy of keeping the details to himself. Nope. He shared them in front of my family and friends. Well, his friends, it would turn out.

"Um, they were already together. They had managed to keep it from me for three months."

Adam arched his eyebrows and shook his head. "What a jerk."

I was surprised he would say that about Kyle. Adam and Kyle were close. I would say Kayla was my best friend and Adam had been Kyle's. Kyle and I used to joke that Kayla and Adam should get together.

The four of us spent a lot of time together. Parties. Binge sessions. School. Weekends. The four of us were always together. Even when we hung out with Kyle's other friends, the four of us always were closest.

"Guessing everyone sided with the golden boy then?" Adam said, his eyes on the happy couple.

How did he know that? I nodded my head. "My friends circle has gotten smaller."

"Yeah, well, they follow Kyle blindly—always have." Adam looked back at me, and I saw anger in his eyes. "You didn't deserve to be treated like that."

Funny. He was only the second person to say that to me. Everyone else wouldn't even speak to me. Like Adam said, they followed the golden boy. He was popular, he was extremely handsome, and girls had always been jealous of me being with him. I think they all couldn't believe their luck that Kyle was back on the market. Pity Kayla spoiled their hopes.

"He is happy. I guess that is all that matters." I put my sunglasses on my head, ready to face another long lunch.

I wasn't hungry. I never was. Some days I didn't eat at all. Then the next day I'd only eat because I was light-headed, and my stomach would growl for food.

"Are you?" Adam asked, his voice gentle and kind. Two things Adam rarely showed anyone. Sure, he was nice. But he had an edge to him. He wasn't the golden boy, he didn't do well in classes, and he relied on my help.

Adam had been forced to go overseas with his parents because they couldn't trust him to be left alone. Last time they did, Adam ended up getting arrested throwing a rage party, trashed their house, got caught on drugs, and on top of all that, defaced a police car because he "felt like it". Like I said, he isn't the golden boy.

But he did just asked me a question. One I wasn't sure if I could answer truthfully.

Was I okay?

I smiled dimly. "Some days are better than others." That was the truth. Some days I would get through painless. Other days I would drown in the heartbreak and feel an indescribable pain when I looked at Kyle.

"Did you lose all your friends?" Adam still wasn't in a rush to go see his best friend.

"They weren't my friends when it came down to it. They were all Kyle's," I replied. "It doesn't matter, I used to love being on my own." I had. But even then, I still had Kayla. She had always been my one steady friend. We were matched up in kindergarten and we grew up together. We went through the awkward years together: the first boyfriends, first kisses, the first times we had sex—we had always shared everything with each other.

Then when I started dated Kyle, we were still close. But one day it was like she woke up and was jealous of my relationship with him. She started saying things like I always put him first or that I would blow her off for him, which wasn't the case.

About six months ago Kayla started to get involved with the drug scene. I tried to talk her out of it, but at the end of the day, I had to support her. I knew what she was doing was dangerous, but I couldn't change it, or make her do what I wanted. I supported her. I was there at the hospital after her first overdose. It had been an accident, but I was there holding her hair back as she threw up because she had mixed the wrong drugs together. I was even there when her last bad relationship went wrong.

I had always been there for her.

How did she repay me? She helped the love of my life break my heart. It flooded me again, the feeling of betrayal.

"Soph, you alright?" Adam placed a hand on my shoulder. He must have seen the emotion in my eyes as I remembered what type of friendship I did have.

"Yeah." I looked him in the eye. "Just need some fresh air before class." It was an excuse, and I saw by his expression he knew I had lied. Adam could always tell when someone was lying or not.

"Do you want me to come?"

I frowned. "I'm not your friend, Adam. You don't have to put up with me anymore." If anything, he had to put up with Kayla now. How unlucky was he…

"Just because you aren't with Kyle, doesn't mean I don't value your friendship." Adam smiled. "Come on, Soph, you really think I'd just blow you off?"

I frowned. "You are Kyle's best friend. He should come first." If there was a line being drawn, Adam shouldn't be on my side of the line.

He shrugged. "Personally, I think he fucked up. He might be my friend; doesn't mean I support what he did."

Was it possible that I still had a friend left? I remained silent, unsure what to say to that. Should I thank him? Not one other person, apart from Josh, said that Kyle was a dick for what he did.

"Can I have your timetable?" Adam said, snapping me out of my thoughts.

"Um, why?"

His carefree grin was back on his face. "So, I can get changed into your classes. It's my first day back and I'm already behind because I don't have you to help me."

I always helped him when it came to school. The teachers never explained it clearly enough for him. He would always have questions but would ask me instead of the teacher. I wasn't exactly excelling in school at the moment.

I pulled out my timetable from my pocket. "I don't know if I'll be much help. I've already fallen behind."

"You've fallen behind?" He looked at me like that was impossible.

Yeah, the old me wouldn't be behind. She'd be ahead.

"What can I say? I'm just not feeling this last year." It was dragging out, and I wanted it over. I would've liked nothing more than to never come back here. Once school finished, once my parents were back, I'd be able to cut Kyle completely out of my life.

"But all the work you've done has led up to this year." Adam frowned. "Don't tell me you're letting Kyle ruin your future? What happened to getting an early acceptance into university?"

That had always been the goal. Now I didn't give a fuck.

I shrugged my shoulders.

"Well, it looks like I'm going to be doing a role I never do and that's enjoy school work."

My lips twitched up. Someone cared. He cared. I thought everyone had stopped caring about me.

"Thanks, Adam." I gave him a full smile. It was forced, but it was a smile. "You should get to the office before they glue you into your original classes."

"Good point. I'll see you later, right?" He stopped leaning the against the locker.

"Yeah, I'm not going anywhere." And I wasn't. Every weekday I would be here. In hell.

"Ok. I'll see you later, Soph." Adam gave me a final friendly smile and left. I turned, watching him walk up the hall, noticing how he ignored Kyle and Kayla, completely.

Kyle noticed too. His eyes were on Adam as he walked past them.

Then Kyle's eyes bounced to mine, and I knew Kyle's emotions well. I knew when he was in pain. I knew when he was upset. I knew when he was happy. Right now his eyes were painted in regret with a tint of anger. I didn't know why he was angry, but I realized it wasn't my problem anymore. I closed my locker door and broke eye contact with him.

But as I walked in the opposite direction, I could feel his eyes still on me until the door swung shut behind me.

SIX

Soph

It was late, after midnight, and I was still up on a Friday night, studying. I used to find studying so easy and now it was like forcing a cat to have a bath—bloody impossible. My body was fighting me one hundred percent.

I groaned when all the numbers ganged up on me and I couldn't solve a single problem.

Then, as if God knew I needed a reason to have a break, there was a knock on my door.

I frowned, wondering who would be up at this time, and more importantly why would they be wanting to see me?

I got up and opened the door. For some reason, I was expecting to see Josh. Well, I was hoping it was Josh. My friendly smile fell when my eyes landed on Kyle.

"What do you want?" My words weren't friendly or welcoming. I was direct, rude, and I didn't feel sorry for it either.

"I need to talk to you." Kyle looked at me awkwardly. "I was hoping you would still be up."

"Why are you even here?" I couldn't stop myself from asking. It was a Friday night, which usually meant a party—which meant by now Kyle should be on his way to a hangover.

"Um, I wanted to see you." He looked me in the eye, and I saw the honesty in them.

I crossed my arms and leaned against the doorframe. "What about?" I couldn't think of one reason why. The way he treated me in front of Kayla said it all. He didn't have time for me. He sure as fuck didn't care about me. And when it came down to it, we weren't boyfriend and girlfriend anymore— we weren't friends. Hell, we weren't even associates.

"I wanted to ask you something." He took a step towards me and immediately I took one back. My brain was screaming run. My body's defences were up. No one had hurt me as much as he had hurt me, and right now that fact had not been forgotten.

I couldn't believe what I was seeing when he pushed my bedroom door wide open and took another step into my room. Like he was more determined than ever to make sure he could get close to me.

I put my hand out. "Don't come any closer." My voice shook with nerves. I swallowed sharply. It was bad enough seeing him but having him close… well, it sent my body into immediate pain, knowing I couldn't touch him and what we had was dead.

"Soph, I need you to trust me." His words came out softly and his voice dipped into honesty. It was seductive and swirled in my ears, pulling me in, wanting me to believe him. "I need you to trust me." He took a step closer and now there was no room between us.

He did something I wasn't expecting. His hand cupped my face, and I saw the pain in his eyes, like he wanted more but couldn't have it.

He dipped his head. "Please, will you trust me?"

I frowned. What did he mean, trust him? Why the hell would I trust him with anything? Why would he be asking this of me?

"I don't understand," I mumbled.

His eyes locked with mine. "I need you to trust me; to not wipe me off. Can you do that?"

What he was asking suddenly registered and immediately I wanted to kill him. "You want me to trust you? Like fuck, Kyle!" I managed to get out before I was interrupted.

"Kyle, what the hell are you doing?" Kayla was standing in the hallway, looking directly at Kyle's back.

Kyle pinched his eyes shut, and I heard him curse. He took his hand off me and I missed his touch immediately. I hated myself for wanting it, for missing it and needing it. Yep, I hated myself a bit more for that. Most of all, I was starting to hate Kyle for making me want his touch.

"I thought you were going to the party?" Kyle turned around, sounding pissing off.

"Well, isn't it a good thing I came to check if you had changed your mind?" Kayla crossed her arms and looked at me. "The one night we're apart, you make a move. Always knew you were a slut when it came to him, Sophia, but even I wasn't expecting you to act on it."

Her words whipped across my body. It wasn't just what she said that hurt; it was that she said it to begin with. For some stupid reason, I thought she would still like me or think higher of me than that.

"Well, he is all yours, Kayla." I wasn't going to fight over Kyle. He was hers. Simple. I was starting to see very clearly how much of a liar she was.

"Stay away from him, Sophia. He's mine." She moved across the hall towards my door. "Don't touch him, don't talk to him, and for fuck's sake, stop looking at him with those pitiful eyes."

Her words were sharp, mean, and sliced open my heart a bit wider.

Instead of shutting down, instead of backing down and just taking it like I had since they became a couple, I found an ounce of courage still in my blood.

I moved around Kyle so I could get a good look at the cheap slut she was. "You know what, Kayla? How about you stop monitoring me? Clearly, you're insecure if you think I can get Kyle back. I don't give a fuck if you are with him or not because, at the end of the day, he still looks at me like he loves me." I stepped out into the hall. "I think that's what really makes you angry because you are just one of the many he will fuck his way through, while I was one of the rare ones he stayed around for."

I saw the disbelief and terror on her face as I pushed past her, heading for the stairs. In that moment, I wasn't the broken-hearted ex-girlfriend anymore. I was finally piecing myself back together, and I realized it that moment, I stood up to her. My breakup with Kyle had given me something that it took months to find… courage. I was a warrior now, and I would never let him, or any man, destroy my heart again.

Once I had my heart back together, I was locking it away. I would never— ever—give someone the power to hurt me again.

SEVEN

Soph

I didn't know where I was heading. I just had to get away. I needed to put as much distance between me and Kyle as possible. I headed for the other side of town.

I knew my normal spots and bars were no-go zones because Kyle's friends might be there. So, I drove to the darker side of town. Maybe I was asking for trouble. I walked into the dimly lit bar and headed to get a drink. It was a shady bar with mainly men inside, but that didn't deter me. I needed a strong drink. Maybe a few.

I most likely would get behind the wheel after this. The old Soph wouldn't have dared. Now I just didn't see any reason for stopping me.

I ordered a drink and ran a hair through my hair. How had I let myself fall for Kyle's charm? I wanted to turn back time. Refuse to let him in.

I threw back the shot glass and got a refill, throwing that back as well. I wasn't much of a drinker. I never was. I knew I would start feeling the effects quickly. Maybe it was best if I didn't drive. I didn't want to kill someone just because I couldn't see the point in life. I put my glass down for another.

"The way you're going, you're going to drink the bar dry."

I turned slightly. I hadn't even realized I sat down next to someone. Or had he sat next to me? I had been so focused on drinking; I didn't know the answer.

I took in his rough looks. He was deadly handsome, tattoos over his fingers, hands, arms, and neck, and a voice that would lure you in. It wasn't just his looks; it was how he was looking at me.

He blew out a mouthful of smoke and turned his body towards me on the stool. "You don't look old enough to be drinking."

I didn't have a threatening or a bad girl image. I never had. I didn't have a confident front like Kayla that made you think she was the girl your parents warned you about.

I didn't know why—fuck, I couldn't explain it, but for once in my life I felt confident. Like I wasn't squirming under his tense eyes.

"You don't look like a guy that follows the rules to begin with," I said, not scared of him.

His lips twitched up. "You read me well."

Yeah. Two words summed him up: bad boy.

"So, if you read me so well, why aren't you running?" He looked at me, impressed. "I'm here every night, I know you don't normally come here."

He must be a regular. Well, if he knew I wasn't normally around here, he would assume this was out of my character—which it was. Still, I didn't find myself scared or lacking confidence. For some reason I felt like I could put a front on, like I could show him a side of me I never showed anyone. A daring side. Because that was what I was doing, wasn't it? Taking a dare. Risking everything by being here. My safety. My reputation—not that there was much of that one left. My limited reputation would go down if I was seen in a place like this with a girl on a pole in the corner, dancing freely to men who weren't even paying her. She must be an employee here because she seemed too good at it for it to be her first time or for it to be a drunken dare.

Most of the men had eyes on her, moving to the seductive beat.

I looked back at the guy, and his attention was solely on me. I saw his eyes run up and down me, maybe deciding what the chances were of him scoring me for the night.

Pity for him I was planning on getting drunk. But I wasn't getting so drunk that I would have a one-night stand.

I knew what I was trying to do was numb the pain in my heart, and I realized that maybe this guy could help with that. Sex was just that, wasn't it? Sex. Not really a big deal. I used to think it was a big deal that had to know and trust your partner before you did it—before you took the step.

Now I was seeing sex for what it really was, how guys see it: just a need, and one that can be filled by anyone. Didn't have to be the love of my life or a guy I trusted with my heart. It could be any man. It could be this guy that was staring into my eyes.

"Bax." He took the cigarette out of his mouth. "My name."

Oh. He was introducing himself. I guess I had made the cut on whether to make the effort.

"Sophia, but everyone calls me Soph." I gave him a smile. It was a forced smile, but hell, at least I was putting in the effort.

"Well, Soph, why are you here?" He turned the empty glass in his hand and then put his hand up for a refill.

I frowned for a second. Why was I here?

"Why are you?" I asked.

"Same reason as everyone else."

"That being?"

"Well, some are here for the cheap liquor. Some are here for the free show that chick puts on every night. Others, like me, well, we are here because this is where business is done." He gave me a small smile. "I'm guessing not one of those reasons is why you are here."

I nodded. He had a point. Was I really that easy to read? "I'm here to forget about my life for a night."

He nodded his head, accepting that as an answer. "You shouldn't have come here alone. Surely, your boyfriend could keep you company? In a place like this you are lucky every guy in here hasn't made a move already."

Boyfriend. Just that one word made me clench my glass tighter. "I don't have a boyfriend." I wanted to make that point clear. I turned, looking at him a bit harder. "I don't believe men are trustworthy. As for guys making a move on me in here, clearly you read that wrong because not even one has glanced in my direction."

He smirked. "Maybe that's because you are sitting next to me, sweetheart. Or did you not realize you sat down next to me?"

"I didn't realize I sat down next to you. I can move?" I glanced down at all the empty bar stools. Moving wouldn't be that bad of an idea.

"Nah, sweetheart." He shook his head as if to say he wasn't letting that happen. "Are you drinking hard because of a man?"

Well, I knew the answer to that, but I wasn't going to tell him, so I shrugged my shoulders.

"Come on, a girl like you doesn't have anything serious to worry about. Guessing your life is as hard as high school." He cracked a big grin and arched his eyebrows. "I'm right, aren't I?"

I scoffed. My life had more twists and turns than the average higher schooler. I put my hand up for a refill. I wasn't surprised that this bartender hadn't asked to see my ID. I think he literally didn't give a fuck whether I was of age or not.

He filled up my glass, and I threw it back. It burnt my throat, and I enjoyed every second of it. The temporary burn took my mind off my heart, which was still beating but broken.

"You want to forget about your life for a night?"

"Yeah, I do."

"Could I tempt you over to the dark side for a night?" He looked up for the challenge, like getting me to follow him would fulfill some of his fantasies.

"How dark is the dark side?" I asked, tempted just to leave with him. One night. One night to escape from my life. I deserved that, right?

He leaned in closer. "As dark as you want it to be, sweetheart."

I had a feeling he could take me to places I had never been and show me a side of life I knew nothing about. The side of life that is dark, cruel, and twisted. Just one look at him and you knew he had a criminal record.

Of course, that didn't automatically make him a bad guy, or someone that would hurt me. Josh had a criminal record. I didn't know what for, but he had showed me that it doesn't mean someone is rotten to the core.

I got off my stool and stepped to his side. "I want it a sinister dark." I had nothing to lose, and there was nothing holding me back. "Can you offer me that?"

The smirk on his face got larger. "Sweetheart, if you want dark, I'll give you dark."

I let him take my hand, and he threw money down on the bar, more than enough to cover our drinks.

I never thought I'd be the type of girl to have a one-night stand. I never thought I'd be the type of girl to go over to the dark side. I knew Bax was dangerous. His tattoos showed a loyalty to something that I didn't fully understand, but as we left the bar I knew, I just knew, that if I wasn't careful tonight, he wouldn't just show me the dark side, he'd pull me into it altogether.

EIGHT

Josh

Sometimes I hated being a vice president. Like right now when I couldn't get Bax to concentrate on what I was telling him. The man had been glued to his phone all week. I didn't know who she was, but she had him more interested in writing back to her than listening to a word I had to say.

Bax had only got out of prison a few months before me, but his parole officer said he couldn't be seen or near a criminal organisation. He was running our associates, taking a silent role in the club. He couldn't wear club colours, couldn't even ride his Harley without being pulled over.

He was doing the things he loved: drinking, handling dodgy deals, and partying. It would seem he had a girl at the moment because he was more interested in whatever she was saying than his monthly update with me.

"Bax, are you fucking listening to me!" I snapped at him.

His eyes slowly came off his phone, and he looked at me with his normal pissed off glare. He didn't like being told what to do, and he hated answering to me because he had been a member longer. We were the same age though, so at least he wasn't older. That would give him another weak excuse to disrespect me.

"You want me to collect rent from the other side of town." He rolled his eyes. "Anything else, Vice?"

"Yeah, who is she?" I snapped, sick of his higher-than-me attitude. When it came down to it, I was the Vice President; he sure as fuck wasn't, so he had to answer to me.

"No one." He put his phone away, and here I was thinking it was glued to his hand.

"Thought you didn't do girlfriends?" I crossed my arms, watching him squirm under my question.

"Mind your own business, Vice."

"If you are bringing her into your life, you are bringing her into the club's life."

"Considering, I'm currently doing the dirty work for the club and won't be bringing her back to the club, I don't see how it's any of your business." He went to get up. "Tell Wolf I'll do it. When it comes to the women I fuck, mind your own fucking business."

With that said, he stormed off, like his normal pissed off self. I threw money down for our coffees and got up to leave. The reason I had to deal with Bax to begin with was because I wasn't in the police's eyeline as a member. Sure, I was linked to them, but nobody knew I was the Vice President. Well, not yet, but it wasn't going to stay a secret for much longer.

Now I had a family dinner to go to. I was being forced to attend because Mom had been complaining to Dad that she never sees me, which resulted in Dad doing something he hated doing, and that was calling me. He hated to ask anything of me, but he did it for Mom, and the only reason I agreed to it was because it would get her off my back for another few weeks.

* * *

I hadn't been home much. The club has kept me busy. I had been coming home late and left early. It was for the best. That way I avoided Dad and Mom and my dickhead of a brother, Kyle.

I shot a glare at my brother who was, once again, trying to make conversation with Soph. My eyes went from Kyle to Soph. She had been giving him one-word answers all night.

Seriously, could Kyle not get the hint that she wasn't interested?

My eyes hovered on Soph. She had always been the centre of conversation and she loved to talk. I swear she used to never shut up. When she wasn't talking, she was laughing. And now... Now she couldn't give my brother more than a one-word answer. Even when Mom and Dad asked her how she was, she just said "fine." Didn't even do the polite thing, like the old Soph would have, and ask how they were.

I had the feeling she was sinking into depression. She looked withdrawn. Actually, when

I thought about it more, Soph wasn't her old self. It was like Kyle had broken her. I shot a glare at my brother. Only he could take a fucking perfect human being and ruin them. Which was exactly what he had done.

I found myself wanting her to treat me differently. I wondered if I spoke to her right now, would she block me out too?

I cleared my throat and sat up, my eyes on her. "So, Soph, how's school?"

Her head snapped up. Her eyes were wide as she looked at me like she misheard me.

"Um. It's good, Josh." She kept looking at me. "How are you?"

I smiled. She asked a question. I had got her to ask a question, and it was directed at me.

"Good, Soph. Haven't seen you about lately."

Her phone buzzed on the table next to her plate. I did a double take when I saw that number and name on her screen. Bax. I knew that number. I knew it so well because I would glare at it for a few minutes every time I was forced to call him.

How the hell had she met him? Suddenly, her lack of conversation wasn't such a serious issue. The more serious issue was who she was spending her time with. Bax was bad fucking news. Surely, she wasn't that stupid or so blind that she ignored that?

I was faced with a decision: let Soph into my world, tell her the truth about me, and tell her what Bax was like—and then protect her from him, or let her go into a situation blind with a man who was deadly dangerous and never respected women.

I reached for my beer and kept my eyes on her as my mind jumbled around the facts. Admitting to her that I was the Vice President of the Devil's Cut, a dangerous outlaw motorcycle group—well, I think whatever she thought of me would disappear immediately.

Seeing her disappointed in the way I lived my life bothered me. It got under my skin. Why did I care so much what she thought? I never cared what people thought. I didn't even care what Dad's opinion was of me, and he was my father.

I wondered why I was suddenly nervous about telling her who I really was and what I stood for. It sent wave after wave of nerves through me. Still, what could I do? Keep my secret just that, or risk it and let the only girl whose opinion I cared about know the type of guy I really was…

NINE

Soph

I closed the front door. It was late. Once again, Bax had kept me out all night. If I could, I would be smiling. Bax was carefree, funny, and I knew he was dangerous, but that didn't scare me away.

I walked up the stairs slowly, stopping and taking my heels off halfway. My feet were aching. Bax decided for us to walk through the busy square. I looked at the long red stem rose in my hand.

I thought Bax would be a one-night deal, but he was determined the morning after to get my number, and when we weren't together, he was always messaging me. I never had to start the messaging with him. It was like he knew when the perfect time was to send a message.

It was dark, and I was heading for my room when I noticed Josh's door open. His door was never open. I frowned and for some reason found myself heading for his room. I knew I shouldn't bother him. I knew he wouldn't like me in his room. But for some reason, I felt like something was calling me to go in there.

I knocked on the door softly. "Josh, you okay?"

It was dark, but I could make out a body on the bed. I heard a groan, and I walked to his bed, stepping over the clothes on the floor. His room was a mess. I dodged the crushed cans and empty bottles.

"Josh, are you okay?"

He groaned. Okay, I was taking that as a no.

"Josh?" I asked softly and moved next to his side of the bed. The curtains were open, and the moonlight helped me to make out his figure, which was on the edge of the bed with a hand over his face. I lowered my voice in case he was hungover and said, "What's wrong?"

His head turned as he took his hand off his face. "Migraine." He sounded like he was in a lot of pain.

He used to get migraines when he was under stress. I noticed the bottles of pain relief next to his bedside. I knew Josh. He wouldn't have anything for it. Getting the bottles out was all he would have done. That was a lot for Josh. He hated the medication because it would linger in his system the next day.

I popped open the bottle and got him a dose out, grabbing an open beer bottle.

"Okay, I'm sorry about the warm beer, but you have to take this, regardless." I took his hand and put the pills in them. He slowly sat up and I saw how gingerly he did it.

He took the beer and threw back the pills. I took it off him and headed for the bathroom.

I ran a face cloth under the cold water and headed back to his bedroom, dodging all the crap on the floor.

"You're back?" He must have spotted me.

"Yeah, you're lucky I haven't broken my neck in this room." I got to his side and gently lifted his hand off and placed the towel down.

He sighed. I walked around to the other side of the bed. I had already abandoned my heels,, and I doubted I'd be able to find them later in this mess.

I laid down on his bed next to him.

"You don't have to stay, Soph." He turned and his voice was soft, as if he spoke any louder, he'd be in pain.

I took his hand and started to massage it. The hand has trigger points to all over your body. My mum used to always massage my thumb whenever I had a headache; she believed it did something, and she was a doctor. If nothing else, it was relaxing.

"Soph, you can go."

I just kept massaging his hand. "Stop telling me to leave and go to sleep." The sooner he went to sleep, the sooner he would recover. He knew that too.

He turned on his side to face me. "How was your date?"

I frowned. I hadn't told him I was going out with Bax tonight. No one knew about Bax.

But when it came down to it, Bax and I weren't dating. "Um, wasn't on a date." I kept massaging his hand. "Sorry I wasn't home earlier. If I had been, you wouldn't have suffered for so long."

I felt guilty about not being here for him. I hated the thought of Josh lying here in pain.

"I'm fine."

"Sure you are." I sighed and closed my eyes. I don't know why, but when it came to Josh, I felt comfortable. Like I could just do what I want in front of him and he wouldn't judge. I wouldn't call it a friendship—it was more than that. Like an unspoken bound of trust.

I turned around, placing my back against his chest while putting his arm around me and having his hand in mine, massaging it. I didn't feel like I was crossing a line. I didn't even think about what it would mean to share the same bed as him. He didn't push me away or take his hand out of mine. Like I said, we had this unspoken trust between us.

I was so focused on the feel of his hand in mine, and massaging it, that at first, I didn't realize he had slipped his arm under my head. For some reason I felt relaxed, calm, and this felt so right. I trusted him as I laid on his arm, and he pulled me back into his chest, as I kept his hand in mine. I didn't feel like I was crossing a boundary by falling asleep next to him in his bed. If anything, I felt safe.

So, I didn't fight it when the need for sleep crept up on me. Didn't think, fuck it, I should go to my room. Nope. I stayed and fell asleep in his bed, on his arm.

JOSH

Sophia was beautiful. I don't think she realizes how beautiful she is. She's the type of beautiful that you would do anything for, just to please her. It wasn't just her looks that had you begging to please her. It was her personality. Right now, I couldn't get over how beautiful she was.

Her flawless skin, her red lips—and it wasn't lipstick; her lips were always red, which stood out against her pale complexion. With all the sunshine here, you would think she would tan, but she never did.

My migraine disappeared slowly over the night once she forced me to take pain killers.

That was the other thing about Soph. You couldn't say no to her. Not that she would react badly if you did, you simply didn't say no because you didn't want to disappoint her.

Like, whatever she wanted, you had to give her—meet her demands.

It wasn't like she demanded much from you. If anything, all she wanted was respect, and that I would always give her.

My brother had broken her trust. I also think he broke something inside her. The old Soph would be full of smiles and glowing with happiness. This version of Soph had her hanging out with men like Bax and coming home at all hours of the night.

She wasn't happy. I think the only thing she was doing was surviving—poorly.

Clearly, she wasn't in the right state of mind to make a fucking decision. Because look where her decisions got her: In my bed, in a dress barely covering her breasts and thighs, showing the black lace that it should be covering.

Her decisions had also led her to Bax. I had hoped she would see it herself. That he wasn't the guy you would waste time on. I had let them go a week, and what was the result? Bax was making excuses to get out of my meetings, and Soph was barely home. When she did come home, it was the early hours of the morning. How did I know?

Cause I was making an effort to track what she was doing. I was even home by nine at night, which was unheard of because the night was meant to be a biker's best time. Best time on the road. And best time to drink and get laid. And what was I doing? Waiting to see if my brother's teenage ex-girlfriend was home.

I didn't know why I was doing it. Wasn't like I loved her. I didn't love anyone. Nor did I ever see myself loving anyone. That just wouldn't happen. I was never giving a girl more than a night again. I was never being forced to be in a relationship with one, and I sure as fuck was never getting involved in her life.

So, what the hell was I doing with Soph?

She was a friend, right? I didn't do friendships either, so I didn't know the boundaries. Didn't know if stalking her bedtime was acceptable. I also didn't know if it was my place to warn her of Bax when she hadn't actually told me about him. So, I couldn't just give carefree easy advice on the subject.

She would have to bring him up, and I didn't see her doing that. Ever.

My bedroom door swung open, and I was so consumed with staring at Soph's flawless and sleeping face, I nearly didn't notice my brother come in.

"What the fuck, Joshua?" Kyle hissed at me, his eyes on Soph and then me.

I rolled my eyes. Of course, he would make a scene. I saw his eyes run down her. And as if she was mine, I covered her, throwing the blanket over her. I should have done that earlier instead of gawking at her perfect figure.

I got up and pushed Kyle out of the room. I didn't want him waking her and he would do that just to be a jerk and get answers on why she was in my room.

"What the hell was that!" Kyle pointed at my bedroom door, which I had closed before he started ranting. His ranting went through my ears. My migraine might be gone, but my ears were still sensitive.

"Nothing." I crossed my arms, standing in front of the doorway in case he thought to charge in there and demand for Soph to explain what she was doing in there to him.

"She's off limits, you hear me, Joshua? She is off fucking limits!" he roared at me, and if Soph wasn't awake, I'm sure that would have woken her.

"You and Soph are finished. What she does is zero of your business." I uncrossed my arms, and in case he wasn't getting a message, I pushed him backward away from my bedroom door. "If anyone will be staying away from her, it's you. You hear me, Kyle? Stay the fuck away from her!"

"She's my girlfriend!"

He couldn't be serious? "Last time I checked you have a new one of them, which means Soph isn't yours anymore."

He shook his head, not accepting that. "She will always be mine. I know what you think of her. Fuck, I've seen how you look at her, but I'm telling you I won't let it happen."

He could say what he wanted and do what he wanted. At the end of the day, what happened between me and Soph would be between us. Not that I was planning on anything happening. At the moment, we were just friends. She was the first friend I had, and I wasn't sure if I was being a good one or letting her down. But still, what happened was between us.

"I know what you are involved in. She will never go for a criminal biker!" Kyle hissed at me. How did he know that I was a biker? The criminal bit, well that was old news, but no one knew about the biker side, unless he has been speaking to Dad.

I titled my head, looking at my brother. We both knew that nothing held Soph back when her heart got involved. But I doubted her heart would ever want me. I was older; I was a criminal, and I didn't care that I scared nearly everyone I met away.

"I'll do what I want, Kyle. Like I always do." I pointed a finger at him. "I think you need to learn your new place, which is in her past—not her future." With that said, and seeing that panicked look on his face, I turned around and slipped back into my bedroom.

Soph had been right when she said she was lucky not to break her neck in my room. It was really bad. I wanted to groan. I hated cleaning. I didn't care if I lived in a mess. If that meant I didn't have to clean, that was fine.

But seeing as Soph noticed how bad it was, I knew I would have to bring myself to the boring task of cleaning. "You're up?"

My head snapped up, and I saw Soph sitting up in the bed, with the blanket over her lap. She was still waking up by the looks of it, which meant maybe my idiot of a brother hadn't woken her up.

"Yeah. How are you feeling?" I moved towards the bed.

"I should be asking you that question." She turned on the bed. "How are you feeling?"

That was Soph for you, always cared more about someone else than herself. I smiled. "I'm better. I owe you one."

"I didn't do it counting on you paying me back." She forced a smile. That was the other thing she did now. Force smiles. Her natural smile was never on her face. Or that carefree grin of hers—that was never on her face either.

"I know you didn't." I looked down at my side of the bed and spotted a rose. I picked it up and looked at her. "I thought you said it wasn't a date?" I wouldn't believe that the Bax I knew would buy her a red rose. In fact, she must have someone else on the cards as well as him.

She looked at the rose. "I thought I had dreamed that bit."

I arched my eyebrows at her. "Who is he?"

She looked down at her lap. "You wouldn't approve," she mumbled, and I started to get a sinking feeling my stomach. Like she was about to confirm my worst nightmare, which was Bax was the one giving her roses and keeping her out all night.

"Try me." I put the rose down on my bedside table and kept my eyes on her. "You know me, I've never judged you."

She frowned and took a deep breath in and looked like she was weighing up telling me the truth or not. "What do you think of bikers?"

The air disappeared from my lungs. I found my mouth dropping open, and I just looked at her like she couldn't be serious. In that second, that one question threw me completely.

Her frown deepened when she saw my reaction. "Forget I asked." She went to get up.

"Stop," I said, putting my hand out like that would stop her from getting up. "How do you know he's a biker?"

"I sort of put together all the facts. But it's strange… it's like he is loyal to it, but at the same time doesn't have anything to do with them." She shrugged. "Maybe I've read him wrong."

She hadn't. She had read him perfectly. He was a biker being forced to have a backseat from a life he loved to live. He loved the drinks, the drugs, and most of all, the women.

"Biker's go through girls, Soph. You shouldn't let yourself be used." Was that crossing a line? I read her expression; she hadn't taken it the wrong way.

She shrugged again. "I've sort of stopped caring. It's not like he will hurt me. Not after…" She swallowed, pausing for a second. "I just mean, like, I'm not in love with him.

If his attention stopped, I wouldn't be heart broken or anything."

Well, at the very least she didn't have her heart set on him. That was something. Still, she was dating him, knowing what type of man he was—the type of man that would never be faithful to a woman.

She deserved to have a man that would always put her first and would always be loyal, respectful, and faithful to her. Bax was only loyal to the club. He didn't respect anyone—not even the people that ranked above him. And he wasn't faithful. Just wasn't in his blood. He was a stereotypical biker.

So why the fuck had he set his sights on Soph?

I ran a hand through my hair, feeling slightly confused by the new emotions that were flooding my body.

"I should get out of you bed and let you rest." This time Soph did get up, and I didn't want her leaving.

"You got plans today?" I asked as I watched her readjust her dress. Her dead straight hair was puffing out, giving her a look as if she had been up all-night having sex.

"Nope." She crossed her arms. "Guess you do, though. Your phone was going off before."

I glanced at my phone. It was dead now. My eyes went back to her. God, she was beautiful. "I don't have plans. Well, apart from cleaning my room."

She grinned just slightly, but it was a real grin. "Why, because I nearly died in here?"

I nodded my head. Yep. She was the reason I was facing down cleaning.

"Well, seeing as it is my fault, you're going to do something you hate, I'll help." She put her hands on her hips. "But I need to change first."

"You don't have to help." That was the last thing I wanted, but at the same time, knowing she would be spending time with me, excited me.

"Just let me change." Her eyes ran over my bare chest. "And you should get dressed too," she said it like me being topless was causing her physical harm.

I realized now if she saw my back, she would see my tattoo. Without thinking about it or caring if it was dirty or not, I picked up the first T-shirt my hand landed on and threaded it on.

She frowned slightly at my abrupt behaviour. She gave me another questioning look as she opened the door and left.

That was a close call. How could I forget about my tattoos? If she saw that, she wouldn't be questioning if I was a biker or not.

TEN

Soph

When it came to life, I had always seen it as black and white: What you can do and what you can't. What you should feel and what you shouldn't. I never saw the grey area. But now I did. I saw a hell of a lot of grey. Like my feelings, for example. If I had to say if I was happy or sad, I couldn't say either. But I could say I was broken, which I think went into the grey side of life where there was a hole in my heart and every day I was trying to fill it… and some days, well, some days I let it get bigger.

Being with Kyle was the thing I did best and now that it was gone, there was a hole in my heart, a hole he created. Some days I could cope. Other days I couldn't get out of bed.

Then there was a rare day when I felt like myself again. But most of the time I felt like a different person. I think that's what scared me the most—that I was becoming a new person, someone colder, someone less happy, someone who didn't smile and saw the darker side of life, not giving a fuck.

I was becoming someone I didn't recognize. The hole in my heart was destroying me — well, the old me. The person I was creating now, I didn't want to be her. Every time I looked in the mirror, I just longed to see the happiness I used to feel daily.

I knew the coldness was getting worse when my razor broke in the shower, and I couldn't think of one reason not to cut my wrists. I didn't. But for a split second, I wanted the relief—to feel something other than numbness.

Sure, Bax brought out a side to me. He made me... well... I don't think I can describe what I felt around him. It wasn't love, and it wasn't friendship. Maybe it was a riskier side to me? Maybe he brought out my wild side? I guess there wasn't much left of me to get hurt if things did go bad, so why not risk it? That was what I thought every time he called me late at night. I knew it was a booty call, but I went.

Then there were the rare nights when he just wanted to spend time with me. Didn't fucking know why he would want to spend time with me. It sure as hell wasn't my personality. Wasn't like I made great conversation either. I just couldn't. I literally couldn't do it. It was like I was relearning how to be around people. Like all my experiences with Kyle had been wiped. The person I was, wiped. The skills I had, wiped. What was this? Was this the heartbreak that song writers sing about? Was this the type of pain romance novelists attempt to describe?

At the end of the day, I knew one thing for sure: no one could describe this heartbreak unless they had been through it. And if they did experience it, live through it, and survive it, I can guarantee they wouldn't be the same person anymore.

No one could fix this hole in my heart. Hell, it wasn't a hole. There was barely anything left of my heart for it to be considered an organ.

I think what was worse was Kyle always knew the right words to say. He always knew what to do—usually he knew me better than I knew myself. I'd grown so tired of putting up a front. I wasn't okay. And I was okay with not being okay. I was just hoping one day, somehow, by some miracle, I would recover.

Just because I couldn't see it happening didn't mean it wouldn't, right? Miracles happen. It was possible one would happen to me. In the meantime, I just had to get through day to day, hour to hour, minute to minute.

I had to admit, right now I was getting through the day thanks to Josh.

I looked up just as he scratched the back of his neck, glaring down at his couch. His expression had my lips twitching up. Nearly a smile, but it wasn't.

"You know, you can't just keep glaring at it, right? You're going to have to sort out the mess," I said. I was sitting on his floor, sorting out the clean washing. His mum had just kept putting basket after basket of clean washing in his room, but wouldn't put it away. It was fair to say he had been living out of these baskets.

He said his mum cleaned everything that ended up outside his doorway. He looked at me like I was stupid when I asked him if he washed them. His response: "fuck the washing." It was enough to get me to nearly smile again.

"This is disgusting," he muttered, picking up a pair of jeans which were covered in grease that had, by the looks of it, rubbed off on his shirts underneath them.

Nothing could make me laugh, but his expression was bringing out the humour in me.

"Fuck, look at this!" He dug out something and then showed me a pizza box. "How the fuck did that get underneath all this?"

"I'm going to say you were drunk and hungry at the time that entered your room." Which was the only explanation on why he would have food in here. He would come back from one of his wild parties or fights. I say fights because he often had a black eye, bruised knuckles, or a cut lip. But the funny thing was, his attitude seemed to imply he wasn't on the receiving end of the beating. That was Josh for you. I think he lived to push his body to the breaking point with exercise. He used to be like that before prison, always running or at the gym. I remember he took up mixed martial arts before prison.

I took in his board shoulders and arms I couldn't wrap my hands around. His muscles were that big. Even the muscles running up his neck bulged out. Honestly, I was sorry for any poor bastard that pissed him off because I think Josh could kill them with his bare hands and strength.

If I had to describe Josh as one thing, one word to sum him up, it would be protector. I think that's why I felt so safe around him. There were other ways to describe josh, like dangerous, a definite violent streak, not emotionally ready for a relationship... even cold hearted. But I think the most frightening thing about him was he was able to tell, with just one look, what you were thinking. Yeah, that scared me the most, and I was trying my best to dodge his glances. I didn't want him to know about the hole in my heart. I didn't want anyone to know.

I watched him throw clothes out into the hallway. He was assuming that his mum would pick them up and wash them. For a twenty-something-year-old man, he was relying an awful lot on his mum.

"Well, look at that!" I said with a tiny smile on my face.

"What?" He glanced at me, still holding the pizza box between two fingers, as if the old pizza would escape from the box and attack him.

"Your carpet is gray." I stood up.

He scoffed. "Well, I'm still unsure what color my fucking couch is."

"Could have a flower pattern."

He shot me a drop-dead look. Like it would be over his dead body that anything with flowers on it would come into his room, which just supported his character: stereotypical alpha male.

"You still haven't told me his name." Josh threw more clothes into the hallway along with the pizza box.

I frowned. "Whose name?"

He looked up at me with determination in his eyes. "The biker."

Oh, that. I should have kept my mouth shut. "I don't know if he is a biker or not."

"How old is he?"

"Old enough to not be interested in me." And that was the truth.

Josh scoffed and shook his head. "Do you see yourself in the mirror?" He waved an arm at me. "You would have any sane man begging."

What was he trying to say? That I attract men? How wrong he was. The only man I wanted found another girl more attractive than me. If I couldn't keep the one man I wanted, how the hell was I meant to keep others interested?

"That's not true," I said firmly. "If that was the case, I wouldn't be…." I clamped my mouth shut and shook my head. "Men aren't worth a second thought." I knew that to be true, yet my mind still would revisit the topic of Kyle often. Even though nothing would change between us, and nothing could change our future and what he did to me.

"Are you happy to cut this one off then?" Josh said so casually you would think he was talking about the weather and not my sex life.

My mouth dropped open slightly, and I found myself stumped by his assumption.

He arched an eyebrow at me, reading my expression. "Is that a yes or a no?"

I looked at him like he couldn't be serious. Finally, I shut my mouth, and the shock disappeared.

"Actually, it's a no." I started to collect the empty baskets.

"So, you like him?"

"I like having sex with him, yes." I found myself being honest. What was wrong with a girl using a guy for once? I wasn't going to be heartbroken if Bax stopped talking to me or suddenly got interested in another girl who showed up at the bar. "Why do you care?" I finally asked, walking towards him. "You use women for sex and don't say you don't because I know your reputation, Josh."

Even two years ago he was known for being a heartbreaker. The devil with the looks and a hand made to grab hearts out of girl's chests and destroy them without feeling one inch of guilt. True to his character, he was the bad boy—the one every girl wanted to try to tame.

I wasn't stupid; I knew Bax was a bad boy, and I wasn't the dumb blonde who thought she could change him. I accepted Bax for what he was, and that was great for sex—but that was it. He wasn't boyfriend material, and he sure as hell wasn't a man I'd give my heart.

"You aren't that cold, Soph." Josh kept his eyes on me as I stood behind the couch in front of him. "You can't say you can just use a guy for sex and feel nothing."

I looked at him, deadly serious. "If you reckon I can't do it, why have I been doing it since I met him?" It was true, my heart wasn't involved. My body was, and that I wouldn't deny. My body was into Bax—his tattoos, his muscles… yep, my body felt him one hundred percent.

After Kyle left me, I'd been holding onto a memory of him, and I'd been so focused on what we had, being stuck in the past, that I couldn't get over him. He was deep in my veins and I couldn't give Bax my heart even if I wanted to, because I didn't have one. I really needed to let Kyle go, but I didn't know. He was like my own personal drug, and I was going through withdrawals.

I was still holding on to a memory, even though he had basically said he was sick of me and wanted nothing to do with me. He wanted me to let him go, and I just didn't know how to do it.

Which brought me to where I was now: openly admitting I was using a guy for sex. The old Soph felt too much to ever do that; she lived to please, love, and feel. The new Soph… well, if anything, I learned just how much I'd changed because the new me didn't live for any of those things.

"I don't like this guy. He isn't good for you," Josh said, his dark eyes staring into mine, locking with them until I felt like I couldn't look away even if I wanted to. Fuck. I was scared to blink. "I want you to end it."

Nobody told me what to do anymore. It was the only thing I got from the breakup with Kyle. Nobody told me who to be with, or who not to be with, and no one could be ashamed or disappointed in me if I didn't listen to them. But Josh was standing here like I had to answer to him.

"I don't tell you who you can and can't sleep with." I crossed my arms, feeling like I needed another reason to back up my response.

Josh picked up a packet of smokes and lit one up, looking like he needed to calm down. Why was he getting so worked up over this?

He inhaled, his eyes still locked with mine. "You need to let him go."

I frowned. "I'm not holding on to Bax." I wasn't. I wasn't clinging to the hopes of being his girlfriend. Hell, I didn't even expect him to be a friend when he was done with me.

Josh shook his head. "Kyle..." He took the cigarette out of his mouth. "You are still letting him control your decisions. You're letting him turn you into this..." he paused and ran a one hand through his hair while holding his cigarette in the other, "someone else," he finally settled on a word. "You are better than this, Soph."

I wasn't better than anything. I wasn't letting Kyle control my decisions. If anything, I was just surviving. I was who I was because that was what was left of me after Kyle was done.

"You want to be my friend, right?" I held my head up high, even though I could hear the disappointment in his voice.

Josh didn't do friendships, so I knew he was going into this one blind. He didn't know boundaries. He didn't know what was right and what was wrong. He didn't know where a friendship stopped being a friendship.

He nodded his head, looking unsure whether he wanted to hear what I had to say.

"Well, if you are my friend, you are meant to be there no matter what. No matter how many times I fail or succeed, you are there to support and encourage and help me pick up the pieces if I do fail." I looked at him a bit harder. "Either way, I'm always meant to be able to count on you. No matter what I do."

That was a friendship, right? The core values of a friendship. Well, that's how I saw them. If Josh wanted to be my friend, he had to be there through the good times and the bad.

"If you can't be there in the good times and bad times, we don't have a friendship," I added. He was staring at me, weighing up what I said. He didn't know the values of a friendship. He was only doing what he did best, and that was protecting someone he cared about. I assumed that was why he wanted me to end it with Bax, because he thought I'd get hurt.

Little did he know I couldn't get hurt anymore.

He inhaled on the cigarette, still staring into my eyes, before he slowly exhaled. "Bax is a bastard, Soph. You will end up hurt." His eyes hardened, and he was looking at me like I was something special and he wasn't about to have me ruined by a man that could never love me.

He also said that like he knew Bax. I shook my head. "Clearly you didn't listen to me when I said through the good and the bad."

"Why should I support the bad when I can stop it from happening?" He had a solid point. A friend would point out a mistake before I made one, but would be there when I made it, anyway. "Soph, you deserve better than one-night stands."

My eyes widened slightly. "How do you know that's all my relationship with Bax is?"

I sure as hell didn't tell him I was Bax's favorite booty call. "How do you know he doesn't hold me higher than that?"

He scoffed and shook his head, dropping the cigarette in an ashtray.

Whatever he was thinking, he was keeping it to himself. He was acting like he knew Bax; like he knew what Bax was capable of and not, which wasn't possible because Josh might be bad, but he wasn't in Bax's league. Well, not that I knew of. As I thought about it more, I began to wonder whether Josh had a double life, one whether his criminal past wasn't the past.

"I should have known you wouldn't listen," he muttered to himself and then looked at me defeated. "Guess I'll just be there when he breaks your heart," he said with so much honesty and concern.

"Thanks, Josh." I wish I could smile. Because what he was doing—letting me go into a situation that was going to end badly—well, it showed he really was going to support me in the good and bad.

His phone went off on his bedside table and I glanced at it. It had been doing that a lot this morning. I assumed it was some needy girl he was trying to cut off.

"Seems like she won't give up." I looked back at him as his phone rang in the background.

He frowned. "What?"

"The girl who hasn't stopped calling you all morning. I don't think she is giving up."

His face was twisted with confusion for a moment, and then it registered what I had said.

"Yeah, I should get this, and you should get out of here. I'm sure cleaning my bedroom wasn't what you wanted to do on your weekend." He looked at his phone, which had stopped ringing, and then looked back at me. "Can I ask something of you?" His tone was serious.

I tilted my head, looking at him. "Sure."

"If he is a biker, don't go to the clubhouse or club parties," he said firmly. "Promise me you won't get involved in that scene?"

I bit my bottom lip. The truth was, Bax was trying to get me to go to parties, which I knew had something to do with a biker club, but they weren't parties at a clubhouse. They were at random houses. I heard him say on the phone to someone he was going to a "supporter's house." It was another thing that had tipped me off to him being in a club.

But the other night, after we had sex, I took in his tattoos with more detail. I don't know why I hadn't looked at them or studied them before. But I could see tattoos dedicated to The Devil's Cut. I knew that was the local biker club in town. I guess I really was playing with fire being near Bax.

"I won't get involved in clubhouse parties," I said it clearly. I wouldn't be going to a clubhouse. But I would go to a party in general, whether it was a supporter's party or not. Josh didn't seem to pick up on my clarification.

He nodded his head and his phone started ringing again.

"I'll, um, let you get that." I gave him a fake smile and left him in his room, closing the door after me and heading across the hall to my room.

ELEVEN

Soph

Ok, I was beginning to think my life couldn't get any worse; that I had suffered through enough awkwardness for a lifetime. If there was a God, one would think that he'd had enough entertainment from my train wreck of life.

But that didn't seem to be the case tonight.

Louise, Kyle's Mum, who I had to admit I had been giving the cold shoulder since I arrived, asked me to stay in Saturday night. I had plans with Bax, but I couldn't say no to her.

She and Jed were putting me up, and it would also seem that Jed wanted me to stay in tonight as well. Josh, however, had disappeared sometime that day, and when I saw his empty spot at the table, I assumed he wasn't being forced to spend Saturday night here.

Jed Hawkins was many things: a man passionate about this city, a true-blue supporter of the Bull Dogs, a family man, and I would say a great dad—to Kyle. It was no secret he had no time for Josh. He had written Josh off years ago. I think even before I came along. But when it came to anything in Kyle's life, he was the golden boy.

I stabbed a carrot as Kayla continued to make small talk with Louise.

Yep, Kyle had been given the order to stay in as well, but he dragged his girlfriend into the family night I was being forced to attend.

I glanced up, and I wished I hadn't because my eyes locked with Kyle's, who was staring directly at me.

I wanted to snap at him, but instead I shoved a carrot in my mouth and attempted to keep a lid over my temper and embarrassment. Just as I went to shove another carrot in my mouth, Louise turned to look at me.

"So, Sophia, how is school going? I bet the universities are hovering," she said so sweetly, like she still cared about my future, even though my future would not include her son. She should really redirect that question to Kayla, her future daughter-in-law.

As the table went quiet and all eyes were on me, I realized I was going to be forced to answer. I opened my mouth to answer, but an annoying and relentless voice spoke before me.

"I don't know about Soph, but the universities' attention is really intense. I was telling Kyle earlier in the week if I get one more promotional letter, I'll never make a decision," Kayla finished with a fake sigh at the end.

Louise turned to look at me. "Are you having the same problem, Sophia?"

"No, I don't get letters." I looked at Kayla. "I get phone calls." Kayla's eyes narrowed, but I continued, "Kayla is right though, it is intense. Then there are the face-to-face appointments—shoving scholarships down your throat."

"Have you picked a favorite yet, Sophia?"

Jed entered the conversation. For some reason, they actually still cared where my future was headed.

"I'm thinking overseas. I got a few good offers from aboard."

"You aren't going overseas," Kyle scoffed and shook his head. He spoke as if what I had just said offended him. If anything, he should be glad to not be in the same country as me.

"Mum and Dad are encouraging it." I frowned, my eyes on Kyle as he glared at me.

"You wanted to stay in the state. What happened to that plan? What happened to you going to Monash? We both went to their welcoming and put them as our first choice. Hell, we even looked for an apartment there. You had your heart set on Monash!" Kyle's words sprayed over the table at me. He was basically a second away from getting up and screaming it at me.

I had never seen him this angry. I just stared at him with my mouth slightly open, speechless.

"Um, well, that was our plan…" I trailed off, not really sure what to say.

The tension at the table was palpable.

Louise and Jed were looking between us, while Kayla's glare was fixed firmly on Kyle.

"Darn straight it was!" Kyle threw his fork down. "Now all of a sudden you're forgetting about our plans and heading over fucking seas?"

"Kyle, language!" Jed warned.

Was Kyle serious right now? He thought I'd be heading to the same university as him? He thought that I would still be following the plan he and I had set?

Gathering my thoughts. "My plans changed when you weren't in my future anymore." I looked into his heated eyes. "I'm sure you and Kayla have discussed where you both will be heading next year, and I doubt it's the same plan you had with me."

I attempted to speak reason, but Kyle reacted like I had thrown gasoline onto an open fire.

"We made a promise, Soph! You and I were heading to Monash. You can't go back on that now. You do realize that once you set your preferences you can't change them? Hell, we set our preferences last year!"

"And I changed them the first day back at school." I shook my head and frowned. "It's not like my future effects yours anymore. At the end of this year, I doubt we will ever see each other again." It was the truth. I didn't see our paths crossing again. Not after high school ended, and we both relocated.

Kyle got up abruptly. "Take that back now, Sophia! Now!"

"Kyle, calm down," Louise attempted to intervene.

"Can you hear this bullshit?" Kyle pointed an arm at me. "She is wiping me out of her life!"

I awkwardly looked at Louise, Jed, and then Kyle, my eyes bouncing from one to the other.

"Kyle, you wiped me out of your life," I reminded him. "Why the hell are you getting upset? We aren't together. We aren't friends. Stop looking at me like I have to be loyal to our old plans." I dropped my knife and fork. I wasn't hungry anymore. Not that I was to begin with. But I was no longer putting on a show of pretending to eat.

I couldn't believe how he was acting! It was as if he thought that come next year, I would be attending Monash with him. Hell, I think in his twisted mind he saw me sharing an apartment with him. Did he really think I would want to share an apartment with him and his girlfriend? Was he that insane!

"If you set your preferences now, then come three months when they are locked, you won't be able to change them!" Kyle yelled a fact at me I already knew from across the table. "You could change your mind and you'd be locked into heading overseas."

"What's going to happen in the next three months that would change my mind?" I stood up, sick of him having the higher ground.

He scoffed. "The election—that's what will happen." He made that sound like it was obvious.

I glanced at Jed. "How would Jed continuing to be mayor, affect my university decision?" I arched my eyebrows at him. He was looking at me like it was obvious why he was getting so upset. But if anything, I was just confused more.

"It will fucking change everything!" he roared. "Don't you dare lock in your choices!"

My mouth fell open. "On that note, I think I'm going to leave." I pushed the chair back. I couldn't believe he was threatening me. I wasn't going to win this argument; I didn't even know why we were arguing! Geez, as if come election day my whole world would change.

"Don't you dare leave Sophia! This conversation isn't over." Kyle followed me out of the dining room, yelling at my back.

God, could he not get the hint? We were over. Where I went to study had nothing to do with him.

I walked into the lounge room. At least his parents didn't insist on me finishing dinner. At the bottom of the stairs, Kyle, still not getting the point, gripped my upper arm and pulled me to a stop. I twisted to look up at him. Rage was painted across his face.

"Are you on drugs or something?" I asked, a hint of concern clear in my voice. "Because you aren't making sense, Kyle. Your decisions aren't making sense."

"Drugs." He laughed sickly, shaking his head. "The fucking cause of all my problems."

I frowned. The Kyle I knew didn't do drugs. I had no idea what he meant by that.

His grip loosened, and he slowly ran his hand up my arm, across my shoulder, and up my neck until he was cupping my face. He took a noticeable step towards me into my personal space. God, he was close.

His other hand went to my hip and slowly moved around until it was on my lower back, and then he pushed me into him.

I would love to say my brain was screaming at me to push him away. But instead my mind was blank. Maybe from shock, I don't know. But it wasn't stopping what was happening. As Kyle handled me like I was still his.

"Can you not make any decisions until after the election? Please, tell me you won't lock anything in?" He spoke so softly. His eyes were painted with concern. "I need you to trust me."

I frowned up at him.

He was speaking like his life depended on the election and my decisions between now and then. Like he wanted to freeze me until that date.

Just as he dipped his head, my brain kicked back in gear, and I pulled away from him. I pushed his hand off my cheek. How the hell did I let myself get lost in his touch?

"I don't trust you, Kyle. And I won't ever be putting my future on hold for you." I stepped back onto the stairs. I was ready to turn and bolt, but hesitated. "You and I are done. There is nothing you can do to get me to trust you again. I will never, ever, let you into my life again." I finally found myself having a backbone. "We aren't in a relationship. We aren't friends. I'm never planning on that changing."

"You love me still. You can't lie to me about that."

I clamped my mouth shut. Yeah, I still did love him. But one day that love would turn into hate. "We are done," I said firmly.

"No, we aren't. We will never be done."

"I'm seeing someone."

His eyes widened. "No." He shook his head. "There's no fucking way you are dating someone else."

"I am, Kyle." I wasn't going to explain that Bax and I weren't really dating each other. I didn't want to ease the worry on Kyle's face right now as he panicked.

"Who?" his voice went up. "Who is it!" he rudely demanded like I had to tell him.

"No one you know." I crossed my arms.

"Try me," he gritted out. "Wouldn't be my brother, would it?" His words dipped into sinister and disgust. "I saw you in his bed. I saw you barely wearing a fucking thing, sleeping in his bed!"

That took me by surprise. "No. It's not Josh."

"Don't lie to me!"

"I'm not."

"You always had a thing for him."

I gasped. I couldn't believe he just said that. "You know what, Kyle, you aren't mine anymore. I don't answer to you. I have to let you go, and clearly you need to let me go!"

He shook his head. "I still remember our first date. I still remember how that red dress clung to your perfect body. I still remember every date we had after that." His hand spread across my cheek like he was holding onto me for dear life. "Every night we spent together, every day I spent with you, it's on repeat in my head. Reliving those memories keeps me going. Hoping."

"You're holding onto a memory, Kyle. You're not mine anymore. You walked out on our relationship. You need to let me go. My love for you is unconditional, but it was you who broke me into pieces." The sadness I felt every day cracked through my voice and he surely heard it. "I still love you. But those pieces are so small that I can't be put back together."

It was the truth; for the first time I wasn't putting up a front with him.

"Don't say that, Soph. Don't say I destroyed you." His voice echoed heartbreak and sadness.

Tears swelled up in my eyes. I couldn't stop them if I wanted to. "You are like my own personal drug, and now I'm going through withdrawals. The only way I am going to survive and get some sort of life back is by letting you go."

He shook his head. "Nope. Not happening. You aren't giving up on me. You have to trust me. You can't give up on me."

The tears fell from my eyes. "You need to let us go, Kyle. You aren't mine anymore, and I'm not yours." How was it possible that he was breaking my heart more right now? I thought he had destroyed it beyond a beating organ.

"I love you, Soph. Please don't walk away from me. I need you." He touched his forehead against mine. "I'll always need you."

I did something I knew I might regret. I reached out for him, my hands running across his shoulders. I didn't know what to say.

"Whoever you are seeing, break it off. Just trust me for three months. Just put your faith in me," he begged, his voice soft, gentle, and pleading. "I've never hurt you."

I felt it hit my core. "Yes, you have, Kyle. You ruined me. You turned me into this cold, hard, empty woman. You took what made me, me, and you destroyed it." I looked him in the eye, tears swelling and falling just as quick.

"I miss your lipstick on my neck and on my tops. I miss the way you would wrap yourself around me when you slept. I miss you, Soph. I miss everything about you. Every day. And every day I'm reminded of what I lost. Whenever I look at you, I'm reminded that I lost you." He gazed was fixed on me, and I was sure he was close to crying.

"You changed, Kyle." I took my hand off him and leaned back. "The things you are missing are easily replaced. I'm sure your new girlfriend will kiss you the way I did and love you the way I do and will have traits that you love about her."

"Fuck Kayla," he said. "Don't give up on me, Soph. You told me once you would always be mine and I need you to keep your word."

"What are you hoping to achieve by making me—no, forcing me to wait for you to change your mind?"

"You said you loved me. You told me it all the time. I'm counting on that love still being there."

My face softened, and I felt pity for him. "I will never forget you, but I can't live in the past. I knew from the moment I met you I would love you until the day I died." Time wouldn't change the fact I would always love him. "You will forever be in my heart, Kyle, but I can't stand here and tell you that I'm able to hold on to you on the chance you change your mind. Can't you understand that holding onto you will kill me in the end?"

It would kill the new me, the old me, and any version of me I tried to create.

I couldn't hold on to him. It wasn't healthy. But more importantly, why was he asking me to when he had a new girlfriend? One he loved. One he spent all his time with. One he was making new memories with.

He wiped the tears away from under my eyes with an expression that reached into my chest and pulled on what was left of my heart. "I love you, Soph. The last thing I want to do is hurt you more." He leaned in and gently kissed my forehead. "I'll let you go."

A dim smile traced my lips. "You already have, Kyle. You just don't realize it." Every day he woke up with Kayla, every day they spent together, he was writing over the past him and I had. He was making a future with someone else, and I had to accept that. I just didn't know how I was going to.

"It's going to kill me you know."

I frowned. "What is?"

"Seeing you move on from me." He gulped like his heart was breaking. "I don't know if I can see you with another guy. Let alone accept you being with someone that isn't me."

"Well, what did you expect to happen when we broke up?"

"I thought I would have fixed it by now." He looked at me honestly. "I thought by now I would have figured out some way to get you back. Not fucking letting you go."

He looked like he was in pain, like letting me go would kill him. I ran my hand across his cheek. I hated seeing him in pain. I knew I should be happy seeing him suffer, but I guess the old me wasn't completely dead.

"If it makes you feel better, he doesn't compare to you. I think you only get the love of your life once, you know? A one shot, one chance deal. And we just didn't make it."

There was a stage where I pictured our life together, right down to grandkids. I knew it was thinking way too far ahead for a high school romance, but I honestly thought we would make it. I thought what we had was unbreakable—was so strong it would see decades out.

He ran his hand down my arm and linked his hand with mine. It felt so natural and I didn't realize how much I missed it until my hand was back in his.

"I know what you mean, Soph. I fucked us up. Our chance. Our future. I just hope that one day you will understand why I did it." He squeezed my hand. "I will regret what I did every day for the rest of my life because it cost me you."

I looked him in the eye. Wasn't he forgetting something? "But at the same time, it gave you Kayla, and she really loves you." I sighed. It was hard to admit that. "You can't regret ending us when it has led you to another woman. One you could very well marry." I put on a fake smile and pulled my hand from his. "You should go back to the dining room. She will be looking for you."

He scoffed but didn't say anything.

I felt like I was missing something, but the more I looked at him the more I didn't see what it was I was missing.

"I need to change 'cause my night plans just got wiped," I said. I had to get out of this house and away from him. That meant I was heading to my favorite distraction.

I couldn't stand here and go over things we couldn't change. Him and I were over. No amount of him saying how much he missed me, or longed for me back, was going to change that. It wasn't like he was going to break up with Kayla and get back together with me. He didn't love me or miss me that much. The future we had planned, well, he didn't want it so badly that he was willing to break up with the girl that filled his every sex fantasy.

"Have a good night, Kyle." I wasn't sure what else to say.

"You going to him?" he said bitterly, stuffing his hands in his jeans pocket. "I'm just meant to let you change and go out with a guy that isn't me?"

Who the hell did he think he was? "Kyle. You ended us. So yes, you are meant to let me change and go and spend the night with another man. That's how a breakup works. You don't see me getting upset with you every time you and Kayla shut your bedroom door."

He ran both his hands through his hair, looking frustrated. "Fucking unbelievable," he muttered under his breath. I don't think I was meant to hear it. "This isn't meant to be happening. I thought what we had would last longer. I didn't see you moving on so soon."

I didn't know what to say, and I could only think of one way to end the conversation. So, I did it. I turned around and walked up the stairs, leaving Kyle at the bottom with a look on his face like it had just hit him. He'd lost me.

TWELVE

Soph

"Soph?"

I felt a kiss on my shoulder.

"Soph?" Bax whispered in my ear and his hand ran down my side.

I groaned but kept my eyes shut as his hands explored my body.

"Come on, darling, you need to wake up." He kissed my earlobe.

"Why?" I complained. His bed was so comfy. It was like a giant cloud that your body just sunk into. I loved Bax's bed.

"It's eight thirty," he whispered as he kissed my cheek.

"Still not seeing the importance," I groaned and kept my eyes shut. I loved the way his hand ran down my side.

As he gripped my hip, pulling me back towards him, I was forced to open my eyes. My hand automatically went out and ran down his jawline. He had a small smirk on his face as he looked down at me. We had done something we never did, and that was spend more than one night together. I thought he would kick me out the door come Sunday morning. Instead, I woke up to him making me breakfast and kissing me.

His good morning kiss yesterday really got to my head. To the point I was forcing him not to break it.

I titled my head, looking up at him, and wondered what he was thinking. I didn't know how to explain that look. I didn't care that I was naked under this sheet. I didn't care that he could see my completely naked body if he wanted to. But his eyes weren't exploring my body; they were locked with my eyes. And again, that look was still on his face, a smirk to go with it.

He moved his head down and kissed my collar bone. "I want to spend all day in this bed with you." He continued to kiss along my collarbone. "Take you over and over." He started to kiss up my neck, and my body was filled with tingles and my neck arched. "All day just you and me." He kissed the corner of my lips.

"I like the sounds of that." I linked my arms around his neck. "But I'm sure you have more important things to do than be with me." I brushed my lips against his.

His smirk got bigger. "I don't but you do."

I frowned. "No, I don't."

He laughed softly and dropped his mouth to my ear. "School starts in twenty minutes, darling."

My eyes went wide, and his laugh became harder as I scrambled off the bed and started searching for clothes.

"Why did you let me sleep in?" I asked as I searched the floor. Bax was always awake before me. How the hell did I forget it was a Monday? I swear sometimes he just woke up earlier to stare at me because every time I woke up, I would be tucked under his arm and he always had a smile on his face, like me waking up had made his day.

Bax got up and dressed. He still had a large smirk on his face as he watched me pull my jeans on. I found my top and groaned. "What's wrong, darling?" he asked as he lit up a cigarette.

"This." I showed him the stained top. "I can't wear this to school!" I doubted that even stain remover would save this white top.

He opened his draw and threw a top at me. "As much as I would love to see you walk around in your bra all day, I don't want any other man seeing it." He gave me a wink.

I threaded the long sleeve top on and used my hair tie to gather the top at the back so it fitted my body better, showing off some of my figure.

"Shit," I cursed just as I remembered my car had a flat. My head was still on the conversation I had had with Kyle and not on the road. So, I popped a tire.

"Guessing you just remembered your car is out of action?"

My head snapped to Bax. "What are you a mind reader this morning?"

"Come on, darling. I'll give you a lift."

I picked up my handbag. "Your reputation could be ruined if you're seen dropping me off."

He laughed. "If anything, being seen with you adds to my reputation." He wrapped his arms around me as soon as I was within distance.

His mouth went to my ear. "Being seen with you is every guy's wet dream."

I rolled my eyes. "No, it's not."

He shrugged his shoulders just as he let go of me and I put my shoes on. He leaned against the foyer wall, watching me. "How not? Every guy's dream is to get a girl like you in their bed."

I wanted to laugh. "Bax, you have an endless list of girls in your phone, and on the nights we aren't together, you are with one of them. So, don't act like I'm special, because I'm not. And I'm okay with that."

His eyes narrowed on me. "You think on the nights we aren't together I'm with other women?"

"Yep." I put my hands on my hips. "And that's fine because we're just having casual sex." Like I expected, I wasn't heartbroken by the thought of him with another woman. If anything, I was used the idea.

"What do I do on nights we aren't together?" He crossed his arms, looking pissed off.

"How the hell am I supposed to know?" I didn't know the answer to his question, and I really had to get moving for school.

"On nights we aren't together, I'm messaging you and calling you. Have I mentioned another woman?"

Well, when he put it like that... no, he hadn't. "Bax, what are you trying to tell me? You and I both agreed this was sex and nothing else." We didn't do feelings. We didn't do love, and this time last week we didn't spend more than a night or a day together. "You and I aren't a couple. I don't expect you to stop your lifestyle for me. Have sex with whoever you want. Hell, if you meet a girl you want more than a casual fling with, you can end what we have."

I was being reasonable, wasn't I? I was giving him what most guys wanted. So, I didn't understand why his expression hardened.

"What if I have met this girl I want more than a casual fling with, but she is the one not wanting more?"

I frowned. "Then I would say that girl is an idiot. You're a great guy, Bax. If she sees what I see, she wouldn't be turning you down."

For some reason what I said made him smile. "Maybe hope isn't lost after all." He looked at me, and again I was stumped on how to explain his expression. It was like he was hoping for me to change my mind about him or something. But our casual fling showed me, Bax couldn't do a relationship.

He reminded me of Josh in some ways — an outlaw that couldn't be tamed. No girl or woman could get an outlaw to truly love them because they were free spirits. I didn't know what Josh got up to, but I would take a stab and say that car he was working on in the shed wasn't legal and he hadn't bought it.

I also assumed he hadn't left his criminal side in prison and learned from his mistake, not that I knew what got him in prison to begin with. Nevertheless, if I had to compare Josh and Bax, Josh would win on who was the worst.

Bax might be a bad boy, but he wasn't deadly dangerous like Josh. Him and Josh weren't even in the same league. I knew where I stood with Bax: just a casual fling. But with Josh, well, with him I was starting a friendship, and for some stupid reason, I had feelings for Josh.

I still wasn't sure what that meant, but I knew I had to put a stop to those feelings. I wasn't going back to the girl that felt everything for everyone and lived on the thought that fairy tales happened. My eyes were open now, and I wasn't going to close them and fall back in love with anyone.

***

Bax's car said a lot about him. I nearly smiled when I first saw it because it just screamed everything about him. It was America muscle—a shiny black and a beast on the road. It was loud and dominating, and it scared other drivers off the road.

In fact, two cars had pulled over to get out of his way on the way to school. When it came to everything that Bax did, he didn't do what was expected of him. Like respect the road laws, or speed limit.

He sped to the school and double parked out the front, ignored the other cars that had their blinkers on looking for a space. His loud engine was roaring when he came to a stop. His eyes went off the road and he took the car out of gear.

"Do you want me to pick you up?" He had a smile on his face. I didn't expect that of him.

"Nope. All good. Thanks for dropping me off."

His hand ran up my thigh. "You busy tonight?"

"Bax, if we spend tonight together that would be three in a row, and you and I only ever do one night." I arched my eyebrows at him. "I know you have a life that doesn't involve me."

He was glaring out my window, and when I turned to see what had his attention, my expression dropped. Of course, Kyle would be out the front, and was standing there, glaring at us.

I wished Bax's car had tinted windows right now—illegal tint, the one you can't see through.

I looked back at Bax and sighed. "Ignore him. He's an ex-boyfriend."

Bax looked at back me. "So you do, do relationships?"

"Yeah, once. Never again."

"Because of that jerk?"

I rolled my eyes. "I have to go." My hand fell on the door handle. "Thanks for dropping me off." I got out, leaving Bax glaring at Kyle.

I walked away from the car. Kyle's eyes were on me and I knew he was going to give me a spray, even though he had no right to give me one. Maybe I should just walk past him and ignore him. I decided to try that.

He didn't deserve my attention. I was so set on ignoring him I jumped when an arm wrapped around my waist. I glanced down, recognized the tattoos, and as I relaxed back into his chest, I slowly turned around.

"You forgot something." Bax smiled down at me. It was a cheeky smile, and I saw his eyes glance at Kyle. When he looked me back in the eye, it was like he had something to prove.

"What?" I frowned. And then his lips were on mine. He pushed me firmly into his chest and held me there as he kissed me.

I was breathless when he pulled back. His hands were still on my lower back, holding me tight to his chest.

"I'll message you." He looked rather pleased with himself. As he let go of me, he shot a glare in Kyle's direction.

I was breathless and my fingers touched my lips—they were tingling.

"So, that's your boyfriend?"

I slowly turned around. I really didn't feel like facing him. Kyle's eyes were heated and the look on his face, well, it was enough to have me take a step back. I heard Bax's car pull away, and as it disappeared in the distance, I wished he was back here, standing behind me because Kyle's face was scaring me.

Kyle looked at my top and shook his head in disgust, pointing a finger at me. "Stay the fuck away from my brother." He spat the words at me like they were bitter and sour.

"What does Josh have to do with anything?" I sure as hell didn't know how Josh just entered this conversation. I was expecting Kyle to be spraying me about the man that had just claimed me in front of him, not bringing up Josh.

"I'm not fucking stupid, Sophia! Your top says it all!" With that said, he spun around and stormed off.

For the first time this morning I glanced down at my top. It said The Devil's Cut and had a logo in the middle.

My frown deepened. Why would Bax's biker club have anything to do with Josh?

If anything, it just proved to me that Bax was involved with them. It dawned on me I was going to have to spend the day walking around promoting an outlaw motorcycle club.

I sighed, wondering if he did it on purpose. I doubt he even glanced at the top he handed to me. I pulled my phone out of my jeans pocket, bringing up his number.

Did you notice what top you gave me? I sent.

My phone buzzed in my hand and I unlocked it.

Wanted everyone to know who protects you.

My mouth fell open and I let out a sharp breath. I was not protected by anyone. I sure as hell wasn't protected by a motorcycle club.

I don't need protecting.

And I didn't. I didn't need protecting from anything. Wasn't like I was one of those girls that attracted trouble or anything.

I started to walk through the school gates and my phone went off my hand again.

You are right, cause I'll be doing it personally. But in case I fail, the club won't.

I stared down at the phone, frozen at the entrance. Suddenly, I had a feeling Bax wasn't looking at me like a casual fuck anymore. He wouldn't want to personally protect a casual woman he is having sex with, would he?

I didn't know the answer. And I didn't know what to write back, so I locked the phone. But his message kept running through my mind.

* * *

I glared at my English teacher as he explained yet another poem, twisting it and turning it from a romance piece into a suicide note.

How the fuck can you go from romance to a poem about death? I sure as hell didn't see it and I was trying my best to give him my attention while the voice that was born to grate on my nerves spoke right behind me.

"Babe, I'm telling you this poem fits us perfectly," Kayla said so sweetly.

Was she even listening to the teacher? He was saying it was a death letter, and she was comparing it to their romance?

I leaned back in my chair, crossing my arms. Last class of the day and it was dragging.

"Babe, how about we skip studying tonight and head to the coast for a few hours?" Kyle's voice shocked me.

I had not heard him once speak to her like that. He normally ignored her or grunted. And he never made plans with her.

"Really?" Kayla's voice went up.

Looks like I wasn't the only one to notice the relationship had been one-sided. The coast. That was where he would take me when he wanted to spend alone time. Just me and him. No distractions.

"Yeah, of course, babe. Some you and me time sounds perfect." Kyle's voice was honest and sweet.

I felt automatically disgusted. Was he doing that on purpose? To make me jealous and piss me off? Well, it had fucking worked.

I immediately entered a dirty mood, and I wasn't just jealous—I was seeing red. How could he take her to our place? To our getaway!

Everything he had said the other night was nothing but a lie.

Why the hell did I even give him a second of my time? Well, I wouldn't do it again.

I made a decision right then and there to never again let Kyle fool me with fake love.

I pulled out my phone. I knew one way to get under his skin: do something he told me not to. Suddenly I felt like a rebel, and I had something to prove. I checked the teacher was at the front, explaining his stupid poem to the front of the class. Yep, his attention wasn't on me. So, I pressed dial.

I listened to it ring, and I hoped this plan was going to work. If he didn't answer, the plan of pissing Kyle off like he had pissed me off would fail.

Just as I thought he wasn't going to answer. Josh barked a very unfriendly hello into the phone and my lips twitched up at hearing his voice.

"Hey, Josh." I put a fake smile on my face. I said it loud enough so big ears Kyle could hear my conversation. He wanted to make me jealous. Well, I could make him jealous. He was the one who had got the idea in his head that I was with Josh. Well, I was going to use that against him.

"Soph?"

"Yep, it's me. I have a favor to ask."

Josh went quiet for a minute and the noise in the background quietened.

"You hurt?"

"Nope."

"Did that fucker of a man you seeing cross a line? Because I'm telling you, Soph, I'll take care of it."

A small smile twitched across my lips, which was real, and then I made my fake one light up.

"It isn't anything like that. I was hoping you could pick me up. My car is out of action."

"Guessing you don't want to car ride with Kyle and his woman."

I scoffed. "I would rather walk on hot stones than get in a car with Kyle and his slut of a girlfriend," I said, loud enough for them to hear. I heard Kayla scoff.

"They're around, aren't they?" If Josh was standing in front of me, he would have a smirk on his face, and I suspect a look that told me he was proud of me. I wasn't the type of person to bad mouth anyone. "You really want to piss him off?"

My eyes lit up with delight. "Yes, I do." Would Josh help me get back at Kyle? My hopes skyrocketed at the thought. Josh was always cleverer than me.

"Repeat the following back to me. I didn't realize your shower was so small with two in it."

I wanted to grin because that was going to eat Kyle up. "I didn't realize your shower was so small with two in it."

"Now say, I love your back tattoo, but I really love what it stands for."

I frowned for a second—I didn't know Josh had any tattoos, but then quickly plastered a fake smile on and even forced a blush. "I love your back tattoo, but I really love what it stands for."

"I think that will do, baby girl. Well done. You have successfully pissed him off," Josh said with a tone of pride in his voice. "I'll pick you up in half an hour."

"Actually, can you head to me now? I really want to escape." I wasn't putting on a show now. I was serious. And Josh would have known that by the way my voice wasn't as light.

"Okay, I'm coming."

"Thank you, Josh. I'll see you soon." I took the phone from my ear and hung up.

I gathered my books up.

"You are dating Josh!"

I rolled my eyes. Should have expected her to have questions. I slowly turned around and kept my fake smile on. I looked at Kayla, for once seeing her in her true light with a heavy makeup facade and her knock-off designer perfume hanging in the air.

"What can I say?" I glanced at Kyle, who was glaring at me. "I like them bad." I picked up my books and stood up. "You know, Kayla, if I was you, I would get a vibrator to make up for the times Kyle leaves you wanting." I shrugged. "I don't have that problem anymore. I found out a boy has sex with you, but a man… he pleasures you." I shot her a final smile. "Just a tip."

And with all that said, I turned around and walked away from Kyle, not feeling even slightly bad for what I did. Payback was a bitch, right? And he had just been slapped with a cold reality check. The old Soph wouldn't have had the guts to do that—fight fire with fire.

It was the first time I fought dirty. And I had to say, it felt good.

THIRTEEN

Soph

I kept wondering why people were staring at me as I walked down the hall and cut through the canteen. When I came to a stop out the front of the school gates, I ran a hand through my hair. I hadn't exactly got ready this morning. I'm sure it showed how I spent my weekend—in bed with a man.

"Didn't take you as a supporter."

I frowned and looked to my right. A guy I had never seen before was speaking to me. I had no idea what he was talking about, so I turned my head back and waited for Josh.

"You know, you have been the news of the school," he continued.

I groaned. Why couldn't I be left alone? I turned to face him, as much as I didn't want to. "I have no idea what you're talking about."

"Come on, you're out of school uniform. That brings attention. But that top..." He stepped towards me, and I noticed that he was also out of uniform, with ripped jeans, a loose T-shirt, and piercings everywhere. Why was he judging me on being out of the uniform when, from one glance at him, I was positive he didn't even own one?

Finally, his words registered. "What am I putting on display?" Tilting my head, I turned around completely and stepped towards him, really interested in the answer.

He nodded his head to my top. "You are a supporter of The Devil's Cut. One look at you and everyone knows you aren't club property. So, you must be dating someone in the club—and high enough up that you aren't looked at as just another girl. Someone's claiming you."

I think all expression was wiped from my face. Was that why everyone was staring at me today? Because they thought I was dating a Devil Cut member and that Bax had claimed me? I didn't realize wearing something with their name on it made you a supporter. I didn't know that this top was screaming, "I'm taken by a Devils Cut member."

There was a beep behind me, and I glanced over my shoulder, seeing Josh in the car, waiting.

The guy laughed, and I looked back at him.

"What?" I asked. This explained why every male I went near today did a double take and then backed away like I was toxic. I let out a frustrated groan when the guy didn't stop laughing. "What the hell is so funny?" I yelled at him.

He nodded his head to Josh's car, his laughter stopping. "I see you've gone to the top of the food chain."

What the hell did that mean?

He was mad. Insane. I was talking to an insane person. With that, I spun around and headed for the car. It wasn't like I was in a great mood all day. But my mood was really foul now. Did Bax know what he was doing with his little stunt? That I had spent the day walking around not just assumed to be a supporter of him and his club, but also his woman.

I was nobody's woman.

I opened the door roughly and got in, throwing my handbag on the floor and slamming the door shut.

"Okay, who pissed you off?" Josh's eyes were on me.

"I'm not pissed off. I'm furious." I turned to look at him. "Can I hire you to kill someone?"

He broke out laughing. "I'm not killing my brother." He pulled out onto the road. "Anyway, who said I'm a violent person?"

"I've known you long enough to know your character." I turned and looked him in the eyes. "And you, Josh, are a hot head."

His laughter continued as he shook his head. "Apart from wanting to kill my brother, how was your day?" he asked easily.

I crossed my arms and glared out the window. I did not want to repeat how my day was. It was crap. Not only did I have to suffer through school, but I also walked around basically yelling to the world that I was claimed by a Devil's Cut member.

I was going to punish Bax for this.

"Come on, what's up?" Josh nudged my arm. "Furious doesn't suit you."

I rolled my eyes and kept glaring out the window.

"Well, if you aren't going to tell me how was school, how was your weekend? Haven't seen you since you disappeared."

I sighed and realized I couldn't be rude. He did stop what he was doing to pick me up.

"My weekend was great until this morning."

"Okay, now we are getting somewhere. What happened this morning?"

I didn't need to nut down and figure out why I was in a bad mood. It was all thanks to Bax.

Josh reached over and put a hand on my thigh, which caused me to look at him. "Soph, what happened this morning?" His words were gentle, kind, and sweet—all things you wouldn't think Josh could be if you glanced at him. Hell, you wouldn't even take a second glance at him, the first would tell you he was dangerous, and if you stared, he was likely to break something in your body.

"Doesn't matter," I finally said. I didn't know how to explain my situation. Josh was in a world much darker than mine. Probably darker than Bax's as well. Josh didn't need to hear my complaints or worry about how my day was. I'm sure he had much more important things to worry about.

"Soph, just tell me what happened." He wasn't giving up.

I didn't know where to start. So, I started at the beginning. "I spent the weekend with this guy." Who I thought was alright until about ten minutes ago... "Anyway, my day started shit. I slept in and my top was stained, so I borrowed one of his. Didn't think much of it. Then school was school… and…" My words dried up.

"And?" Josh asked.

I didn't say anything. My temper was going up thinking about it.

Josh gave my thigh a squeeze, and I sighed. I didn't know how to say it, so I just showed him. Hell, he would notice when I got out of the car, anyway.

I unstrapped my seat belt and turned, "What does this tell you?" I said, putting my shirt on display.

Josh's eyes glanced from the road to me and then he did a double take. His expression dropped, and I saw his knuckles slowly turn white as he gripped the steering wheel tighter.

"Did you pick that top?" Josh's words were coming out ridged and forced, like he was controlling what he was really thinking. I was guessing that whatever he was thinking was on the line of disgust.

"No, he gave it to me." I turned back around and strapped in. "All day I've walked around wearing it, not having a clue what it was telling people. How I could I not know that wearing a top like this said something?"

I was frustrated with myself, I was pissed off at Kyle, and I wanted to wrap my hands around Bax's neck for doing this to me.

Josh's eyes narrowed, and he shook his head, looking nearly as furious as how I felt.

"All day I've been wearing this! I can't believe Bax would do that to me. We have a casual fling. Nothing else. Then he goes and basically puts a claim on me. Somehow, he managed to tell the whole world I was dating a member of the Devils Cut, and I'm not even dating him!" As soon as one word escaped, I just kept blurting words out. My frustration was getting the best of me.

"You sure about that?"

My head flung to the side to look at Josh. "What do you mean?"

"You sure you aren't dating him?" Josh said again, confirming where I thought he was taking this conversation.

He pulled up in front of his house and I shook my head in disbelief. My eyes locked with his and the anger I was feeling towards Bax was all redirected at Josh for asking that question.

I got out of the car and headed for the house. I didn't give a fuck if he followed me or not.

"Soph!" He got out and called after me. He could go get fucked. Everyone could go get fucked.

I heard him getting closer as I reached into my handbag, feeling for the spare key Louise gave me. Of course, this would be the moment I couldn't find anything inside.

Josh stood behind me. "Soph, come on, it's a reasonable question."

Oh, he did not just say that! I flung around, giving up on finding the keys, and I shoved him back. "How dare you! How dare you assume I'm some stupid girl who doesn't know if she is in a relationship or not!" My rage was coming out.

His hands landed on my shoulders.

"Soph, calm down." He said it like it was an order. Who was he to give anyone orders?

"No. You can fuck off because you're a male and I'm finished with males!" I spun back and started searching my handbag again.

Bax could piss off, Kyle could go jump off a cliff into shark-infested waters, and Josh, well, he can take those assumptions and apply them to a girl who was going to be more than a friend to him.

Josh reached around me and put his key in the door, unlocking it.

I was quick to push it open and bolt, but he wrapped a hand around my upper arm as soon as we entered and pushed the door closed.

"Come here, Soph." He was being kind and gentle and sweet again, even though I had just told him to fuck off. Did he miss the part where I said I was finished with all males?

He took my handbag off my shoulder and dumped it in the foyer floor. His hands went behind my back and he undid the hair tie, which was holding the T-shirt. Then his hands went under the top and my eyes went wide. What was he doing? He slowly pulled the top up and then gripped it, gently taking it off me.

I threaded my arms out of it, and then the realization that I was standing just in a bra in front of Josh hit me. I should have been scrambling away. I should be panicked. I shouldn't have felt calm and confident, like I was comfortable with him seeing my body. I never have been ashamed of my body, but I was always nervous showing it.

But that didn't happen in front of Josh. This was the second time I felt those two things in front of him: calm and confident.

His eyes ran down me; I think it was only naturally for them to.

"The shirt was the problem. The shirt is going. Problem solved." He gave me a reassuring smile. "Maybe next time don't let your boyfriend dress you."

I bit my bottom lip for a second and then looked up at him, meeting his eyes. "Bax isn't my boyfriend. I'm never being in a relationship again. Ever." My heart was locked up — what was left of it—and I wasn't willing or prepared to ever risk what I had left.

Josh kept staring into my eyes. "Soph, you can't wipe every guy off, just because Kyle was a dick." Josh dropped the shirt on the ground and his hands landed on my hips as he frowned. Then his eyes ran down my body, like he was inspecting it. "You still not eating?"

Suddenly I wished I was still wearing that stupid shirt. I crossed my arms and took a step away from him, his hands falling off my hips.

"Thanks, Josh." I forced a smile and turned around and headed for the stairs.

I left him standing down there. Not answering his question. Truth was, I wasn't eating. I really didn't see the problem anymore. I was still surviving. My body was still working. When it really wanted food; I would eat.

I closed my bedroom door. It was only Monday, and I already knew it was going to be one long ass week.

FOURTEEN

Josh

I lit another cigarette. I was down to my last few because I had been chain smoking since we got to the strip club. Didn't matter which girl was in front of me. Didn't matter if she was stripping or dancing naked. My head was somewhere else. Somewhere it shouldn't be. I ran a hand through my hair, the frustration getting the best of me. I was frustrated with myself. I never had this... feeling? I didn't even know what to fucking call it.

Why couldn't I get lost in the naked girls like everyone else? All the boys seemed to be enjoying it, throwing money and getting lap dances. And what was I doing? Fucking feeling like this. Most of the guys paid the strippers to lie to them, most of the guys were willing to pay them for an easy lay.

When we weren't at the club, we were here. I had never felt more disconnected. I glanced down my phone. Her number was up, and it was taking all my will power not to message her.

The normal questions ran through my mind:

Was she okay?

What was she doing?

Is she asleep? She should be, but it was a Saturday night. She could be out.

Who was she out with?

Did I have a right to ask that?

Questions liked these continued to flood my mind. Soph was literally stuck in my head. Ever since Monday I hadn't been able to think of anything else but her. It wasn't like her and I had a special moment. It wasn't like we fell in love or anything. When I really thought about it, hell, she literally got stuck in my head as soon as I saw her again in that bathroom after all those years.

But since Monday, she had withdrawn completely. She wasn't home—she never was. And by Bax's attitude, I knew she wasn't spending time with him. He was in the worst mood. I looked up to see him glaring down at his phone.

I don't know what happened between Soph and him, but whatever had happened caused him to be even more of a dick. He was here even though he wasn't meant to be seen with us. It was like he didn't give a fuck anymore whether he got locked up or not.

All week I had been busy with the club. All week my mind was meant to be focused on our business. Instead, every spare second, my mind was drifting to Soph. That look in her eyes as she stood half naked in front of me. That look... it had me. I couldn't explain why she would be looking at me like that. I didn't understand what the look meant. It was as if she felt safe. I had never seen a girl look at me like that. It was messing with my head.

Cold stares, jealous glares, and a pleading look of need or lust—I knew those looks and dealt with them regularly around the club from girls.

But the look Soph gave me was... I couldn't fucking explain it. It was driving me insane.

I butted the cigarette out and immediately lit another.

My phone was still in my hand, and I was thinking of one reason, one good reason, to message her after one in the morning. I didn't want to wake her up, but something was telling me she wasn't asleep.

I looked up at Bax who had just threw his phone on the table and grabbed another beer. He was drinking heavily tonight. He was throwing down a lot of cash as well but wasn't one bit interested in the girls.

This was the only time ever that Bax and I had something in common. We both had our minds on something else. I didn't know who was controlling his thoughts. But mine were on a tiny blonde with the most dazzling hazel eyes and red lips. Her skin was so soft. The type of soft one ever believes is real. And while she was small, I had never seen a more perfect body. Her laugh just made you smile. Even thinking about it had my lips twitching up. When it came to Soph, she brought out another side to me. A side I didn't know. The feelings I felt for her were a fucking mystery to me.

I unlocked my phone. Her number was already on my screen, but I couldn't think of one excuse why to message her.

Was it normal to message after one in the morning asking if she was okay?

Nah, I couldn't do that.

I started to shake my knee up and down, thinking. Come on… one reason that was all I needed.

The guys got louder as the group of girls increased and it started to piss me off. I didn't give a fuck about those naked girls.

Maybe I could just head home and hope she was there?

Yeah, that was an idea. An accidental run-in.

But what if she wasn't home and was out at a party? I'd just spend the night hoping she would come home and then when she didn't, I wouldn't be able to stop my mind running with all the possibilities.

I decided I was messaging her. I unlocked my phone again.

I'd just keep it simple.

R u up? I sent it. Bloody hell, it was just a message, but my brain went into overdrive. What if she was serious when she said she was done with males and had cut me off already? What if she moved on from Bax and she was way too busy with the next guy to check her phone.

My mind went wild with ideas as it tended to do when Soph was involved. It was like she injected my brain with drugs which causes it to race and over think every little detail.

My phone buzzed in my hand and I looked down. She actually wrote back, which meant she was up. I just stared at her name on my screen for a few more seconds before I unlocked it and opened the message.

Just got home. U?

She had been out. I stared at the screen a little longer. Well, if she was home that was a solid reason to head there. Then again, she could be heading back out. I sighed. I didn't know what she was up to this week.

I guess I had one question, so I started to type it.

U staying home?

I stared at the screen, seeing she had read it. I knew for a fact Kyle had taken Kayla to the coast for the weekend, and Mum and Dad were out of town.

That meant if I head home right now, it would just be me and Soph.

The speech bubble appeared at the bottom of the screen. She was writing back to me.

"Hey, Josh, you want another round?" Gazza barked at me, causing me to look up.

"What?"

"Another round? Do you want on?" He looked at me like I was stupid.

The fact I had hadn't been paying attention had managed to get everyone else's.

Even Wolf was giving me an odd look.

I glanced down at my phone.

Yep.

That was all I needed to know. I stood up. "Nah, I'm heading home. But I'll pay." I pulled out my wallet and threw down a bunch of fifties. I looked at Wolf and he gave me a head nod which meant he wasn't questioning me as to why I was bailing on their Saturday night.

I walked out of the darkly lit strip club. I had to go back to the club, change the bike to the car, and take off my vest and leave it in the dorm room.

I knew one day I wouldn't be able to hide how I spent my time, or who I really was. The word was starting to get around now. But that didn't mean I was about to tell Soph tonight.

* * *

The house was dark when I pulled up to it. I locked my car and walked up the porch steps, the security light coming on. I twisted the doorknob. At least it was locked. I unlocked it and entered to the foyer that was dark.

I was about to go up the stairs but stopped when I heard a noise, which sounded like it came from the kitchen. I walked through the lounge and saw the lights on in the kitchen, and I heard her curse as I walked in.

"What are you doing?"

She jumped as she spun around, dropping whatever she was holding.

There was white powder across her cheek.

"Are you doing drugs or something?" I asked as I walked towards her, feeling the most relaxed I had felt all week. Just being in her company relaxed me and I didn't know why.

She stepped out of the way of whatever she was trying to hide from me. I frowned, seeing the large tub.

"The school nurse reported my weight to the counsellor. Apparently, I'm too thin." She crossed her arms and shot a glare at the large tub of protein powder. "Honestly, they are making it out like I'm a second away from being anorexic."

I looked at her. She was wearing a long black singlet that showed off her figure. She was thin, but she hadn't entered unhealthy yet. I think she was only a couple of kilograms away from it. They clearly had noticed this as well.

I asked her if she had been eating on Monday. She hadn't given me an answer then. "So, you are doing protein powder?"

She sighed and picked up the scoop from the floor. "Well, I got told if I exercise, I have to have a protein drink. I ran for nearly two hours, so I'm just doing what I'm told."

My head snapped to look at her. "You ran for two hours!"

She shrugged. "I can run for nearly three. I'm getting fitter."

She couldn't be serious right now. "Soph, running for two hours isn't fucking healthy."

She rolled her eyes. "I like how I feel after a run."

Suddenly it wasn't just her eating patterns that were setting off warnings. She was exercising aggressively like she was punishing her body.

"What have you eaten today?" I crossed my arms, standing in front of her. I saw her squirm.

"Um, stuff."

"Start naming what you've eaten, Sophia."

She groaned. "Please don't call me that! Why must you be on my back too? Everyone else is already on my back about it. God, I'm not that thin!"

I gripped her shoulder and gently pushed her around to face me. "What have you eaten today?"

She sighed and looked up at me. "I can't remember."

"Well start trying. Breakfast, what did you eat?"

"Didn't."

"Lunch?"

She frowned and then looked like she remembered. "An apple. It was a green one, they're my favorite."

Just don't snap at her. She clearly doesn't see what's happening. "Ok, what about dinner?"

"Skipped it because I went for a run." She shrugged.

"So, all you've fucking eaten all day is an apple!" I gritted out, trying to keep my anger in check. She couldn't be serious, standing in front of me saying she didn't have a problem when all she had eaten was an apple!

"Well, and this shake I'm making." She looked up at me, frowning. "It's not a big deal. Some days I have less."

"Less than an apple?"

"Calm down, Josh." She rolled her eyes and turned around, picking up the lid to the protein powder and twisting it on. "God, you are acting like I've just told you a horror story."

"What are you doing?"

I watched her pack up. "I'm going to bed."

"No, you aren't!" I snapped. I would admit that came out rude and controlling. I assumed she had taken it that by the way she turned around and looked up at me. Yep. It had come across exactly the way I had said.

Well, she needed a rude awakening.

"We are ordering takeout and you aren't going to sleep until I've filled you up with carbs." I pulled my phone out.

"No! Not happening. I am not stuffing my face!" She reached for my phone, but I held it above her head. She didn't have a chance of getting it from me.

"It's not stuffing your face. It's called eating."

"I don't eat junk food."

I rolled my eyes. "The old Soph did." Her hazel eyes sliced through me.

"Well, the new Soph doesn't eat shit. I admit I'm not eating much. But it's not like I go weeks without eating—maybe a day or two and then my body will remind me I haven't eaten."

My expression dropped. "You go days without eating?"

She exhaled slowly and then nodded her head. "It's not a big deal."

What the fuck had happened to her? What the hell sort of damage had Kyle done? How can she stand here in front of me and say she doesn't eat for days but everything is fine? It wasn't a big deal?

I knew she was struggling with the breakup, but clearly, I didn't realize how much. She was putting on a good show for everyone. And fuck, I fell for it.

But she wasn't okay. She sure as fuck wasn't coping—she was punishing herself. The sad part was she didn't even see it.

"Well, if you don't want junk. What do you want?" I was going to be reasonable. If she hadn't been eating and had been avoiding all junk food, that meant her stomach couldn't take the greasy food I had planned for.

"It's okay, Josh. I can just go to bed. Start fresh tomorrow." She gave me a small smile, like the last thing she wanted was to bother me.

Didn't she see by now that she wasn't a bother? It wasn't like she was forcing me to care; I just did. I realized that in that moment I cared. I cared if she ate or not. I cared if she was abusing her body.

As a friend. This was what a friendship was like, right?

"Name it and I'll get it for you." I took a step closer to her, blocking her between the kitchen island and me. "Anything, Soph, what do you want?"

She bit her bottom lip. "You'll think it's stupid."

"Try me." Whatever she wanted she was getting. And then, as of tomorrow, I was going to make sure she ate breakfast, lunch, and dinner.

"I feel like Nutella on toast." Her lips twitched up.

Getting something overly sweet into her sounded like a good idea.

"Let's go."

"What, where?" She frowned, and I took her hand. God, she was cold.

"You cold?" I asked.

"Um, yeah. It's another thing I do these days. I don't dress appropriately for the weather."

"You don't have the heating on either." I shook my head. "Why?"

"Because I didn't see a point in running up your parent's electricity bill when I'm the only one home."

It was one of her best qualities the way she cared for other people. But it was also one of her biggest weaknesses. I let go of her hand and took my hoodie off.

"Josh, you don't have to give me your jumper. I can go up and get something from my room." She looked at the jumper I was handing her.

For some reason, I didn't know why, something inside me wanted her to take it. As if her wearing my hoodie meant something more than just her wearing it to keep warm.

"Arms up," I said when she still was hesitant about wearing it.

She sighed and then put her arms up. I took pleasure in her doing something I wanted, and it flooded my whole body. I shouldn't have been so pleased with her, just for doing something I asked, but I was. Still, I wasn't sure if that was out of friendship or not.

It swallowed her, dropping down below her knees.

She pulled her hair out and smiled at me. "It smells like you." She pushed up the sleeves.

"Good or bad thing?"

Her smile got wider, and I wasn't sure if it was one of her real smiles or not.

"Great thing," she said. I wasn't expecting that. Then she did something else I wasn't expecting—she slipped her hand in mine.

I was always the one to touch her. She never touched me. Her eyes ran up me until they locked with mine. She looked like she wasn't sure if she had crossed a line or not.

I couldn't stop the smile and it was automatic to link our hands. I heard her exhale slowly, like she had been holding on to her breath, while she waited for my decision on whether she had crossed a line or not.

When it came to Soph, there wasn't any boundaries or rules she could break. Well, not when it came to me anyway. My normal rules when it came to women didn't apply to her. I glanced behind me as she followed me through the house, looking at the ground.

Maybe my normal rules didn't apply to her because she was a friend? Was that the reason? Something in my gut told me there was another reason. I was either too stupid to see it, or I was right about the friendship thing?

***

"What were you doing before you took pity on me and came home?" Soph asked, munching on her toast.

She was eating. Thank fuck for that. Now I was just going to make sure she kept doing it. She was used to her pattern of not eating for days and exercising intensely. I was going to have to break that habit. How do you go about making someone eat? I couldn't force the food down her throat. She wouldn't eat anything loaded in carbs, which told me she was watching what she ate.

"Earth to, Josh." She clicked her fingers in my face.

Right, she asked a question. "What did you ask?"

She rolled her eyes and swallowed her toast before answering. "You really aren't listening to me, are you? You know you can go to bed. It is late."

"Nah. My mind was just somewhere else. What did you ask?" I turned on the bar stool to face her.

"What were you doing before you came here after taking pity on me?" She turned on her bar stool to face me too, forgetting about her food.

"You keep eating and I'll tell you."

She rolled her eyes. "I've eaten half a piece!"

"And I want you to have both pieces." I nodded towards the food. "Keep eating."

She sighed and picked up a piece of toast.

"You are forcing me to eat." Yes, I was.

She took a bite. "Okay, tell me what you were doing." She turned back to face me, her toast in hand.

What could I say? I couldn't really tell her what I was doing. I hated lying to her, but I didn't see another option.

"At a friend's," I lied, and I hoped she didn't press me on it.

She arched her eyebrows and slowly chewed a piece of toast, and I knew by her expression I was in trouble.

"So, we lie to each other now?" she said, looking at me unimpressed. She also did something I didn't want her doing, and that was stop eating.

I sighed. "I was with my friends."

She looked at me a bit harder. "Uh huh. You are leaving parts out…" She chewed her bottom lip and glanced down at her toast, then looked me back in the eye. "But that's okay. You don't have to tell me everything." That had me wanting to groan. I did want to be honest with her. I did want to tell her where I was and who I was with. But I couldn't, and it was for her own good.

"What did you do tonight?" I tried to change the subject. I guess I shouldn't expect her to be honest with me when I couldn't be honest with her.

I think that thought ran through her head too as she looked at me. Yeah, she was weighing up if she was going to tell me or not.

"I was…" She sighed and put her toast down. "You wouldn't believe me."

No. She wouldn't believe me if I told her what I had been doing tonight. I doubt anything she could have done would surprise me. "Try me. Keep eating."

She groaned and then took the tiniest bite she could take and swallowed it. "Promise you won't judge?"

Hell, I should be saying that to her. "You know I won't." That was the truth. I would never judge anything she did, but I would help encourage her to make better decisions.

"I was stripping."

"You were fucking what?"

"I told you, you wouldn't believe me." She took another bite of the toast, not seeming one bit fussed by my reaction.

I couldn't form words. I couldn't wrap my head around what she just said. "You were like... stripping at a club or something?" The words just fell out. I couldn't, no, I wouldn't believe that she was doing that. She was too far above that. Surely, she had more respect for herself?

No man deserved to be able to see her naked. It should be a sin. In fact, I'm sure it is. It was sinful to take in her perfect body, her well-shaped breasts, and the way her body had this perfect curve.

"Wasn't like it was in front of men." She decided to now only add that detail. "God, wipe that look off your face!" She pushed my shoulder.

"So, it wasn't at a club? You aren't becoming a stripper or anything?" I think I was still panicking.

She shrugged. "Well, I don't know."

"What do you mean?"

"Well, it is for a job bar tending and dancing. But it's not like I'll be stripping."

"You aren't fucking doing it." Nope. Never. Ever. Happening.

"Why?"

I scoffed. She wanted to know why I wouldn't let her dance and strip and fall into that side of life. "Because I said so," I replied firmly. "You aren't doing it. If you need money, I'll help you."

"I don't need money! God, I have like three credit cards and a bank account in the thousands."

"Well, if you aren't doing it for the money? Why do it?"

She looked down at her feet and then slowly lifted her head. "You ever wanted to do something risky to see if you can do it?"

Yes. But I was a hopeless case. I was a wipe off. No one was expecting anything of me or my life. She wasn't a wipe off. Her life was just beginning. Her life wasn't being framed by bad decisions in her past like mine was.

I knew what she was talking about. But I couldn't let her do what she wanted to do just to get some life experience that could cost her the perfect life she deserved.

"Soph, you are better than all that. You don't need to know if you can face that type of life when it isn't where your life is heading." I tried to speak clearly to her. "Hell, you're heading to early acceptance to a university of your choice and you can have any man you want. Why throw that away for some cash you don't need in a job that is degrading?"

She looked at me torn, like there was something she was keeping to herself. I didn't think, fuck, maybe I should have, but I found myself pushing up my jumper, so my hand was on her bare knee.

"You not sure what you want to study?" I took a stab in the dark.

She looked down at my hand and chewed her bottom lip again, and again. I found myself just acting and not thinking, and I pried the lip from her grasp with my fingers.

"What's up, Soph?" I asked gently and leaned in closer to her. My hand was still close to her face. I didn't stop myself as I tucked her hair behind her ear. "Come on, it can't be that bad?"

She looked me in the eye, and I saw something she normally kept hidden: emptiness.

"Dad and Mum are forcing me into the medical field. It's been expected since I was ten. It's what I've worked towards. The offers are rolling in and I've stopped answering my phone and stopped opening the letters." She gulped, and again emptiness was in her eyes.

"What changed? Is it Kyle? Has he made you stop wanting your career?"

She shrugged her shoulders. "Maybe it is part his fault, but it's mainly mine. I realized something and realizing that made me see…"

"See what?"

She shook her head. "You wouldn't understand."

She kept saying that. "Come on, Soph, just tell me. I can help." I didn't know how I was going to; I wasn't smart like her. I'd never had a heart to heart with someone. Or helped someone make a decision. Fuck, no one came to me for advice, unless you include my club brothers. I didn't see helping out a brother the same as helping Soph out.

Her eyes glanced down and then back up. "No one can help me."

Why would she think that? "Well, at least tell me what you realized?" I was going to work away around her closed answers. Get her to open up to me.

She stopped looking me in the eye and fiddled with the sleeve of my hoodie. She finally sighed. "Being a doctor means you care for others. It also means you feel for others." She was looking me in the eye, but I had never seen her so distant. "I can't look after myself and... I don't feel anything anymore." She dropped her toast on the plate. "How can I go into a field where I don't have two of the essential skills?"

Kyle. It was all Kyle's fucking fault. I had never wanted to hurt my brother more. How stupid was he? How could he do this to the most perfect woman? How could he not see what I saw? And if he did see what I saw, how the hell did he let her go?

He hadn't just broken her heart; he had destroyed who she was. I was seeing that now. She had been hiding it well, but I was starting to see what Soph was hiding from everyone. My Soph—the Soph I knew for years—was loving, carefree, happy and cared for everyone. And now, well, she was sitting here saying she couldn't even look after herself. Hell! She was saying she didn't feel anything for anyone anymore. The girl that would go out of her way to help others.

I found myself unable to say anything. I couldn't accept the fact that my Soph was saying something like that. That the girl I knew was gone completely.

"Yeah, see, there isn't much to say to that, is there?" she said dimly, sounding like a broken woman. Her eyes were glued to her lap. "Thanks for dinner, Josh. I'll, um…" She looked up and again what I saw I hated seeing in her eyes. She finally gave me a fake smile, like everything was okay and her world wasn't falling away. "Night, Josh." She pushed away from me.

I stood up and stopped her. "You aren't heartless, Soph. You're just going through a hard time." That was it, right? She would snap out of this... because I didn't want to believe that Kyle had destroyed her completely. I didn't know much about feelings, or what happens when you break up with someone. So, I didn't know what she was going through. But I was hoping, for her sake, that her old self would come back. It had to. The Soph I knew couldn't just be... gone.

She was looking down at our feet. "It doesn't matter anymore. I am who I am. The one good thing about it is I didn't feel heartbroken when I told Bax to stay away from me."

I frowned. "You told him to leave you alone?" Was there a chance her brain was still working even though her world was falling apart?

Her hazel eyes looked up and that dim, barely even considered a smile, was on her face. "Yeah. At least for a week."

I thought it was too good to be true. She hadn't wiped him out of her life altogether. He didn't deserve a second of her time.

"You can do better than him." I didn't stop myself when I reached out for her, grabbing her hips and pulling her towards me. "You know that, right?"

I just had to touch her. It was like… if I touched her, she would feel something and come back, not be so cold or distant. I wanted her to feel again. I wanted her to laugh again and the thing I wanted the most —the very most, was for her to be herself again.

Her hazel eyes were still looking in mine, and while I knew she heard what I said, she was keeping her answer to herself.

"Soph, did you hear me? You can do better than Bax." My hands spread on her hips. "You deserve better, you know that, right?"

She shook her head. "I don't deserve better, Josh. That's where you are wrong."

She couldn't be serious. "You deserve a relationship. Not one-night stands."

"But that's all I want. I made it very clear to Bax that that was all I was capable of. I don't do love. I don't do feelings. I don't do relationships. He knew all that, and what does he do? He wants more." She clenched her fists at her side. "I thought every guy wanted a girl to sleep with whenever and have her happy, hell, even supportive of him seeing other girls."

She was right, most guys would love that. It would be their dream come true. What Soph wasn't factoring in was... well, her. When you got a taste of Soph, you didn't want anyone else but her. Bax wanted to lay claim on her before anyone else did. Because he knew, like I knew, she could do better than him.

She would have billionaires begging for her attention. Men that wanted for nothing their whole life, even they would want her. They wouldn't give up until she was theirs. But it didn't matter what you promised her, what you could give her, she wasn't interested because in her head, she wasn't worth a second thought. In her head she wasn't worth anything. Someone had to make her realize she was worthy. Someone had to make her feel again. Someone had to get her to risk her heart again.

But I knew I wasn't capable of helping her with any of those things. Just wasn't in me. I wasn't that type of person. I was the type of person to use my fists instead of my words.

But I could still try to be her friend.

Her phone buzzed on the kitchen island and she was more interested in staring up at me than getting it.

For some reason, my grip on her tightened. I didn't want her leaving.

When the phone stopped ringing, it started again right away. She sighed and looked at it. A small groan left her lips.

"What's wrong?" I asked, and she unclenched her fist and picked it up.

"I told him earlier to leave me alone." She looked down at the phone. "Again, he just ignores what I want."

Bax. It had to be him. "You going to answer?" I knew what Bax wanted. He wanted her. Not just for sex. He actually wanted her to be his. It only took him a few weeks of being with her for him to see what I saw. She was priceless and deserved a life better than what he or I could give her. But him being the selfish bastard he is, he was going to claim her regardless of whether she deserved better or not.

"He will be drunk and just want sex and I'm not interested after the stunt he pulled." She blocked his call and then turned her phone off. "He can speak to my voicemail."

I smiled. I was proud of her. She might not think she deserved better, but all hope wasn't lost.

"You going to sleep?" she asked. Her hands ran down my arms as my hands still clung to her hips.

"Aren't you?" I pulled her in closer. Friends touched, right? Because I had to touch her. I couldn't explain it… it was like a need—a desperate need to touch her. I'd never felt like this for a woman before. Never wanted to touch a woman as badly as I wanted to touch her.

It was even the small touches I wanted. Like when we were in the supermarket, I had to have my hand on her lower back as she decided on whether she wanted whole wheat or white bread. Then when her hands didn't have something in them, I had to have one hand locked on hers.

She didn't seem to mind either. She didn't pull away. She didn't even flinch when I wrapped an arm around her and pulled to my side. She didn't care either when we were at the cash register and I wrapped both arms around her waist like she was mine and pulled her back to my chest.

Anyone could make the mistake of thinking we were together. But we weren't. We were just friends. Friends did that type of crap.

"What are you thinking right now?" She ran two fingers down my jaw, looking puzzled as she looked up at me.

I wasn't telling her what I was thinking. If I did, she would think I was mad. Having an obsession with touching her—she would think the worst.

"Nothing. You going to bed or not?" She grinned, and I think it was a real one. "Nope." She shook her head. "I'm watching reruns of The Young Ones. They are on the BBC from two am to four am."

I groaned. "The music in that show is terrible, Soph. How can you still be obsessed with it?"

"But the comedy is priceless." She suddenly seemed hesitant. "Um, are you interested in joining me?"

She was asking me to join her? I could tell by the way she stopped running her finger down my jaw and looked like she was holding her breath that she was nervous.

"Your room or mine?" I smiled at her.

She inhaled a breath. "Mine because my electric blanket is on." She started to back away, her hands gripping my arms, gently guiding me to follow.

She didn't have to convince me to follow her. I let go and then I spun her around, wrapping my arms around her waist.

"You still cold?" I asked, walking behind her. God, she was tiny.

"Not as cold as I was. Not with your hoodie." She pulled her hands into the sleeves as we walked up the stairs.

We came to a stop at her door and she twisted the doorknob. Then she stepped out of my arms, her arm searching for the light switch.

FIFTEEN

Josh

The light came on.

Her hand went out for me, and I grabbed it just as she balanced on one foot to take her heel off. She sighed with relief as she removed the other.

"God, you have no idea how amazing that feels." She kept holding my hand. "Now I just need to get out of this lingerie."

My expression dropped, and she let go of my hand and took my hoodie off.

"What did you say?" I asked, not believing she had just said what I thought had escaped her lips.

She titled her head. "I've got to take the lingerie off. It was for the job interview. You know, you have to dress up to strip."

Yep. She had said what I thought she said. God. Please. Don't be cruel. Don't let her do it front of me. I was silently begging a higher spirit above not to torture me.

She was reading my expression, as if she could pick up on the tiny bit of panic I was feeling about her stripping in front of me, she should know not to do it. I wouldn't be able to control myself. The need would overcome me. The need to explore her body, naked and in front of me. Fuck, it would kill me to not to act on those feelings and I'm a man of control.

A cheeky grin appeared on her face as she took a step closer to me. "Do you want to undress me Josh?" Her voice went up with a hint of teasing.

Why the fuck would she say that? Just don't let her see how badly I want to do it. Because yes, I did want to undress her. But then I also wanted to explore her naked skin. She linked her hand with mine and pulled me into the room, moving me back to until I was against the bed. When my legs hit the edge of the bed, she gave me a firm push, landing me on my ass.

She stepped in between my legs with the most alluring look on her face. If I wasn't already stiff, that look would have done it alone.

She had me ridged, scared to fucking move a muscle. Not trusting myself near her.

She gripped the hem of my hoodie and pulled it off. Then she dropped it beside me. She hadn't just abandoned it. She placed it down, like it was special to her.

Then I gulped as her hand went to the strap of her long singlet. "You know what the girls said that I stripped in front of?" Her voice was low, alluring, and so fucking sweet. It would send a diabetic into a sugar coma.

She pushed the other strap off her shoulder, threading her arms out.

Please don't do it. I prayed as her hands went to her breasts and she slowly pulled the fabric down.

She dropped her mouth to my ear. "Still no idea on what they said, Josh?" I could hear the smirk in her voice.

She was getting pleasure out of this.

"No," I forced out, as she picked up my hands. She placed them on the fabric of her top, on the sides of her breasts. Not on her breasts, but so fucking close—my thumbs nearly touching them.

Slowly she pushed my hands down, causing the fabric to go down with them.

I hissed, seeing her low-cut black bra, and the top of her breasts spilling out. My eyes couldn't move off them. She kept moving my hands down, pulling the fabric down, showing more of her beautiful snow-white skin.

She was going to kill me. Tempting and waving a drug in front of me. That drug being her body.

The singlet got to her hips, and she took her hands off mine, and my hands stilled on her hips.

She leaned in towards me, linking her arms around my neck. "You going to finish the job, Josh?"

I was breathing in sharply and out even sharper, trying my best to keep my shit together.

"Come on, Josh, I've done most of the work." Her words were like velvet to my ears.

Don't do it. Don't fucking do it. I kept repeating over and over in my head, telling myself to take my hands off her. But what do I do instead? Instead of fucking listening to myself…

My hands started to push the fabric down. I don't think I could believe my luck. If you had told me hours ago, I would be stripping her, I wouldn't have believed it. I wouldn't believe that I, Josh Hawkins, would get to see Soph in her underwear again.

I moved the singlet down her thigh, and I took a staggered breath in when my fingers brushed over the straps connecting to her stockings. *Why? Why was she doing this to me?*

I looked up at her and her eyes were on me. She looked so calm. My hands kept pushing down the singlet until it fell down on its own.

She dipped her head, her eyes locked with mine. She unlocked her hands from around my neck. My hands were back on her, gripping the back of her thighs and pushing her closer to me in between my legs. My hands ran up her thighs, over her ass, and paused on her lower back.

She didn't stop me. She didn't even push me away. She pushed her hair to the side and then cupped my face. I knew it was going to happen. It had to happen. The kiss was coming, and once her lips touched mine, I wouldn't be stopping with a kiss. It wasn't in me.

I would give myself a challenge as soon as she kissed me. That challenge being having her gasping and moaning, clenching. Fuck, yes. She would regret ever teasing me.

Her mouth went to my ear again, and I wanted to groan because I wanted her lips on mine.

"They said I wore black well. What do you think?" She put her hands on my shoulders and smiled at me. "No words?" She was a bloody minx!

I held my breath. *Was it her mission to kill me with temptation?*

She stepped back, and she laughed. "Clearly I've made you uncomfortable. Don't worry, Josh, I won't ask you to finish the job." She leaned across me and picked up my hoodie, giving me a large grin. "How about you find the remote? I'll only be a sec."

She walked off with my hoodie in hand. My eyes just followed her, glued to her ass, seeing the lace shape it perfectly.

She thought I was uncomfortable? Fuck, she had made me feel everything else but that.

She slightly closed the door to the wardrobe, but it wasn't enough. I knew I should look away; I knew it was the gentleman thing to do, and it was the right thing to do, but my eyes were stuck on her.

I watched her unclip her tights and roll them down. I had never seen anything as sexy as that. Then her hands went behind her back. It was too late to look away. She took the bra off, and I was reminded just how perfect her breasts were.

Even from here, I could admire the shape, and the perkiness to them. Then my view was ruined when she pulled my hoodie over her body. I got up quickly and my eyes ran over her bed and bedside table, spotting the remote on the floor.

The last thing I wanted was for her to walk back in here and see me gawking at her. "Did you find it?"

I straightened up from picking it up. "Yep." I watched her as she went to the side of bed and threw the blankets back.

"Awesome." She shot me a smile and got into the bed. "Oh my god, this bed is so warm." She tucked her legs under and pulled the blankets up. Seems like she's sleeping in my hoodie. I suppressed my smile and pleasure of seeing that.

I threw the remote into the middle of the bed. "I don't know which channel is which."

"But everyone knows the free to air channels?" She picked the remote up.

"Yeah, and then they went digital while I was in prison." I informed her and kicked my shoes off. I couldn't take my top off in front of her. I wasn't ready for that.

She was having a fling with Bax. But when she realized who I was and what I stood for, that wouldn't be changing. Well, she wouldn't want to be friends with that type of person. I knew her. I knew, when it came to Soph, she would stand on the side of the law. She might be flirting with danger at the moment, but she would come to her senses and she would ditch Bax.

Well, at least that was what I was hoping for because the other option was she ended up with Bax. I wouldn't let that happen. She deserved better. Better than what she could get from this town. I saw the envelopes from overseas on the kitchen island from colleges and universities all over the world. She was going to achieve great things.

I wouldn't let Bax be the man to stop that.

"You going to get into bed, Josh?"

I looked up, seeing her eyes on me.

"I forgot about the channels doing that. Must be difficult adjusting to things out of prison," she added, with a frown. "I guess a lot things have changed for you."

That summed up my life. I nodded my head. I didn't want her pity or the awkwardness that came along when anyone talked about my prison sentence.

She leaned across and threw the blankets back for me.

Whenever someone mentioned my prison sentence the same question always followed: "Why?" Why did I go to prison? So far, Soph hadn't asked, but right now she had a perfect opportunity to.

Instead she looked up at me with a smile. "Your electric blanket isn't on. I never sleep on the left."

That was Soph for you. She would surprise you. I was grateful she had changed the subject. I didn't want to lie to her, but I didn't know how to tell her the truth at the same time.

I hated bringing up why I went to prison.

I was going to waste four years behind bars all because something in me made me do the right thing. Christine didn't even stick by me for a month after my sentence. Hell, she didn't even waste a day. That's women for you.

But then I looked at Soph. The small smile on her face. The blushed cheeks. Her red lips. Her blonde hair pulled to the side. I didn't see her as I saw every other woman. I was thankful she had changed the subject. I gave her a smile. "Are you planning on wearing my hoodie to bed or something?" I asked as I climbed in.

"Yep." She pushed the sleeves up. "Do you want to come to my side where it is warm?" She grinned, carefree.

I shook my head, at least she was covered. "You know you'll get hot." I got in the bed. I knew she wasn't wearing a top under it.

"Nope. I freeze in here every night."

"Why don't you put the central heating on?"

"Don't know how."

I rolled my eyes. "So, you've just been freezing every night?" Why didn't Mom and Dad show her how to put on the heating?

"I use the electric blanket." She glanced at the television. "I love this episode."

"You love every episode." I didn't know if I should move more into the middle of the bed, closer to her, or keep to my side.

"Rick is my favorite."

"I remember." Why she loved such an old show was beyond me.

"Kyle used to hate watching it with me, too." She sat up in the bed. "You can go if you want. I know how much Kyle hated it. Maybe it's a family trait?"

Her eyes were on the television, but I knew what she was really doing. She was giving me an excuse to leave—to leave her. cause that's what she was used to: men leaving her. My brother was the reason why she was expecting me to leave right now. She didn't think I'd want to suffer through this, just to be with her.

I got my answer on whether I should move closer or further away.

I slid into the middle of the bed. "Bloody hell, Soph, you're going to cook yourself."

That had her taking her eyes off the television and looking at me. She leaned forward, sitting up. A small yawn escaping her lips. "You are going to stay?"

"Yes, and watch the hour and a half of musical torture." I put my arm behind her, but I wasn't touching her. It was up to her whether she wanted me touching her or not. She could make the decision.

"It's not all music. It has like one music feature. You are forgetting about all the comedy." Her eyes kept locked with mine. She didn't lean back into my arm, or snuggle into my side. I wanted her to, but I wasn't going to make her. She tucked her hair behind her ear.

"Did you know the actor Rik Mayall, who plays Rick, died three years ago?" She was still sitting up, and she seemed nervous.

"Nah, baby girl, I had no idea," I said gently. When Soph loved something, she knew even the small details about it. I was waiting for her to make a decision, to pull away from me, fall back into my arm, or move back to the edge if her bed.

"Does it bother you if I wear your hoodie? I don't want it to be awkward. I get it if you don't want me to. Kyle hated me wearing anything mildly male." Her voice was pulled back like she was expecting to be in trouble.

Was it wrong that I wanted her to be wearing something that was mine? It was probably unhealthy and a sign of something else, but she was the only woman I wanted to have something that belonged to me.

"Nope, doesn't bother me." It was the truth. "You can have it if you want."

Her head snapped to face me, her attention on the television gone. "You serious?"

I shrugged. "It's not a big deal, Soph." Was it? "It's just a sweater," I added, more for myself.

The smile on her face was tiny, but it was the first real smile I had seen. It wasn't fake. I didn't have to think about whether it was it real or not. I knew it was a real smile. Not a big one, but it was real, and it was directed fully at me.

I made her smile.

She didn't say anything and slid down the bed before curling into my side.

Automatically my arm wrapped around her, pulling her closer. Her head was on my chest and my hand was running up and down her side.

"If I fall asleep on you. I'm sorry." Sophie yawned and cuddled in closer to me, hooking one of her legs over mine.

Last time we slept together I was in a world of pain, but tonight I wasn't. I was going to enjoy every second of sleeping with her.

I kissed the top of her hair as her eyelids grew heavier.

SIXTEEN

Soph

I slowly woke up, feeling relaxed and comfortable. So comfortable I didn't want to move or open my eyes. I just wanted to lay there all day. His hand was under the hoodie that I was wearing. I wouldn't lie and say I didn't love this hoodie. A guy had never given me something of theirs to wear before. I had worn Bax's T-shirt, but that was different; it was an emergency. Like, Kyle hated it if I wore his T-shirt or sweater. Then Josh goes and gives his hoodie to me.

His fingers were running up and down my side, and he was slowly putting me back to sleep.

"You know that is amazing." I sighed into the pillow. My body knew it was time to wake up, but Josh was putting me back to sleep. I felt him kiss the back of my head.

I pushed back into him. I hope he didn't mind me sleeping on his arm. I had slept on it all night.

"Is your arm dead? I'm so sorry, Josh. You should have pushed me off," I said and lifted my head. God, I had slept all over him all night. He wasn't my boyfriend. He didn't have to put up with that.

With his hand on my side, he pushed me back down.

"It's fine." His voice was low and close to my ear.

"I've slept on you all night. That's not fine." I rolled over onto my back and his hand was now on my stomach. I was sure that if I was with any other guy, I would be very self-conscious of the fact that the blankets were the only thing covering my bottom half. The hoodie was up around my waist, and I wasn't wearing pajama pants. I was, however, wearing underwear that didn't leave much to the imagination. I moved to my side to face him, and his hand moved smoothly across my body.

"You sleep alright?" He asked that like I wouldn't have slept perfectly with him.

I smiled, taking in his concerned face. "I think that's the best night sleep I've had in a while."

The corner of his lips twitched up.

"Good."

I knew he was always touching me, but I found myself, like last night, wanting to touch him. So, I moved my hand under the blanket and slowly traced my fingers up his arm.

"What are you doing today?" I asked, getting lost at the feel of his skin. His fingers traced circles so gently on my lower back. My eyes slowly closed, overwhelmed with his touch.

"Got to fix the throttle on my bike."

My eyes opened wide. "You have a bike?"

His eyes had been shut and I don't think he realized what he said until I questioned him. Then his eyes were open, like he had just told me his life secret. "Um…" Was all he managed.

I arched my eyebrows at him confused. Okay, something was wrong. He had a bike, what was the big deal? Why was he looking so… horrified?

"Josh, what is with the expression?" I asked, his fingers had stilled on my back and he looked scared. "Are you okay?" Suddenly, I was concerned for him. I wondered if I upset him. How was having a motor bike a secret? He used to ride dirt bikes when he was younger. "Josh, are you okay?" I repeated.

"Fine," he staggered out and frowned.

"Then what is with the expression?" I frowned.

"I'm not." He wiped the expression I was talking about off his face. "I should go." His words were firm, and he looked so distant. In fact, I liked the horrified expression more than the one on his face right now. He was looking at me like… well… I had seen that look before on his brother's face, when Kyle told me he would never love me again and wanted nothing to do with me.

Yeah, Josh wanted nothing to do with me. His expression was telling me that. He wasn't hiding it either, he was looking at me like I was nothing but a fly in his life.

Suddenly, he wanted to run away from me. That for some reason hurt. I don't know why, but I really cared about his opinion and I felt so comfortable and relaxed with him. I had hoped he felt the same. But right now, he wasn't comfortable with me and he sure as hell wasn't relaxed. He wanted to run. I nodded my head.

"Sorry," I said. I didn't know what else to say. I was making him want to bolt. I didn't know why, but it was me who was scaring him away. I guess sorry was the only word to say.

He didn't need to tell me he wanted nothing to do with me. His facial expression told me everything. It told me he was regretting ever speaking to me. It told me wanted to be anywhere but here. But what was hurting me more than it should, was well, the regret in his eyes. Was he telling me that he regretted last night, when I had enjoyed it so much? I had hoped that our friendship was growing in a positive direction.

Hell, I never had a male friend that cared as much as him. The friendship developing between Josh and me, it was deeper and stronger than the friendship I had with Kayla. I never had a male friend I felt so comfortable in front of. That brought out another side to me.

Josh brought out things in me I thought were dead, like laughter, confidence, and faith—I had faith in him, trusted him.

But that friendship that I was enjoying, that friendship I was starting to count on, well, I think Josh was putting an end to it.

It was like I had touched a subject that made him pull the eject rope. Wish I knew why he wanted out of my life. But I guess I should be used to people, especially Hawkins, coming abruptly into my life and departing just as abruptly, giving no real reason.

I stopped touching him. I got off his arm and sat up. He wanted to run, and I wasn't going to stop him. I had no right. As much as I would love for him to tell me why he wanted to run and what was scaring him, I had to let him go.

"Soph." He was saying my name like he was trying to undo something. There was nothing to undo.

I was averting my eyes, looking everywhere but in his direction.

"Soph?"

He must have read my reaction. He must have realized I had read his reaction well. I had got the point he wanted out that he wanted to run.

"Like you said, Josh, you should go." I pushed the blankets down and went to get up. I knew I was going to have to look at him, so I wiped my expression. I gave him a fake smile. "Go fix whatever needs fixing." I didn't need to know the details, wasn't my place. "Like I've said before, you don't have to explain yourself to me."

He knew that by now, right?

"Soph, come back."

I was forced to look at him again and kept my expression neutral. "Josh, you should know by now, you don't have to explain yourself to me. You don't have to tell me anything." It was a simple fact. I didn't expect anything from him, but every little thing he gave me I was so grateful for. I forced a smile, keeping what I was really thinking to myself: "Go start your day. Thanks for last night."

And I was thankful. I was so thankful for him being with me last night. I don't know why he came home, but he had, and he had spent the night with me. He had made me eat; he acted like he cared. No one really cared about me anymore, so just a small dose of it, well, it went straight to my heart.

He groaned and got out of bed. "I don't want to lie to you."

My lips formed a tight line. To be honest, it sounded like he meant that, like he really didn't want to lie to me, but it was like he was in a position where he had to.

Whatever. He didn't answer to me. Didn't have to tell me one honest word.

I looked up from staring into the carpet, facts went through my head on why he didn't have to tell me the truth. I was surprised to see his eyes on me. I wondered why he was looking at me so intently. God, it was intense. Please, I begged silently to whoever was above me to make his eyes snap off me. Please, oh please stop it.

I couldn't move and at the same time couldn't look away from him.

His expression earlier, which was telling me he didn't love me, never would, and didn't want anything to do with me, was gone. Now his face was serious; his emotions were hidden, so he might still be thinking all those things, but not putting them on display for me to read.

Then finally his eyes snapped off me, and I took a deep breath in.

"What are you doing today?" he asked, totally changing the subject. But I heard the edge in his voice; he was angry. There was a hint of anger to his tone, and it was loud enough for me to pick up on it.

"I might answer one of Bax's missed calls." I crossed my arms. I don't know why, but I suddenly felt like I needed to be on defence and Josh's head snapped up after he pulled on his pants.

"You going back to him?" Geez, he didn't hold back the judgement in those five words.

"I guess." I frowned. I told him I wasn't judging him, and he didn't have to answer to me, yet he wasn't returning that to me. He was judging me, and he spoke like I had to answer to him. "Why are you so angry?"

"He's a biker," Josh spat those words out and crossed his arms. "He stands against the law. The law your parents love, that you love. Every value you hold dear well he gives it the finger. He goes through a different woman each week. He will never love you, respect you, or really care about you. So why the fuck are you going back to him?"

I was taken back by that. He had just listed a stack of facts that should stop me from going to Bax. Josh hadn't listed one fact that wasn't true. But he was demanding that I explain why I would go back to Bax.

I looked harder at him. Yeah, he wanted to know. He wasn't dropping subject. So, I stood a bit taller. He wanted an answer, a real answer, then I'd tell him exactly what I thought.

"I don't care what he stands for, or what he doesn't. Yeah, he is a biker, but that doesn't mean he is rotten to the core. Just because he is one thing, doesn't mean you give up on him completely! God! What type of person do you take me for, Josh?" I shook my head frustrated. "The values you are talking about, that I hold dear, well, he does stand for them—loyalty, fairness, he has a love for a club, one that he is willing to protect with his life. Those three things say more about his character than the fact that he is an outlaw biker."

I wasn't finished there. Josh had mentioned a few other things I wanted to cover; I couldn't stop myself from pointing a finger at him.

"I encourage him to go to other women. I don't want love, and I don't need his respect. I also don't need him to care for me. I don't expect anything from him."

Yeah, he wanted an answer, well I just gave my answer to him!

But his judgmental eyes stayed on me, narrowing as they locked on to mine. I thought Josh was angry before, but the look on his face now went from pissed to offended to furious.

"You deserve so much fucking better than that! You deserve better than some low life criminal, who isn't going to contribute to the world! You deserve everything, Sophia! Why are you settling for a man that will never love you! Never put you first. Never..." His lips tightened. "He won't care about your health. He won't care about your future. All he cares about is fucking you—literally."

I couldn't argue with one fact that Josh had just said. But I did have a minor adjustment to make to his statement. "Just because you view him as not contributing to the world, doesn't mean that's true." I wanted to stand firm on that. "He affects other people lives, that's contributing to the world. Even if those people are other bikers and women, they are still people and his life still matters. He is contributing to the world."

I couldn't explain the expression that captured Josh's face; it was like I had just rewritten a rule he had put in stone. "You think he contributes to the world?" Josh repeated what I said like he had misheard it. He repeated it like it couldn't be true.

"Sure, he does." I shrugged but felt frustrated at the same time. God, why were people so quick to judge someone's image? "Everyone does in their own way."

"You really don't care that he is a biker, do you?" He looked shocked, surprised, and something else as well. I would have to pick as amazement, he was looking at me like I was the perfect female and he was seeing it for the first time. I didn't understand why he was looking at me like that, I was far from perfect. "You really think even a biker's life contributes to the world?" he added.

I softly smiled at him. I felt like he was turning what I was saying about Bax and putting it on himself. He wasn't a biker, though. But the criminal part, he did wear that. He had been to prison and I think deep down, he didn't think much of himself. He couldn't believe that someone else would accept his flaws and also see the light he gives the world.

Josh thought his life meant nothing. That's why he lived day by day. I think he thought just because he went to prison his life was worthless and he wouldn't leave an imprint on this world.

He wore his prison scars well. The scar of being cut off from society. The scar of going to prison to begin with. I knew he hadn't learned his lesson while in there. I didn't have proof of that. He had never confirmed if he was or wasn't in the criminal underworld.

Still it didn't matter. His life matters. He was leaving a mark on the world. Hell, he was leaving a mark on my life.

"Of course I do," I finally said and his expression turned back into amazement. "Just because Bax has a criminal record, doesn't exclude him from being a good person." I thought about Bax for a few more moments and a smile crept across my face as I remembered something. "You know he likes to gamble. It's his thing. He loves it." I shook my head, I never got it. "Anyway, whatever he wins he gives it to a homeless dog charity, and if he loses, he matches whatever he lost and still donates. Little things like that say more about him than just some record the police have on him."

Like I said a while back, I wasn't seeing the world as black and white anymore. I saw grey. I saw the good in someone, even when everything about them told you they should be a bad person.

"You know, Josh, you shouldn't be so hard on other people. Everyone has their own issues and problems weighing them down." I uncrossed my arms and I think I had made my point to him, but I had something I wanted to add—something I felt like he needed to hear. "You also shouldn't be so hard on yourself. Stop thinking your life means nothing and you won't leave a mark on the world. Because you have left a mark on me, and I'm sure I'm one of many." I gave him a real smile. "Sorry for holding you up. You better get going."

He was just staring at me. I didn't know what about. It was almost like I had shared the most detailed and private fact about myself to him and he couldn't wrap his head around it.

I didn't know what to do, and the more I stared at him, the more I realized that I didn't think there was anything I could say to make him snap out of it. So, I turned and went to my wardrobe, pushing opening the door and leaving it ajar.

I took off his hoodie and couldn't stop the smile on my face as I looked down at it. I don't think he realized how much that meant to me. It was perfect too. It kept me warm, smelt like him, and like how I feel when I'm with Josh, I felt safe. His hoodie gave me a small dose of that safety. I couldn't compare it to a hug by him because his hugs just blew my mind. But his hoodie surrounded me with his scent and that was comforting.

In that moment, I wasn't sure if I was wrong to be feeling that.

I just put on my bra when the door burst open. I turned, but as soon as I did, I was off the ground.

"Josh, what the hell are you doing?" I asked alarmed. He kicked closed my wardrobe door, still holding me in the air. He lifted me like I weighed nothing at all. I was thin, but I still weighed something. He shouldn't have been able to be balance my full body weight with one arm. I wrapped my legs around him, because I was guessing that was what he wanted by the way he was holding me. He wanted me close; he didn't want space between us. I could tell that by his actions.

He leaned me back against the closed door, an intense look on his face like his will power had snapped. His other hand moved up my side, exploring my revealed skin. I knew I wasn't wearing much, but I wasn't uncomfortable or nervous like I should be.

I saw his eyes flash to my lips, and he slowly moved in closer, like my lips were pulling his lips to mine. I knew what he wanted, but I also knew he wasn't ready for it. I moved just before his lips made it to mine and kissed his cheek. I felt like my lips were leaving a mark on his skin, as if I had branded him.

I looked back into his eyes. So blue, so enchanting, so magical that I could get lost in them. Actually, I was getting lost in them now. Did he know how incredibly good looking he was? Before he went to prison, he couldn't walk into a café without every girl's eyes going to him. He was "that" guy. If you were a girl or a woman, you couldn't not look at him and admire and daydream.

Now I think the pull he has on women is stronger. He was so well built, but it wasn't just his body that women would drool over and gawk at. It was the whole package. The sharp blue eyes, the way he carried himself, he didn't give a fuck what anyone thought of him and that was very appealing.

He wasn't just your normal bad boy. He was a man. A man that didn't give a fuck about society or what was expected of him. He did what he wanted, when he wanted. He wasn't a bad boy: he was a dangerous, deadly man—that would give you an overdose of lust and then depart your life as quickly as he entered it, not caring what he left behind.

"Josh, you should go start your day," I said gently and linked my arms around his neck. "You don't have to explain yourself to me, remember that."

His masked expression dropped, and he looked so torn. "I want to be honest with you, Soph. I really do."

"But you don't have to," I added. I titled my head, staring into his amazing eyes. "You don't have to explain your life to me. I don't expect that. You are a very private person. I've always known that."

I didn't go into this friendship with Josh thinking he would be telling me every secret. I knew him. I knew he was private and the walls he had up never came down. He was carefree, but at the same it was a show; he wasn't showing his real self. He never had.

He shows the world he doesn't care, he doesn't need anyone, and he had this confidence that couldn't be shaken.

But on a rare occasion—very rare—you get a glimpse of what he is hiding from the world. Like how he was so concerned last night hearing I hadn't eaten. He hadn't hidden his reaction. He cared about me. It showed last night. Not just care about me like he has to put up with me because I'm staying at his house but like he cared for my physical health.

Josh didn't think he was capable of showing emotion or expressing it, but he had shown concern last night, real concern.

"Can I ask you something?" His words were low and so soft, as if he was hoping I wouldn't hear it.

"Always."

He looked at me hesitantly. "What do I have to do to make sure I don't lose you?" His tone dipped into nerves and anxiety. He had just asked a question, and I could tell he was really worried about the answer.

I couldn't stop the smile. "Josh, there is nothing you can do that will result in you losing me." Out of all the things for him to be worried about he didn't have to worry about that. "Seriously. There is nothing you can do."

"Not even things about me?" His hand paused just under my bra. "Not even what people say about me?" I thought about what had been written in the papers about him. I had read one article about him, and it didn't say why he went to prison, but listed all the reasons why a man like him or any criminal shouldn't be given early release.

I found myself smiling at him, and I unlinked my arms and my placed my hand over his cheek. "Josh, you could be a mass murderer, guilty as fuck, and I'd still be standing beside you." I kissed his other cheek that I wasn't cupping. "I don't give a darn about your money either, or how you spend it. All I want is a friend." I knew money was a sore point with him, because he had a lot of it. His granddad, who he was really close to, left Josh his estate —everything.

As soon as word got out that Josh had money, that wasn't his family money, it was fair to say, girls were promising him everything just to get money out of him. I think that's one of the reasons he didn't trust women.

"Can I ask something of you?" I wasn't sure if this was about to cross a line.

"Yeah, sweetheart. You can ask anything of me and I'll try my best to be honest," he said, like he wanted to tell me every detail about his life, like he hated not being able to share whatever it was that that he couldn't share with me.

He was still holding all my weight, but it was like I was a feather and he could hold me up all day and all night.

I took a nervous breath in. Okay, I was going to be honest with him. "Start living like your life matters." My hand stilled on his cheek and I tried my best to give him some advice. "I know you don't express emotions well. I know you don't do friendships. I know you don't do relationships. But that doesn't mean your life doesn't matter."

Did he not see how important he was to this world? He contributed to it, even if he didn't see it. Hell, he contributed a hell of a lot to my life. I think anyone that met Josh was marked by him and that grin of his—the grin he tried his best to hide. It impacted your life thinking you might never see a grin as big, and as loving as his.

I leaned my forehead to his. "You matter. You leave a mark on me, every time you spend time with me. And I'm positive I'm not the only one. Every woman and man that comes in to contact with you, well, they are marked by you."

I don't think he believed what I was saying. Perhaps he was too far gone for that to be the case. I sighed. Yeah, he really wasn't believing it. I could tell by his tight expression, like he had a list of reasons behind him why that wasn't the case.

Maybe over time I could make him see it.

He kissed the corner of my mouth and then pulled back. I think he knew as well as I did, he wasn't ready to kiss me.

"Are you busy tonight?" he asked as his hand moved to my back and his other held me up. "Do you have any plans?"

"Maybe a run. Oh, and there is an earlier showing of *The Young Ones*. Like, the episodes I missed during the week." My face lit up remembering that. I didn't hide my smile, and then my expression soured. "Then your family dinner, which I'm guessing you're bailing on."

I didn't see why I had to attend their family dinners. I was a guest. But Louise said, before leaving, she really wanted me to make plans around the dinner she had planned for tonight. It would be fine if it was just Louise and Jed, but the devil and the devil's assistant would be back from the coast.

"There is a family dinner tonight?"

"What did you not get told to make plans around it?" I scoffed. I wasn't Kyle's girlfriend anymore. It wasn't like Louise and Jed were going to have me as a daughter-in-law. So why they were still making sure I felt like family I didn't know.

Josh frowned. "No. But by your reaction you were told to."

"Yes." I sighed. "I swear I'm turning into that annoying ex-girlfriend. I mean, Kyle has to put up with me at his house and family dinners. Like, how awful is it to have to have dinner with your new girlfriend and your ex? I'm like the pathetic clingy ex-girlfriend."

"Soph, stop." Josh's hand moved off me and he cupped my face, forcing me to look him in the eye. "You aren't pathetic."

"Yes, I am! I'm the pathetic ex-girlfriend that he can't get rid of." That was putting the situation nicely. I looked Josh in the eye. "How would you like it if you couldn't escape your ex-girlfriend and she moved into your house and was suddenly at all family dinners?"

It wasn't a normal situation. It wasn't healthy and it sure as fuck wasn't fair to me or Kyle. I deserved to move on, not being forced to see him with his new girlfriend. And he deserved a clean break from me.

Then Josh said something that surprised me: "I think it's good that you are around."

"What?"

"Every day Kyle is reminded of his mistake. I know my brother; he regrets what happened between you and him." Josh gently tucked my hair behind my ear. "He hates that you are talking to me too." Josh smiled, a full-blown cheeky smile. "I love watching him squirm. When he looks at you, I think he hates himself a bit more each time."

I rolled my eyes. "Trust me, he doesn't hate himself. He hates me. I think Kayla is going to kill me at one of these family dinners with her steak knife."

Josh suppressed a smirk. "I think Kyle loves you too much to let that happen."

"Are you insane?" Seriously, had Josh lost his mind? "Do I have to remind you of our breakup? Do I have to remind you he has a new girlfriend? That he just spent a romantic weekend with his girlfriend?"

This time he didn't suppress his smirk; he let it spread. It was like he knew something I didn't.

I huffed. "Well, if I die tonight at the hand of Kayla, remember to turn my electric blanket off."

Josh laughed. "Awe, sweetheart. I've missed your humor." He leaned forward and kissed my cheek. "I'd love to say I could save you tonight, but I've got something I can't get out of."

"Yeah, yeah, whatever. You just want to attend my funeral." I winked. "Okay, Hawkins, put me down. You have places to go and people to see who aren't me."

I couldn't hold up his day anymore.

He pulled me back away from the back of the door and I slid down his body. It looked like he didn't want to let go of me and his hands froze on my hips as soon as my feet hit the ground. Yep, he didn't want to let me go.

I thought it was a bit cute. I looked up at him, smiling, and his eyes ran up and down me.

"You know that job you were thinking about taking?" His eyes slowly moved up my body until he was looking me in eye. I nodded my head.

"You aren't taking it."

"Why?"

"Because I don't want another guy seeing you like this." He swallowed sharply, a tint in his eyes that I didn't understand. "I have a need to kill Bax and Kyle just because they have seen you like this."

I laughed. He couldn't be serious? I slowly sobered up. "Josh, Bax and Kyle have seen me in less than this." They had seen completely naked. I frowned for a second. "But then again, so have you."

"So, that's it, Kyle, Bax and me, that's everyone who has seen your body naked?" He questioned me like I held the million-dollar answer.

"Are you asking who I have and haven't had sex with?"

"No." He shook his head. "But if Kyle, Bax, and me are the only ones who have seen you completely naked, I already have an answer to that question and don't need to ask it. So, the question stands, are we the only three?"

I could lie? But he most likely would pick up on it. "It's pathetic that I've only been with two guys, right?" I said deflated. Compared to Kayla, she had more experience, and knew more about sex than me. God, she was probably wowing Kyle with all her experience. "I bet Kyle is loving the upgrade." And that's what Kayla was to me: an upgrade.

"Baby girl, look at me."

I shook my head; I didn't need pity. "It's fine, you should go." I couldn't pull my eyes off my feet. I felt behind me, twisting the doorknob and opening the door. "Thanks for last night, Josh."

His hand lifted up my chin and he forced me to look up at him.

"You aren't a car. Kyle hasn't upgraded from you. If you are anything, Soph, you are the grand prize, the woman every man would fight each other to death just to get you."

I rolled my eyes. "You are my friend; you have to say that."

He arched his eyebrows. "Have I ever come across as the type of guy that would lie to make you feel better?"

I frowned. No, he wasn't. Josh would never lie to make anyone feel better—not even me. It just wasn't in him. A dim smile graced my lips. "Thanks, Josh." I took a step out of his way, chewing my bottom lip.

He paused in front of me and then moved slowly, as if giving me time to stop him if I wanted to, and he gently kissed the top of my head, lingering for a second. "I'll see you soon."

He really was a good friend. He walked out the door, and I turned. "Oh, Josh?"

"Um?" He turned back to look at me.

I crossed my arms with a smile. "Don't be a tight bastard and try to repair that throttle. Just replace it with a new one."

He frowned and then I watched as he understood what I was talking about. "You know me too well, Soph." He gave me a wink, and he didn't seem completely terrified at the mention of the throttle, even though earlier it sent him into a meltdown.

I watched him leave and I admit I was disappointed when I saw him close my bedroom door. Now I was faced with one question: did I call Bax or not? For some stupid and unexplainable reason, I felt like I would be betraying Josh if I called Bax.

I didn't know why I had this feeling. I didn't know where I got that idea from. Josh and I were friends, that was it. Nothing more.

Seriously, I never ever would Josh see me as more than a friend.

So why was I worried about what he'd think?

SEVENTEEN

Soph

Had I been blind for years? Kayla was obnoxious. Her hair. Her makeup. Her perfume. Her personality. Everything about her was obnoxious. Why was I only seeing it now?

Now, as she gushed over every single detail of her weekend away with Kyle. I would throw up, but I haven't eaten anything today apart from bits of this potato, which I was busy destroying but not really eating.

Kyle and Kayla had spent the weekend at Kyle's sex house. Well, it wasn't his sex house. It was his parent's house on the coast. But Kyle was the only one using it. We used to escape down to it and stay for the weekend.

Walks on the beach, lounging around in the hammock, and then sex in the ocean, in the master suite, in the bathroom, hell, everywhere in the house. Yeah, it was fair to say it was his sex house.

So, I knew right now as Kayla told Louise how much she loved their unique dining table, she must have experienced it up close and personal.

Sex on the dining table, classic Kyle.

My eyes bounced off my plate and, what do you know, Kyle was looking directly at me. When it came to these family dinners, he always took the chance just to stare at me.

"Kyle and I had so much fun on the beach, and Kyle is such a good surfer." Kayla put her hand over Kyle's on the table.

God, they were making me sick. Were Kyle and I ever that in love? It was sickly. Their relationship was just as obnoxious. I guess it should be expected. Even she would take a normal relationship and twist it and turn it. I was suddenly disappointed a shark hadn't taken Kyle off his board.

"But I guess our weekend was boring compare to Sophia's." Kayla turned all attention on to me, a tint of vengeance and pleasure in her eyes.

What the fuck?

My weekend had been uneventful. I auditioned for a job that I now couldn't take because I think Josh was serious about no one else seeing my body. But not just that, Josh said I was too good for it. He made a lot of good points, proving that he really was a good friend and had my back when I was about to make a mistake.

Usually I liked to make a mistake on my own —you know, trip over, face plant. I never listened when someone told me I was about to make a mistake. Not when my parents told me. Not even when Kyle would warn me. I viewed a friendship as meaning that you are there in the good times and bad. Sometimes, you couldn't prevent me going through a bad time, even if you knew better and advised me from it.

But this time, just this once, I was going to take Josh's advice and not take the job.

I narrowed my eyes at Kayla. She would have to know I spent the weekend by myself.

She sipped her water and then put the glass down, an evil glint in her eyes. "You know the rumor around school is you are into the drug and party scene now, right? So, I'm guessing you spent the weekend doing what now do best?" She added a concerned pout to the end of her sentence.

Again, I was thinking what the fuck? She was the one in to the party scene! She was the one experimenting with drugs.

I glanced at Kyle, but I couldn't read his expression. Meanwhile, Kayla was enjoying me being examined like I was a dead bug on a glass plate under a microscope.

Louise and Jed's eyes widened in surprise, and I knew what was coming next. A lecture.

"Actually, she spent the weekend with me."

Every head in the room snapped to the doorway. My mouth fell slightly open.

"Josh, what are you doing here?" Louise got up in a hurry, sounding so happy. "Sweetheart, I thought you were busy today, otherwise I would have invited you for dinner." Louise moved so quickly around the table to hug her son.

Josh hugged her back, but his eyes were on me, like he was silently telling me not to panic.

He had told me he had something going on tonight that he couldn't get out of, so what was he doing here? Josh was a busy guy, and I knew for a fact he hated these dinners. Every time he was forced to come to one, I would watch him hate every second of it as he sat across from me.

Louise pulled back from him, looking delighted. "Your father said I wasn't allowed to make it mandatory that you came tonight. You know let you live your life." She rolled her eyes. "He thinks I baby you. But a mother can't stop worrying about her son."

A small grin spread across Josh's lips. "Yeah, I love you too, Mum." Josh let go of her.

"I'll get you a plate," Louise said and headed for the kitchen.

"Kyle, move over and make room for your brother," Louise said from the kitchen.

Kyle rolled his eyes and wasn't in a hurry to get up to move down. Josh and Kyle always sat next to each other. I think they were brought up sitting next to each other.

Though for some reason I had noticed Kyle was even more of a jerk to Josh than normal lately. Sure, they never got along—complete opposites. But they usually made more of an effort with each other. Like, as much as they disagree on things, they always came together.

Josh walked to Kyle's side and did something that made Kyle do a double take. I watched, startled, not believing what I was seeing as Josh picked up the chair next to Kyle and walked around the table with it, placing it next to mine.

Not just on my side of the table, but right next to me. Like, as close as Kayla's and Kyle's chairs were together. Josh casually sat down next to me and extended his arm on the back of my chair like it was no big deal.

I could nearly hear Kyle grinding his teeth as he gave his brother a death glare.

Josh's eyes were on me. He gave me a wink and then he turned his attention onto Kyle.

"So, how was your weekend, Kyle?" Josh asked casually. Louise placed a plate of food in front of Josh and gave him a frown, most likely questioning why the hell Josh was sitting next to me.

"Fine," Kyle snapped and leaned back in his chair, looking like he wanted to kill his brother. "So, you and Sophia," he spat my full name out as if it was sour, "spent the weekend together?"

Kyle wasn't asking nicely, politely, or because he wanted to know. No, he was asking with judgement in his voice and daring his brother not to say yes. As if Kyle would launch across the table and kill Josh if he did.

Josh glanced at me and gave me a small smirk, and then he looked back at Kyle. "Yeah, Soph and I had a good weekend, if that is what you are asking?"

Tension. That was all I felt. Tension between Josh and Kyle. It was tight and bloody thick.

Kyle scoffed. "I can't think of one thing that you two could do together." Kyle waved a hand at us. "The nobody and the criminal. Seriously, what do you two have in common?"

Then it hit me.

Kyle was right. I was a nobody. Kyle had made me someone, and then he took it away. My eyes suddenly dropped to my plate. Yeah, Kyle was right. The nobody—that summed me up. Josh shouldn't waste a second me with, not because he was a criminal, but because anyone could see I was a nobody.

I didn't think one word could hurt me.

But I shouldn't be surprised. It was a word off Kyle's tongue after all. Kyle always knew how to get to my heart and twist the knife he had dug in there. God, he had me nearly in tears with just one word!

I was going to get up and leave, let them have their family dinner. I wasn't hungry to begin with. Yep, I was leaving. I dropped my knife and fork and went to push myself away from the table. But then Josh's arm that was on the back of my chair dropped around me.

"Soph and I have shit load in common." Josh's voices wasn't friendly. I didn't know the expression he was giving Kyle because I wouldn't look up from my plate.

I literally was a second away from tears.

I knew Kyle didn't think much of me. How could he? I wanted to run. I wanted to leave. Now.

"More than what you and she had in common." Josh's tone hardened. "You wanted to know how she spent her weekend? With me. In her bed. That enough of an answer for you?"

"In her bed? Since when do you sleep in any woman's bed?" Kyle's voice had an edge to it. "Everyone knows you don't sleep in any woman's bed because they might get clingy," Kyle said it so confidently.

I went to get up. I didn't need Josh explaining himself. But his hand went around my shoulder, pushing me back down. He wasn't letting me go anywhere.

"Yeah, her bed because she loves her electric blanket, and I didn't have one." Josh's kept control over his voice, but not well enough; you could hear the tint of anger. "But I fixed that today, little brother, so don't you worry about it."

I frowned and looked up for once this evening. "What do you mean you fixed that today?"

Josh was so busy having a glare off with Kyle, he didn't answer straight away. Then finally their glare broke. Josh's eyes landed on mine, and the anger that was in them slowly disappeared.

"I brought you an electric blanket."

"But I already have one."

A smirk spread across his lips. "For my bed, sweetheart." He leaned in, his mouth going to my ear. "My bed is bigger and so is my TV," he said softly, but loud enough for everyone to hear. For some reason, he wanted to give the impression to everyone that we were sleeping together.

I guess we had spent two nights together. He pulled back slowly, a carefree expression on his face, but I noted nerves as well. He was worried about my reaction. Was he thinking I would declare I would never sleep in his bed or something? Yeah, right now, reading his expression, he was worried about that.

A small smile appeared on my face and I turned my body into him. "Bigger screen to watch *The Young Ones* on, and a bigger bed? You're just better when it comes to everything, aren't you?"

"It's on tonight, right?" he asked, acting like our conversation wasn't being listened to by everyone. For some reason that made my small smile get bigger.

"It is, but you watched it last night. I'm going to force you to watch it two nights in a row." I continued our charade of being the only ones at the table.

Josh smirked, and he turned completely to face me, his hand going to the side of my face, gently pushing my hair back over my shoulder. "What can I say, I'm a sucker for a comedy." His words were soft and kind and had me by the heart.

He was a really good friend. But he was proving to me he wasn't just capable of being a friend, he was capable of being a great friend.

I was getting lost in his vibrant blue eyes again. God, I was a sucker for his eyes. They weren't just a bright blue; they had a hint of dark blue to them too when you looked closer. But it wasn't just any type of dark blue; it was the type of dark blue the ocean turns when the moon is cast over it. Yeah, that type of dark blue.

I was so lost in them—loving them, that I sighed in frustration when he broke our eye contact.

"Have you eaten a thing?" His eyes were on my plate and then back on me. I could see the annoyance in his expression. "You've stabbed a potato, that's it?"

I rolled my eyes and looked back at my plate. Okay, everything was not untouched apart from the potato which did look like it had been stabbed to death. Well, what did he expect? I had to take my frustration out on something listening to Kayla.

I looked back at Josh. "Not hungry."

He arched his eyebrows. "Do you really want to say that to me?" There was a threat in his tone, a threat that he would call me out and make me list everything I've eaten today, and if I did tell him the list, which was coming up blank, I didn't want to see his reaction.

"Um. It's cold now." I pushed the plate away from me, turning and giving him a full smile. "I only liked the potato, anyway."

His eyes widened, "Really, so you love potatoes?"

"To death. Pity there was only one." And just like that, I dodged the whole 'no eating' thing.

Josh pushed himself away from the table slightly. I looked back at him. Was he leaving? Well, I guess he had made one heck of an appearance. My eyes were still on him when he looked back at me. Why was he looking at me like that?

"Up," he said, and gestured with his hand for me to more. "Now."

I frowned. "What?"

"Up. Now."

I didn't understand why I had to stand. But doing as I was told, I pushed myself away from the table. Just as I stood, his arms wrapped around my waist and he pulled me down to his lap. Surprised by the sudden move, my arm wrapped around his neck automatically to catch myself. I heard Kyle scoff like it was unbelievable, but my attention was on Josh as he repositioned me.

One of Josh's hands stilled on my side, holding me in place as the other reached around me, pulling his plate closer.

"Start eating," he said firmly, and his hand went to mine, which were locked around his neck. "Now, Soph."

I groaned. So, this was why I was on his lap. "I am not eating your dinner," I even pouted a little. There was nothing wrong with me not eating. Nothing at all.

"Just so happens I don't feel like potatoes and mum has given me heaps. So, you can either start eating them, or I'll start feeding them to you." He was serious right now, his tone, his expression both deadly and fucking serious. He didn't care who was watching; he didn't care who saw him feed me. He wasn't backing down.

I huffed. "Fine." I turned on his lap and picked up the fork. "But just for this, Josh, I'm sleeping in the middle of the bed. With both electric blankets on." I smirked a bit at my plan. I knew for a fact he thought the temperature I kept my blanket at was too hot.

Then he did something I wasn't expecting, he kissed my bare shoulder. I turned just slightly to look at him, and all I saw was pleasure. He was happy right now. Him getting me to eat made him happy.

Louise and Jed got up and entered their own conversation. Seems the attention was finally off Josh and me. They went into the kitchen talking about something. My eyes were glued to Josh. So was my attention.

"Soph, you aren't eating." He nudged his head towards the plate. "Eat."

I sighed and turned my attention back to his plate. "You know I think your bed is more comfortable than mine." I started to chop up the potato.

"It is and from now on you are sleeping in it."

I wanted to laugh, but then I began to wonder whether he was serious.

Kyle laughing caused my eyes to snap from off Josh and on to him. "So what are you going to do, Sophia, when you go to sleep in his bed one night and wake up to him and another woman?" Kyle's eyes hardened with annoyance but also enjoyment.

Kyle had taken what Josh said as a fact, like I would be spending every night in Josh's bed from now on. And if you looked at Josh's expression, you might have thought that, too.

But I doubted that Josh was serious about me sleeping in his bed every night.

Kyle was right, Josh did sleep with other women. I wasn't having sex with Josh; we were only friends. Josh would need to have sex at some point, so Kyle had a point. But I wasn't about to gush over how awkward it would be if Josh kicked me out of his bed so he could have sex with another woman.

Nope. I wasn't doing that.

I sighed casually. "Well, who knows, Kyle? I am in to the drugs and party scene now. Doesn't sexual exploration come with that?" Seeing the shock on Kyle's face was priceless and with that said I put the fork in my mouth and took the potato off it.

Josh laughed, and it hummed through my body as I sat on him. I think Josh had never seen his brother so fucking speechless. *Ha. Take that, Kyle.* For once he had nothing to say. I glanced at Kayla and her expression mirrored her boyfriend's.

Did Kyle really think he could put me in a position where I would feel awkward and he would control and know my feelings? Yeah, I think he did. I think in his world I was still his little Soph, the one that would shy away from an awkward situation or at the mention of sex.

Seeing as he was in shock, I decided to use that to my advantage. I pointed my fork at him after swallowing my potato. "You know what you should do, Kyle, you should get tattoos. I know it goes against your whole golden boy image. But trust me, they turn girls on." I looked at Kayla. "You always had a thing for tattoos, right?"

They both just stared at me with their mouths slightly open.

I shrugged. "I never really liked them until I saw Josh's. Now I don't even glance at a guy that doesn't have them." That was true now. I loved the work in tattoos. But I loved Josh's tattoos the best. And I hadn't even seen all of them.

Kyle shook his head, snapping out of shock. "So, you are telling me you stand for everything my brother does?" He looked at me like that was impossible. "You are actually saying that not one of his tattoos offend you? That you, Sophia, would accept his type of life?"

I frowned, what the fuck was Kyle going on about?

"So, you are saying that you would stand by him even though he is worthless criminal?" Kyle added, and just those words made my blood boil. "His life is going nowhere!"

I had spent so long being hurt by Kyle that I was never really mad at him. I never thought I deserved him in the first place. But for him to sit there and degrade another human being, especially his brother, had just sent my body into overdrive with hate towards him.

I could not believe that the Kyle I knew would think so little of a person. Let alone his flesh and blood.

I felt Josh's hand go still on my back, and I didn't need to see his expression. I already knew what Josh thought of himself, which wasn't much. Josh was most likely thinking Kyle was painting his life with more color than he deserved.

"Clearly, you and I have a different understanding of worthlessness. I value Josh more than I value men like you—spineless, gutless shits that treat women like they are nothing but a sex symbol." My glare hardened on

Kyle, the lid on my temper gone. "Your life is the one going nowhere, do you know why that is?"

He didn't answer, so I took the chance.

"Because you will never have a woman that truly loves you for you in your life. You will have the degree, you will have the expensive car, house, and successful career, but you know what else you will have? A wife who will never love you for you without those things, and who will care more about the dollars in the bank than about you." I held Kyle's eyes. I wasn't finished. "Do you know what your brother will have?" I arched my eyebrows. "A woman who stands by his every decision, who loves the dark and the light side of him, and who won't just fight for him but also beside him. He is going to have a woman that loves him for him. No matter what. He will have a family and he also will be there for his children, not working in a pointless corporate job. So, remind me again, who will have the worthless life?"

Just like that, I shut Kyle down. I shut down everything he thought about himself. He really thought he was better than Josh.

Well, he was wrong. Josh was so much better than him. Josh was the one that was going to have the great life. Josh was the one that would have the woman who loved him. Josh was more of a man than Kyle would ever be.

Kyle just stared at me and then finally opened his mouth. "Well, at least now I know which brother you think more of."

I shook my head. "It's not that at all, Kyle. It's about which brother is more of a man." I dropped my fork. "Maybe one day you will actually realize how much of an example your brother is. Until then, I guess your future is looking as bright and happy as a funeral march."

I didn't feel bad when I saw the hurt in Kyle's eyes because only moments before, he was trying to put that hurt in Josh's. Kyle looked at me so hurt, I thought he was close to tears, like my opinion really mattered to him. That me saying I thought Josh was going to have the better life didn't just hurt him, it shattered his heart.

Well, if he didn't like where his life was heading, I guess I had just given him an eye opener. Now he could do something about it.

I hated it when people put others down because in their head, they thought they were better. Just moments ago, Kyle thought he was better than Josh. Why? Because he judged value on material things. On what society thinks of you, and on the opinion of narrowed minded people.

I took my eyes off Kyle and as I turned in Josh's lap, I saw his expression. He looked just as shocked as his brother. Maybe even more. He had heard every word I had said, and I think he just didn't know how to react. I knew Josh; he wouldn't think that one word I had just said was possible of happening.

But I knew different. I knew he would get all those things. Why? Because Josh had a good and pure heart and when he decided he was ready to open it up to a woman, she was going to be one hell of a lucky girl and she would be giving him all those things I've listed.

Josh didn't see it, but I did. And so would the woman that he let into his life.

I put my hand on his cheek. "So where is this electric blanket? And I'm totally claiming the right side of the bed." I smiled at him, hoping that he would snap out of just staring at me.

The shock slowly disappeared from his eyes and an emotion painted in them I had never seen before. Not in his eyes, or any man's eyes. I didn't know if it was amazement, hatred, love, or disappointment.

I couldn't help but grin. Truth was, Josh was going to have a great and successful life. Society might not approve of how he lives it, or how he earns money, but Josh would be happy, and that is all that mattered. Isn't that what everyone wants, happiness?

I opened my mouth, ready to pull him from this state, but my phone buzzed on the table. I reached for it. Then I saw his name and nearly rolled my eyes. He still wasn't getting the whole silent treatment I was giving him. I unlocked my phone, opening up Bax's message.

Babe, I'm so fucking sorry. Just tell me what I need to do to get u back.

My eyes ran over Bax's words a couple of times. I had blocked him out for over a week. I had told him I didn't want anything to do with him, and yet he wasn't ready to give up on me.

I hit reply just as the phone was snatched out of my hands. I frowned, and it took me a second to realize what had happened as I looked at Josh, my phone clenched in his hand, and an expression I did know —jealousy.

"Um, Josh, you have my phone?" I was very calm about it, casual, like we were fooling around, when really, he was being a control freak.

He had given me reason after reason this morning why I shouldn't go back to Bax. And all day I hadn't reached out to Bax because I couldn't get "what would Josh think" out of my head.

I wondered what it would take for Josh to snap out of the state I put him in by me telling the truth to his brother about him, and the life he was going to have. But I hadn't expected him to go straight into jealousy.

It wasn't like Bax would ever come in between our friendship. Maybe I needed to tell him that?

"Josh, give me the phone," I said calmly and put my hand out. "You and I had this discussion this morning, and we both know where we landed on the subject."

I was not going to rehash this morning fight with Josh in front of Kyle and Kayla and within earshot of his parents.

"Nah. The answer to his question is nothing. You hear me, Soph? Nothing he can do." Josh never told me off or talked to me like he was in control of my life or anything. Actually, Josh never cared what anyone did with their life as long as it didn't impact his.

So why the fuck did he just say that like he didn't just care, but I couldn't argue with him?

"Josh give me the phone."

"No."

I scoffed. I couldn't believe it.

That was when I heard Kyle laughing.

I turned to look at him. "Why are you laughing? Something snap you out of the depressive life you are living?"

"My brother has competition for you." Kyle pointed a finger at Josh with a wide grin. "How does it feel, big brother, to finally meet a girl out of your league? Soph might think you are a better man than me, but you still aren't man enough to have her." Kyle looked at me with hope. What the hell was wrong with him?

"Josh, give me the phone. Don't you have somewhere you need to be tonight, anyway?" I reminded him of the busy night he did have planned this morning.

"Yeah, that was until I realized something." He kept clenching my phone so tightly I was waiting for the screen to start to crack.

"Let me guess, Soph is more important than another night on the piss at the strip clubs?" Kyle piped into the conversation.

I turned and threw a glare at Kyle. "Shut up, Kyle. We all know I'm not important enough to stop anyone's plans. I'm nobody, remember? I'm not the woman you drop plans for. I'm not the woman you do anything for. You said I was a nobody, and you were right." I turned my attention back on to Josh. "Now give me the phone."

Josh's eyes hardened; his gaze focused on Kyle "See what you fucking did?" Josh yelled across the table at his brother. "You happy with yourself?"

Josh completely ignored me. Instead, he started yelling at Kyle. "You are fucking toxic. I meant it when I said you stay out of her life. That means no talking to her." Josh was yelling, and even his parents looked up from the kitchen to see what the problem was.

Kyle narrowed his eyes at Josh. "You can't ban me from talking to Soph! She was mine to begin with!"

"There you go again, forgetting that you are in her past, not her future!"

"And there you go again, hoping to be in her future!" Kyle snapped back at Josh just as quickly. "Soph and I will always have more than whatever fucked up relationship you have with her."

"Oh, for Christ's sake!" I roared and slapped Josh's arm off me and got up. "You both are acting like I matter! I don't!" I never yelled, but here I was screaming at them. "So, stop fighting! You are brothers!" God, I wasn't worth an argument. "I don't have one fucking idea why you two want to compete on who will know me better when we all know there is nothing about me that anyone would want."

I didn't get it. I didn't get what they were talking about when they were saying futures and pasts and shit. I wasn't in anyone's future because I wasn't worth a second glance. I wasn't even worth a first glance. I was a nobody. No one important, and as much as I went on about everyone contributing to the world, I knew my mark wouldn't be great, inspiring, or deep. It would be a scratch.

"Sophia dear, are you okay?" Louise said from the kitchen.

No. I wasn't okay. But I didn't need Louise's pity.

I forced myself to take a steady breath and turned to face Kyle and Josh's parents. "Thanks for dinner, Louise and Jed. I'm heading out now." And with that said, I walked behind Josh's chair and through the house.

Bax wasn't a guy that would love or respect me. I knew that. But I also knew I wasn't worth being loved and respected. Sex. That was all I was getting from Bax, and that was all he was able to give me. And while I had sex with him, it filled some need inside me. It gave me all I needed.

I picked up my keys for my car from the foyer table and opened the front door and closed it swiftly behind me.

Josh and Kyle would make up. They were brothers. I don't know why they were suddenly thinking I was a rag doll in between them. I wasn't. I wasn't worth a fight.

Kyle would get a trophy wife. Maybe Kayla.

And Josh would find the love of his life.

When they both did that, they would realize how pointless it was to fight with each other, especially over me.

As soon as I was not living in the same house as them, they would forget all about me.

I was walking down the garden path when I heard the front door close.

"Soph!"

I picked up my speed.

"Soph!"

I just pressed the button to unlock my car and my lights flashed. I opened the driver's side door and then Josh's hand went to the corner and shut it.

I wanted to groan. Couldn't he just let me leave? His hand was still on the door and he was trapping me between the car and him. I could feel his strong body behind me, pressing into my back. I was breathing sharply and trying my very best, to not show how upset I was.

"Sweetheart, please turn around?"

I crossed my arms and kept my back to him. I would not turn around. Then his hand went off the door and I took my opportunity. I uncrossed my arms and my hand went to the door handle, and just as I opened it his hand forced it shut again.

I huffed in frustration.

"Sweetheart, I'm not letting you go to him." Josh's words were firm, yet soft, which made me frown and I turned around.

"Why?" I looked up at him, and he was staring down at me again with a tint in his eyes that confused me.

He took a step towards me, closing the small gap between us. I took one back.

"Because."

"That's not a reason."

"I'm not going to be the one that drives you into his arms."

I rolled my eyes. "You aren't."

"You are going to him right now because of me." Josh pulled his hand off the car and his hand went to my side; he dipped his head. "I'm sorry for upsetting you."

Josh never said sorry. He didn't believe in the word sorry. So, I knew right now he was only saying it cause he didn't know what else to say.

I shook my head. "Don't do that. Don't say sorry when you don't mean it."

"I do mean it."

I scoffed and couldn't help myself. I pushed him firmly back. "Piss off, Josh."

Josh grabbed my hands, trapping each one in one of his strong hands. "Sweetheart. I mean it. I'm sorry. Now please don't run from me." I heard the change in his words, pain crept into them. Like me leaving would hurt him.

I stopped and looked at the situation. Josh was standing here saying sorry. He never said sorry. He was standing here stopping me from going to a man that Josh thought wasn't worth my time.

He didn't want me to run from him. He thought he was driving me into another man's arms. What was he scared of? Why did thinking he was driving me to another man bother him so?

I didn't have an answer.

Josh did realize that if I left tonight to go to Bax, it wouldn't change mine and his relationship, right?

Okay, I didn't have an answer for that either.

"Soph." Josh's pulled my hands and forced me to come to him. "Please don't leave."

"If I do, what does it matter? It's not like me going to him will affect our friendship. I'm thankful you came home when you did, but that doesn't mean I'm expecting you to stay for the night."

Yeah, I gave him an explanation. His night didn't have to change. I'm sure his phone hadn't stopped ringing since he left his friends. His phone was always ringing.

"It fucking matters." Josh's words were sharp. "Fine, I tried talking to you, you leave me no choice."

I frowned and then squealed as he threw me over his shoulder.

EIGHTEEN

Soph

I knew Josh was strong. He looked like a walking UFC beast. So, I wasn't surprised that he was carrying me like I weighed nothing. I squirmed. I wiggled. I yelled at him. And he ignored all of it.

He even walked us past his parents who were in the foyer and they didn't seem to care that Josh had me over his shoulder like I was doll he just pick up and carried around.

To say I was furious with him when he shut his bedroom door was an understatement. And mind you, he was assuming I wanted to be near him and didn't mind being carried to his bedroom.

My feet hit the floor, and as soon as I got my balance, I pushed him hard on each shoulder.

"How dare you just carry me around like that! Who the hell do you think you are just to carry me away from my night's plans?" I wanted to punch him, but I knew I would be the one that ended up sore. I would have a sore fist and he would end up laughing.

"Calm down, sweetheart." He didn't seem fussed that I was furious.

I took a step towards him and pointed a finger into his chest. "I'm leaving and you can't stop me." I was serious. I was leaving. I wasn't staying here just because he had dragged me here. He might have carried me in here, but I had legs and could walk out, which was exactly what I was going to do.

I made one move to go around him and he blocked me.

"Sweetheart, I'm not letting you go to him." He said it like it was the most obvious thing in the world.

What was with men and thinking they could tell me what to do? Kyle always told me what to do. It was because of him I learned to rely on him in my life, like he was the gravity to my world. Bax thought it was acceptable to declare to the world I was his and had me wearing a top that told everyone I was hooked up with a biker, and it was serious. And then there was Josh, who thought he could stop me from going out. First, he took my phone and then, when I went to leave, he literally picked me up and carried me back into the house.

My eyes narrowed at him. "Josh Andrew Hawkins, if you know what is good for you, you will get out of my way." My words gritted as they came out, the anger I was feeling was overwhelming. I was sick of people telling me what to do—how to feel. I was hoping my threat would cause Josh to step out of my way and let me go. So, I was surprised when he took a step towards me, his hands spreading out on my cheeks, cupping my face.

What was he doing? Had he gone mad? Why was he looking at me like that? He had that weird look in his eyes again that was there after I listed all the reasons his life was going to be better than Kyle's. I was thinking, if I was any other female and he was giving the current look he was giving me to them, they would think Josh was in love with them. Hell, you would think all of a sudden Josh's life depended on you.

I opened my mouth to question him on it, but he moved quicker, his lips covering mine. At first, I wasn't sure what to do. Push him away, pull him in? I was shocked for longer than a second. I had been kissed before, but I had never felt this electricity spark through every one of my blood vessels before.

Suddenly, I snapped out of the shock and I wanted my blood vessels to explode by this electric spark he was giving my body.

My lips moved against his, and I felt the corner of his lips twitch up for a second, like he was pleased I wasn't pushing him away but demanding more.

I would have to say, when it came to being intimate, it wasn't natural. I was always nervous at first. Then my brain would drown out the nerves. But this time I wasn't nervous at all.

It hadn't been my brain that drowned out the nerves.

I didn't have nerves to begin with.

It was like my brain switched off as soon as his lips landed on mine, and my body took over.

He lifted me up, my hands locking around his neck while our kiss went up a notch from being demanding to complete raw need. It was like his need for me overcame him. My legs had just wrapped around him when he bit my bottom lip, causing me to gasp. He took the opportunity to explore my mouth. He wasn't gentle and he sure as fuck wasn't soft.

And I loved it.

His hands went to my top, and our kiss broke when he took it off, and then before it even hit the floor his lips were back on mine.

I knew where this could be heading, so why the hell wasn't I panicking or stopping him?

His hands were exploring my skin while he held me up with his body. He slowly lowered me to the bed, and his lips went off mine. He kissed along my jaw and slowly started to kiss down my neck.

It was like he was worshipping me. Each kiss was more intimate.

I couldn't stop myself from arching my neck to him. I was so lost in the feel of his lips on my skin, I hadn't realized his fingers had unclipped my bra until he was dragging the straps down my arms. I knew I should be nervous. I knew I should be experiencing warning signs. But I wasn't.

As soon as my bra was out of the way, his kisses started to go lower.

"Josh?" I managed to say. I had to stop him before he did something he would regret in the morning. "You need to stop." My fingers were running through his hair. I wouldn't lie, I loved his lips on me. I loved how my body reacted—the pleasure that flooded my blood stream—I hadn't felt like this before, so it was going to kill me when he stopped.

He ignored me. If anything, his kisses got more intense, firmer, and lower. I knew where he was going, and it sent wave after wave of need through my body.

Suddenly, I didn't want him to stop. I knew he should. But as his kisses got lower, I didn't want him to stop. I knew it was selfish, and I knew that if we had sex right now, our friendship would be ruined, but I needed him. Now.

His lips went off me, and I realized my words of telling him to stop may have just registered. "Soph, I have to tell you something. It's not fair to you if I don't. Especially considering where I want you and I to go."

I was still high on the pleasure he had just given me to really listen to whatever was so important. I nodded my head and opened my eyes, but seeing his serious expression made me lean up.

"Josh, are you okay?" I couldn't stop myself from asking. He looked scared.

He unlocked my hands from around his neck, linking them with his, his eyes still on me. "I just don't want to lose you, Soph, and I know once I tell you this you are going to want nothing to do with me."

I saw the pain in his eyes for a split second before he masked his expression.

"You know how I know Bax?" He sounded so hesitant, like he was about to tell me something so important that he was positive I wouldn't take it well.

I nodded my head. But before he could say another word, I leaned up and kissed him on the lips, this time soft and gentle. Pulling back, I saw more pain in his eyes. I unlinked one of our hands, my hand going to his cheek.

"Stop looking so worried, there is nothing that will result in you losing me." I was honest. I didn't care about his criminal record. I didn't care that he most likely was still adding to that record.

"You can't say that until you have all the facts." He dismissed what I said. "I know you, I know once I tell you this you are going to think all I did was lie to you and I know how much honesty means to you."

He was right there; honesty meant a hell of a lot to me. But still, I already knew Josh had secrets. I knew he hadn't been in a position to tell me about them, but it would seem tonight he was going to open up to me.

"You don't have to tell me anything, Josh. I understand there are parts of your life you can't share." I tried to gently tell him. I didn't care. I understood completely. "Just because we are going to have a one-night stand, doesn't mean you have to open up your soul to me."

"That's just it. I don't want a one-night stand. I want you to know what you are getting into with being with me."

"Being with you?" I frowned. What was he trying to imply?

He opened his mouth, but there was a banging on his door. I heard the doorknob twist and I clenched my eyes shut. Just fucking perfect.

But the door didn't open. I exhaled slowly. Josh must have locked it.

I opened my eyes in time to see Josh glance at the door, but then his attention was back on me, his eyes running down me. He had me topless and willing to have sex with him, but he was the one stopping us.

"You are so fucking perfect, Soph." He kissed in between my breasts. "Which is why I won't settle for one night." He looked up all serious. "I need you to know everything, and if then you still want this, I'll promise not to hurt you. Fuck, I'll promise you anything."

Now there was a banging on the door. Whoever it was wasn't giving up.

Josh groaned. "Don't move, okay? I just need to tell whoever it is to fuck off." Josh pulled away from me completely, and as soon as his hand left mine, I felt like I was missing something.

In case it was Josh's parents, I sat up and searched the floor for a top, putting on the first one that my hand found.

"What the fuck do you want, Kyle?" Josh's tone was anything but nice. I think he was more pissed off with Kyle because it had pulled Josh from me.

"I need to speak to Soph." Kyle didn't even seem fazed by how Josh spoke to him. "I'm guessing she is in there with you."

I gulped. Why would Kyle want to speak to me?

"Fuck off, Kyle." Josh went to slam the door in Kyle's face, but Kyle stopped him.

"Let me rephrase that: Soph's parents want to talk to her. They've being trying to get a hold of her all night, but you took her phone."

Immediately I was up. My parents would only call Kyle if something was wrong, seriously wrong. They never called me when they were overseas. Maybe on the odd time when I had accidentally set the house alarms off. But that was it.

I squeezed in between Josh and the door.

"Did they tell you what was wrong?" I wasn't hiding my panic. "Did they say why they called?"

Kyle looked somewhat smugly at me. "No, they didn't. Said you would only understand." Kyle handed me the phone. "It's on mute. Didn't want them hearing you fucking my brother."

I rolled my eyes. But right now who and who I wasn't having sex with wasn't important.

I took the phone off mute and put it to my ear. "I'm sorry I haven't had my phone on me—"

I started to explain, but Dad's rushed voice cut me off. He was speaking so fast and in two different languages, which is something he would always do when he called. It would be English and whatever language of the culture he was currently in.

"Okay, Dad, slow down and speak English," I said, unable to make sense of anything.

Then Dad spoke very clearly. And my mind was focused on two words: Ryan and lock up.

"Okay, Dad, I'm leaving now." I hung up and handed Kyle back his phone.

"Everything alright, Soph?" Kyle asked, sounding concerned.

I was back in Josh's room searching the floor for my car keys as soon as I found them, I grabbed my shoes and darted out between them.

I turned just as I was about to bolt down the stairs to look at Josh. "I'm sorry, Josh, but I have to go." I couldn't tell him why. I couldn't even explain what was happening if I wanted to.

I saw all the questions he had, but I didn't have time to answer them. Instead, I ran down the stairs. The same two words ringing through my mind...

NINETEEN

Soph

There was a detail of my life I didn't really share with anyone. Well, it wasn't a detail. It was a person. Ryan Butcher. My parents adopted him when I was a newborn. He was five at the time. His parents left him at the hospital with a letter.

It was Dad who was his treating doctor. It was Dad that read the letter saying that his parents weren't coming back for him. Ryan was malnourished, skinny, covered in bruises, and was a clear case of abuse.

Mom was due to have me any day. But Dad couldn't hand Ryan over to the system. So, they made a decision that most people couldn't and wouldn't ever do. They adopted Ryan. And they may have greased a few palms to make it happen.

The adoption went through the day after I was born. I still don't know how my mom did it. She managed to raise a newborn and a child who didn't trust her.

But Mum and Dad never gave up on Ryan. They treated him like he was blood because, in my parents' eyes, he was.

Ryan slowly accepted them. He had never been shown love, or simple things like a meal three times a day. I still remember Mom telling me she had never cried as much as she did when Ryan couldn't stomach food cause his body wasn't used to it.

His body was used to liquids and sometimes the odd meal.

Mom and Dad had him under every specialist to help Ryan learn to eat. Mom always said Ryan's biggest fear was they would leave him, like his parents left him. He would have nightmares about it every night. His biggest fear: being left by himself again.

So, they did something that goes against Mom and Dad's image of professional surgeons. They both got Ryan's name tattooed on them.

Ryan, I think, was around seven when Mom and Dad did it. Mom told me from the day Ryan saw those tattoos he stopped having nightmares.

Mum and Dad supported Ryan in everything he did, just like they did for me.

Then on his eighteen birthday we had a family party. I was thirteen. Ryan and I were always close. He was there for me as I grew up. Every photo of me had him in it. He was my brother. And he saw me as his sister.

We were best friends. And I thought he would always be there for me. But the day after his eighteenth birthday, he left my parents a note thanking them, and that was it. Not telling them why he left. Not one word directed at me. No I'll miss you. No I'm sorry. Nothing.

Just two words: thank you.

My parents were heartbroken. Mum stopped working, and for the first time in her life she stopped doing what she loved — helping people. Dad threw himself into work, started to miss important events in my life, sports games, achievement awards. Then on my first day of high school, Mum didn't even get out of bed for it and Dad, well, he was working a double shift and seemed to forget his only daughter was facing the biggest fear in her life.

It was on the first day of high school, when I had to walk there in the rain, I realized my parents loved Ryan more than me.

I can't remember how long that went on. We were a fractured family. Mom and Dad weren't even sleeping in the same room. My love for Ryan turned to hate because he had cost me my parents, and most of all my happy family.

Instead, I had a mom that was dosed up on prescription pills and a dad that lived at the hospital. And then there was me; I had never felt more lost than in the first year after Ryan left.

Thank god for Uncle Kane.

One day, I can't remember how long it had been, but I do remember the day clearly it was a Saturday, I walked downstairs ready to have another breakfast alone when I found

Mum and Dad talking and cooking breakfast.

That was the day I got my parents back. They sold the house and wanted to start fresh, so we moved closer to the hospital and my school. Then it was about a month after we were settled in and I started to think things might go back to normal, but at the same time I was grieving for my brother. Ryan that left a hole in our family. I wasn't the only one who realized that there was now a hole in our family.

It so happened to also be a Saturday when my parents told me they were going to do mission work. They left for Pakistan the following Monday. And they hadn't stopped doing mission work since.

It was like they needed to do it—helping others—to fill the hole Ryan had made in their hearts.

I didn't blame them. If I could have filled the hole that Ryan made in my heart somehow, I would have too.

But I never did. I just learned to live with it. I wasn't heart broken when Ryan left. I felt like he took half my heart with him.

And now, in the dead of the night, my parents call me, telling me Ryan was locked up, and the police had called them.

My parents didn't hold a grudge towards Ryan. They loved him. So tonight, when there was a chance for them to help him again, they took it. Dad was so panicked on the phone. He knew that Ryan wouldn't have wanted them to be called.

It had been five years since Ryan left. I was now eighteen. And he would be twenty-three. I didn't say a word to him. I signed the bail information; I paid the money, and then I was handed the court date. I knew I had to make one phone call to make sure the charges were dropped.

Even though he had chosen to stop being my brother five years ago, I was still going to call and get the charges dropped. I knew if mom and dad were here right now, they would be making the call.

I pulled away from the station, keeping my eyes on the road. Not on my brother, who was sitting in the passenger seat. I didn't know what to say to him. Sure, over the years I had questions for him, but as the years went on, I realized I didn't want the answers anymore.

So, I didn't speak to him. I didn't make eye contact. In fact, I hadn't even really looked at him. I just walked straight to my car, and he followed.

I wasn't going to talk to him. He had no idea what impact he had on my life and my parents when he decided to leave. Every birthday of mom's I knew she waited for a card from him or a phone call. And every birthday of Ryan's, Mom and Dad would be extra quiet.

Even though it killed me to see pictures of Ryan throughout the house, Mum and Dad had still put them up in our new house. I hated walking up the stairs, seeing pictures of Ryan and me together.

I lost my best friend, my brother, and my family the day he decided he didn't want to be a part of it anymore.

So, what the hell was I meant to say to him now? How has the last five years been? I wanted to scoff. Nope. I had nothing I wanted to say to him.

The car was silent.

I think he finally realized I wasn't going to speak. I hoped he respected me enough to keep his empty words to himself.

I heard him sigh, and out of the corner of my eye I saw him run his fingers through his black hair. Something he used to do when he was facing an awkward situation. Then I felt his eyes on me.

"Well, you've grown up, Soph." He decided that was the best line to break five years of silence.

I ignored him.

"Guessing the parents must be real pissed with me not to show up. I don't blame them. Still, you didn't have to take pity on me and bail me out." He was speaking like my parents would actually ignore him.

I didn't want to say it because I didn't want to speak to him. I knew I had to correct the flaw in his reasoning. Mom and Dad would have been at the station bailing him out if they were in the country.

"Mom and Dad are in Africa," I said. I really hadn't wanted to, but I did. "So, I didn't get a choice in picking you up or not."

I changed lanes, putting more focus on the road than him.

"What, on a holiday? Mom and Dad don't do holidays." Ryan sounded surprised as well as interested. He knew our parents never took time to relax and a holiday would be a nightmare for them. Not helping people. Not having a purpose every morning. Yep, they would hate it.

I glanced at him. I couldn't stop myself. The expression on his face told me he cared. He cared where Mom and Dad were.

"They aren't." I put my eyes on the road. "They do mission work."

Ryan was silent for a minute. "So, they fly all around the world helping people?" Seemed Ryan did have some idea of what mission work was.

"Yep."

"So, you'd be left on your own a lot then?"

I glanced at him with a blank expression and nodded my head.

"When did they start the mission work? Was it not by choice? Because Mom and Dad wouldn't want to leave you behind."

I gritted my teeth. Yeah, the version of our parents, back when he was still in our life, couldn't see Mom and Dad leaving me at all. But Ryan wasn't factoring in they stopped being those types of parents when he left. I didn't answer him. I wasn't going to tell him that he sent our mom, the strongest, bravest, smartest woman I know, into a depression so bad she didn't get out of bed for a year. All she did was take pills and sleep.

Then there was Dad, the family man, who made sure to be there for big and small events in your life. He would even turn surgeries down if that conflicted with whatever was going on in our life. Then when Ryan left, Dad stopped being the family man. He worked and worked and worked. And when he wasn't working, he was trying to convince Mom to eat something. Then their relationship fell apart. Dad started sleeping in the guestroom on the rare occasion he was home. Mum wouldn't even leave the house to get her pills, she sent our housekeeper.

The parents, Ryan was referring to, died the same time he left us.

"How often are Mom and Dad in the country now?" Ryan was still talking about them like he actually gave a fuck.

"A couple of months or weeks of the year," I answered simply with no emotion. "They try to be here for holidays, but usually Christmas and Easter is when they are needed the most."

"You can't be serious."

I glanced at Ryan, seeing his shocked expression. "What?"

"Mom and Dad aren't even home for Christmas and Easter? You are seriously telling me they are barely in the country? Did they forget they have a daughter?" Ryan's words had heat to them. I think in his head he really thought Mom and Dad would have accepted him leaving their life.

Should I give him a reality check?

"When did this start happening?" Ryan's words were firm. He really wanted to know.

I looked at him, and I couldn't stop my eyes from narrowing. He couldn't be fucking serious. Was he really that bloody dumb?

I took my eyes off him and back onto the road. "What did you expect to happen, Ryan?" My words were cold. "You left."

"So, what happened... I left and suddenly they headed overseas?" Ryan was trying to piece together the last five years with only limited facts.

"Nope." I felt the rage boiling. "First Mom went into depression for a year, didn't get out of bed, and just popped prescription pills. Mind you, she wouldn't leave the house to get them. Our house keeper's list of jobs went up." I was trying to resist the urge to yell at him. "Then Dad threw himself into work, stopped coming home. And on the odd occasion he did, he slept in the guestroom."

I glanced at Ryan; whose face was blank of expression. "Then one day, Mom got out of bed and Dad came home from work and they told me they had joined the mission. They left the following Monday and have been coming and going since."

I saw his fists clench. "So, they just forgot they had a fucking daughter! They just left you?"

I slowed the car down. "No." I didn't hold anything against my parents because I knew what they were feeling. "They were grieving a son and found a way to cope." I pulled in the driveway and looked at Ryan. "The way they found to cope didn't include me." I put the car in park.

I saw the frustration in Ryan's eyes. But what did he expect? He left our parents, causing them to fracture into pieces.

Ryan looked me in the eye. He was about to open his mouth, but I didn't need to hear him say the word sorry. We both knew he wouldn't mean it.

I opened up the glove box, grabbed the envelope and handed it to him. "Mom and Dad wanted to make sure you got this." I let go of the envelope as soon as his hand gripped it. "There are two checks in there. One from the apartment they bought you in New York. The other from a beach house they bought you." Then my eyes landed on the house we had pulled up at. "And the titles to this house. This one Mum couldn't bring herself to sell on your behalf. All your stuff is here."

I sighed and looked back at him, seeing his shocked expression.

"They bought me houses?" He had opened the envelope. Shock wasn't just on his face, it was in his voice.

"One when they adopted you. One when you turned eighteen. And another when you turned twenty-one." The memory of Mom and Dad purchasing his house for his twenty-first birthday ran through my mind. And then the pain on their faces when the private detective they hired told them they couldn't find him.

All Mom and Dad wanted was to give him money. To make sure he had money behind him. They didn't expect him to come back to the family; they respected the fact that he wanted to lead his own life. But they wanted to make sure he had money behind him so he could follow his passions and not just have to work for the sake of it.

"They only ever wanted to make sure you wanted for nothing. These houses are investments, to be sold when you wanted the cash. But people kept making offers. Mum and Dad had this delusion that if they sold them and got in contact with you and gave you the money, you wouldn't end up on the streets." My hands tightened around the stirring wheel. "But they never found you."

Ryan was extremely quiet. I guess if he was like any other human, he would be feeling guilt right now. But this was Ryan; he didn't give a fuck when it came to other people's feelings. Him leaving the way he did proved that.

"You can get out of my car now." I wouldn't look at him. The rage I was feeling was unhealthy, and I knew if he gave me even just one excuse on why he left, I'd kill him.

Because, if he had a real reason to leave, he should have told us. Hell, if he didn't want everyone to know he should have at least told Dad. Dad could have comforted Mom when she realized her son left, instead of hiring every person possible to find him.

Ryan made sure not to be found, and he had been successful.

"Give it back to them. I don't want it." Ryan dropped the envelope in my lap. "And I'll pay you back for the bail you posted."

He could not be fucking serious. I was forced to look at him and he was about to get out of the car when I pressed the automatic lock button.

"You've hurt them enough. Don't you dare insult them again." I couldn't stop the anger I was feeling from creeping across my face. "You have dragged them through the mud. You wanted out of their life. Fine, you got it. But they never let you leave their life. They fucking hoped and prayed you would come back."

I was so angry. The word angry didn't even cover what I felt right now. "You really think that not taking their money will prove something? Like you are too good for them? All they ever did was love you, and how do you repay them? Fuck off as soon as they weren't legally responsible for you. You may have stopped loving them the day you left, but they didn't stop loving you." I threw the envelope back at him. "You know, I used to imagine what our first conversation would be like when you came back. Then after a few years I stopped because I never wanted to fucking see you again. So, take the money and get the fuck out of my car." I unlocked the car. I wanted him gone, out of my car, and back out of my life.

I was so upset, so furious that I couldn't stop the tears if I wanted to. He never understood how much I depended on him. How much I loved him. How much I needed him. How I needed him in my life. He was my best friend. He was my brother.

And he left.

When it came down to it, it was his fault that I was so hurt over Kyle. Losing Kyle reminded me of losing Ryan. I had been fooled again. Ryan said he would always be with me. He left. Kyle said he would always be there. He left.

"Soph." Ryan's hand went to my knee. I didn't want him touching me. I wanted him gone.

"Just fuck off, Ryan. Don't take these tears as sadness." I pushed his hand off me. The sooner he left, the sooner I could forget he existed.

"No."

My head snapped towards him. "I said fuck off. You fuck off." I spoke very clearly. "I paid your bail. I'll call the judge and get the charges dropped. All I am asking in return is for you to fuck off."

The hate in my voice was clear, but also was the pain. The pain he caused me. The pain I felt every time I looked at a photo. The never-ending pain when it came to him.

He still wasn't leaving, and I couldn't keep myself together much longer.

"Please, Ryan, just leave." My tears were flowing down my cheeks. I was so used to crying these days. Usually over Kyle, though. I had stopped crying over Ryan a long time ago. But it looked like, when it came to it, I still had tears left for him.

He looked like he was in pain himself. I didn't understand why. He left. Not me. His fingers ran across my cheek.

"Please don't cry, Soph. You know I hate it." He leaned in closer to me. "I never wanted you to cry over me."

I scoffed. "What the hell did you expect, Ryan? You were my brother. There one minute, gone forever the next! You didn't even say goodbye!" I pushed his fingers off my face. I didn't need him to comfort me. Well, I did need him to—years ago. "You wanted out of our family. You got it." My words were bitter and covered in hurt. "Stay in the house. Don't stay in the house. Cash the checks. Burn the checks. Just do whatever you want."

Because when it came down to it, Ryan always did what he wanted.

He sat back in the car seat, looking like he wasn't getting out.

"You moved," he said firmly. "All your numbers changed. Mom and Dad weren't at the hospital anymore. I tried, okay, Soph. Every one of your birthdays I tried to reach out for you. But I couldn't find you." He turned and looked at me, honesty painted on his face. "You think I didn't hate myself every time I couldn't find you? Every time your birthday came, every Christmas, every Easter, I hated myself a bit more. Cause I knew I was letting you down."

I couldn't believe what he was saying, so I just stared at him. Silently the tears rolled down my cheeks.

"On your eighteenth birthday, I drank myself into a fucking coma. I knew I had let you down. More on that day than any other because we had plans. I remember every detail of what we had planned." His eyes were locked on mine, and I saw his pain—actual pain. "I made promises to you, and on that day, I knew my time to make it up to you was over. You wouldn't need a brother anymore." His eyes dropped to the envelope. "I failed you, Soph, and I am sorry. But I can't make up for five years of broken promises to you. I'm not that stupid to even try."

I nodded my head. He was right. He couldn't make up for being absent for five years.

"The last conversation we had was about you starting high school." He looked at me, then paused. "I always wanted to know how that went. I guess you most likely don't remember it. You would be in your final year now, right?"

I just blinked, tears dropping down. I remembered my first day of high school really well. It had burnt a permeant memory in my brain. I opened my mouth, and I wasn't sure if I was making a mistake by telling him.

"Mom hadn't got out of bed for months. She wouldn't have known if I went or not. Dad forgot, which I understood because he hadn't been home for a week. So why would he come home for my first day? I walked the hour to school, in the rain. When I got there, I didn't have textbooks." But that wasn't what I remembered the most. "Mom and Dad forgot to pay my tuition, so I wasn't officially enrolled. I ended up paying my tuition with my credit card. And Uncle Kane came and signed the papers."

Ryan looked speechless. He opened his mouth and then closed it, like he didn't know what to say. He was most likely thinking how unbelievable it was that Uncle Kane was sober enough to do anything involving paperwork.

"I don't know what to say. I just can't believe Mom and Dad would do that."

I shrugged. "Wasn't a big deal. It turned out alright. For that year Uncle Kane took care of me."

"Are we talking about the same Uncle Kane? The alcoholic?" Ryan looked at me with disbelief.

I nodded my head. "He basically took care of me when he realized how messed up Mom and Dad were. He stopped drinking to the point of passing out. He used to have a 'Soph limit,' he called it, where he would drink a certain amount and stop, in case I needed him." I opened the compartment in the middle and pulled out a photo that I kept in the car and handed it to Ryan. "That was the opening of his first bar. It's called Sophia's." I smiled just slightly, remembering that night. "He has made it into a chain now and he has bars up and down the coast. Still bar tends at that one though."

Ryan was staring down at the picture.

"When was this taken?"

"I was fifteen." I remembered it clearly. "Mom and Dad never made it. Dad was working and Mom wouldn't get out of bed." Those two facts didn't change for a full year.

Dad was always at work. Mum was always in bed.

And Uncle Kane went from the no-good alcoholic to the only family member I had. Uncle Kane thought it was best that Nana and Grandad didn't know how Dad was coping. He also decided not to tell my other grandparents that Mom, their daughter, was battling depression.

Mom hated anyone seeing her weak. So, I understood why Uncle Kane made sure that my parents' behavior was kept to ourselves.

"I really fucked them up, didn't I?" Ryan's words were coated in disbelief. "I thought they would be okay. I thought, they would be relieved not having to pay for my university or my way of life anymore."

I frowned. "You were taking a gap year? You weren't heading to university?"

He scoffed. "Yeah, exactly, as if they would ever want their son not striving to make a career."

"They bought you a year tour of Europe," I said the words and his eyes snapped off the picture and on to me. I smiled. "You were meant to leave the following week."

"They were actually going to let me go overseas?" He sounded so shocked.

I shrugged my shoulders. "You know, all they ever did was support you. I think Mom was counting on you being a drummer. They just wanted you happy. Didn't care what you did." I took the photo away from him. "Anyway, you didn't want that." My eyes ran over the picture and then I put it back in the compartment. "I should go."

It was late, and I knew once he got out of this car, he would disappear from my life again.

"Don't."

My eyes snapped to him and I frowned.

"Don't what?"

"Don't go."

I was puzzled for a minute. Was Ryan seriously asking me not to leave? I couldn't believe it. Ryan had lived the last five years making sure we weren't a part of his life, and now he was asking me to stay?

I just stared at him. I don't know what was more shocking: him wanting to spend time with me, or that I was actually thinking of going inside.

TWENTY

Soph

I wiped the tears away, but they just kept falling. It was a song. A stupid fucking song! That was all it took for me to become this blubbering mess.

I can't believe a song could get this reaction out of me. It wasn't just any song. It had a memory attached to it. A memory with Kyle. I thought after all this time I had fixed myself—you know, got myself together to the point I was over him. But just hearing that song reminded me I was so far from being back together.

I was like a broken mirror. I was trying to put myself together, but you could see the cracks, and while I was trying to put that broken mirror back together, I was cutting myself on the broken pieces.

My tears were slowing just when the bell rang, and I knew I had to get out of the car.

I was trying to ignore the heartache. But I couldn't get that memory of Kyle and me singing and play fighting in his bed to that song. The way he touched me. The way he kissed me. The way my heart pulsed when he took my top off…

I clenched my eyes shut. I guess today was going to be one of my weaker days.

I cracked open my car door and got out. I just had to get through the day. I knew I wouldn't get the pleasure of not seeing Kyle. Kayla and Kyle were in all my classes. Thank god I didn't have art with him today. Cause I honestly don't think I'd be able to ignore him being nice to me.

It was like I needed him to be kind to me right now, like I was craving his attention.

Today was one of those days. I didn't want to face that I had lost him and that what we had was over.

I walked like a ghost through the halls to get my books. I didn't care that people were shouldering their way past me, heading for their classes, as the second bell had rung. I literally didn't care, not even when I had my books and a boy ran past me, knocking them out of my hands.

I dropped to my knees, gathering them up. My weekend was intense, and I felt like a shell today. A shell of the person I was.

Ryan was back in my life. I didn't know for how long for, but he was back in my life. My brother. And there was only one person I wanted to tell. And that was also the one person who said they would never, and could never, love me again. Yet it was still Kyle who I wanted to tell.

A tear dropped from my eye and fell on my textbook.

God, not more tears. I quickly wiped under my eyes and then I glanced up, hoping no one saw it, that no one saw Sophia, the pitiful thing, crying in the hallway. I realized the hallway was empty, just like my life.

I got up, and I knew I couldn't blow off class. But it was like I was invisible, not just to other students but also to the teachers.

So, I wasn't surprised when the teacher didn't even acknowledge me as I walked ten or so minutes late.

I walked to my normal seat, like a zombie, and then when I came to a stop at my chair there was someone fucking in it. I quickly snapped out of my zombie mode and scanned the classroom.

This had to be some sick and twisted fucking joke.

There was only one seat empty.

Only one bloody seat!

I glanced at Kyle, and it would seem he was aware of the situation. I wanted to groan. In fact, I wanted to turn and walk out of the class.

The teacher wouldn't notice. The students didn't care, and as I looked at Kyle, I think he would be relieved if I didn't take the seat next to him.

"Sophia, can you please take a seat?"

I clenched my eyes shut. Great. The teacher had noticed. I guess I was standing in the middle of the classroom.

God darn it! Why the hell did I have to be late?

I slowly walked towards the last man on the planet I wanted to be near right now. There were four seats. First Adam, then Kayla, then Kyle, and then the empty seat which unfortunately had my fucking name on it.

I could feel Kyle's eyes on me as I reached it.

He pushed his things to his side, but he didn't move closer to Kayla. He had his chair more in the middle of the desk, and I didn't have the guts to ask him to move down, closer to his woman.

I slumped in the chair; my eyes glued on the desk. His arm brushed mine, and it sent a million sparks through my body. I think what was worse was that my body was craving his touch, bathing in the memory of his arms and the touch of his lips. It was fucking cruel!

I wanted to groan. What had I done to the universe to deserve this?

I opened my textbook. I had no idea what we were meant to be doing and to be honest,

I didn't care. I just had to get through the hour or so of being tortured by being near him.

I think what was making this worse was that I had spent the weekend with my brother. My brother was back in my life, and I couldn't tell Kyle. I couldn't bring myself to tell Ryan about Kyle either. I kept asking about his life, and when he asked about mine, I just kept redirecting the conversation back to him.

I heard all about his crazy adventures. I laughed and laughed and even cried a bit out of laughter.

When I left his house this morning, I wanted to tell someone—anyone—that my brother was back. My brother who I never thought I would see again.

I then did a count. Josh didn't even know I had a brother, so he wouldn't understand how important it was that Ryan was back. Bax wouldn't give a fuck cause all he wanted me for was sex. He wouldn't want to hear about how my brother was back. There was only one person who would understand how important it is to me and how much it meant to me, and that was Kyle. I snuck a glance at

Kyle and was surprised to find his eyes on me.

My eyes snapped back to my open textbook. My leg was nervously shaking up and down. It was a sign I was close to losing all control and burst out crying.

I then started tapping my fingers on the desk, trying my best to try to get myself together. I couldn't keep thinking about Kyle, but oh my god, being near him was killing me. It wasn't like I didn't crave him sexually. I just needed him emotionally.

Fuck, I needed anyone. Right now, I needed someone to calm me down.

I was about to get up and leave because I was positive the lack of sleep and the emotions flooding my body was going to cause me to go into meltdown mode. Then I felt it and my whole body stilled.

I looked down at my knee and saw Kyle's hand.

I looked up to see him turn slightly towards me.

"You okay, Soph?" His words were soft.

I don't know what Kayla was doing to not notice that Kyle was talking to me. I couldn't pull my eyes from Kyle. He was looking at me like he was worried.

He started to move his thumb in a circle on my knee. "Breathe, Soph." His directions were low and soft.

I didn't even realize I was holding onto my breath, and I exhaled quickly. His lips twitched up slightly as if he was pleased, I was listening to him.

He leaned in closer to me. "Move your chair in."

I frowned, not understanding why I had to, but I did as I was told. His hand went off my knee and I thought maybe he just wanted me to get under the table, so he didn't have to see my leg shaking up and down.

Then his hand was back on my leg, but this time moving up my inner thigh, pushing my dress up slightly. My breathing hitched just when his hand stopped, and his thumb started working in a circle again.

I was instantly reminded how he used to always do this when we sat together. I couldn't believe he was touching me right now after all the things I had yelled at him at the dinner table.

I needed him to be there for me emotionally and he was doing just that. He was calming me down. I couldn't help but look back at him. Why? Why was he doing this?

He smiled at me softly and leaned in. But then Kayla called for his attention.

He turned and started talking to her, but his hand stayed on my inner thigh and his thumb kept moving in the delicious circle.

I was flooded with all the memories of how he would touch me as if I was fragile. How gentle he was. I was getting lost in his touch, in the feel of his hand on me. As much as I knew it was wrong, I wasn't stopping myself. I couldn't stop myself from just enjoying it.

"Oh, Soph, I didn't see you there."

My stare snapped off the table, and I looked up and to my side, looking at Kayla. She was speaking to me? Why?

"Hi, Kayla," I forced out, trying my best to not sound nervous. "Sorry for crashing your table. There was no other seat."

She was smiling at me, but it was bitter and sour and forced. The fact Kyle had one hand under the table and on me seemed to have gone completely unnoticed by her.

"It's okay. Feels a bit like old times, right?" She kept that forced smile on her face.

We both knew she had the upper hand here. She was the queen bee, and I was a nobody.

I went back to staring at my textbook, while all my attention was on Kyle's hand. How it flooded my body with memories and how much I had loved him.

"You know there is actually this thing on tonight." Kayla was speaking, but I assumed it wasn't to me. "Kyle and I are going. Adam, Soph, do you want to come, you know, for old time's sake?"

My eyes snapped up. Did she just invite me out with her and Kyle?

I looked at Adam, who was staring at me. It was no secret that Adam hadn't gone back to being Kyle's best friend. He did however still hang around them. But he had told me multiple times he wouldn't hang out with them because Kayla, well, according to Adam, was off the rails and a troublemaker.

"I will go if Soph does," Adam said, putting all the attention on me.

Kyle hadn't looked at me, even though his hand was still on me and his thumb was moving in soothing circles.

I opened my mouth, and I wasn't sure what my answer was.

"It's a beach thing." Kayla turned her whole body towards me and Kyle. "I won't be swimming, but I will be drinking." She kept smiling at me.

Was she plotting to kill me at this party? Was that why she wanted me to go?

"The four of us—it will be like old times!" she added, and this time she gave me a smile that was actually real. "Come on, you three can make sure I don't go drunk swimming or something."

I didn't know what to say. I doubted Kyle wanted me anywhere near him. Though he was touching me right now, and he was hiding it from Kayla.

I frowned. Could I hang out with them like old times? Today I was weaker. Today I needed my old best friend and my boyfriend.

I was craving my old life. The temptation of just a night with them… I was actually considering it.

Kayla sighed and turned back in her seat. "Don't worry about it. Clearly you would rather be with bikers." Her words were bitter and, if I was honest, it sounded like I had hurt her feelings.

"I'll come."

Kyle's head snapped in my direction, his eyes slightly wide.

I realized Kayla and Adam were also staring at me.

"For old time's sake, right?" I added.

Kayla nodded her head, giving me a real smile again. Adam gave me a grin, but it was Kyle's expression that had me. The smile on his face said it all. He was happy. As if me coming meant something more than just us hanging out as friends for old time's sake.

Our moment was ended quickly when Kayla started to ask him questions on what she should wear, and what she should get to drink.

I forced my attention back to the book in front of me. But while Kyle was answering Kayla's questions, his hand was on me. I knew I should stop it. I knew it was unhealthy and as soon as I got out of this mood, I would want to slap myself for letting him touch me. Yet, I didn't push his hand away, and silently I was trying to think of a solid reason why he would want to.

* * *

The beach was packed, and the drinks and bonfire were roaring. The mood was casual, and everyone was enjoying themselves. I was having fun with Adam. He was in one hell of a playful mood which usually always revolved around annoying me, and that was exactly what he was doing, but I didn't mind.

In fact, I had missed it.

The fact that Kayla hadn't stopped touching and making out with Kyle between throwing back drinks didn't really bother me. Adam had been entertaining me until a girl caught his eye. I had to give him a push to go after her. She hadn't stopped looking at him, so he was in luck.

Kayla was peeling herself off Kyle. I didn't mean to be spying on them, or keeping an eye on them, but I had. And I had noticed Kyle's attention was on me, not his girlfriend who was busy making out with him frantically. She was kissing him like she was trying to prove something.

Kayla's eyes were slightly glazed over, and I knew it wasn't just alcohol that caused her to look like that. She was still using.

Just as I thought that, I caught sight of a guy I had been glad wasn't in my life anymore. Greg, or as Kayla and everyone else calls him, Gaz. He was the local dealer, and Kayla noticed he was here.

She gave Kyle a peck on the lips and then was quick to sprint off in his direction. Gaz gave me a wave which I didn't return.

"God, I hate that guy." I couldn't stop myself from saying it. It was just me and Kyle now. We were slightly away from the full-on party. I looked at Kyle in time to see him nod his head.

"Fucking dick of a guy," he muttered, picking up his beer from off a rock.

"I can't believe she still sees him." I shook my head and went to stand next to Kyle. I was looking back at Gaz as he dragged Kayla off into the dark. I'm guessing to do lines.

Kyle let out a long sigh, but one that sounded more like relief, and turned his attention to the ocean. Then he leaned back against the rock, his shoulders sagging, and drank the rest of his beer. I had to admit, this was the first time I was willing to be alone with him. I leaned against the same rock. My mind flickered back to how he calmed this morning in class. I still hadn't thanked him for that. I didn't really get a chance because Kayla was glued to him for the rest of the day.

"Um, about today..." I awkwardly brought up the subject and turned my full body to face him. I didn't know if he had done it out of pity or something.

His eyes had been on the ocean, but now they were on me.

He didn't say anything. I took a sharp breath in. I was incredibly nervous all of a sudden. I opened my mouth.

"You know what I think?" He spoke before I could say anything. His eyes still on me. "Every time I look at the ocean, you know what runs through my mind?"

I frowned, not sure what to say. I went to open my mouth again.

"You. The night I told you my plan." He moved closer to me. His eyes glued to mine. I saw the honesty in them, and I saw the memory playing in his mind.

I didn't know what was worse, the way my heart was pulsing instantly, or that I knew which night he was talking about.

I kept watching at Kyle as he approached me. Then he stopped, getting closer to me, but not too close.

I was biting my bottom lip, and I finally nodded my head. "I remember the night." Then I remembered the night even clearer because he told me that I was his forever. I loved him before that night, but that night I gave him everything I had. I wanted to be his forever. All those emotions I felt all day. All the emotions I had kept under a lid all day. Well, they flooded me.

But I knew it, tears were falling and this time I wasn't by myself.

"Soph." His voice broke, and he stepped towards me. "Please don't cry."

I scoffed as he wiped away my tears. "I.." My words dried up in my throat.

"I know, Soph. I know." He cupped my cheeks; pain was painted across his face. "I fucked up, and one day I'll be able to tell you how much.

I then felt his lips on my forehead and his arms wrapped around me, just as the tears overcame me. Kyle had no idea how much damage he had done to my heart. Right now, he was getting a glimpse of what I was really like.

"Every fucking day I'm reminded of what I lost. Every day I'm reminded how fucking lonely I am now." He spoke so softly as his hand ran down my back, smothering me, while he held me so tightly to his chest. All I could hear was honesty in his voice.

"You gave me a taste of heaven, Soph. I miss you falling asleep on my chest. I miss the way your back would arch just as I took you." He pulled back to look me in the eye.

And then before I could say a word, before I could point out he was the one to end us, his mouth was on mine.

Immediately, I was given a dose of a flavor I was once addicted to. It was like tasting your favorite candy that you hadn't tasted since childhood.

Crazy. Complete madness. That was what was happening.

I didn't push him away. I couldn't even say that my lips were still against his. As soon as his lips touched mine, before I knew it, my tongue was exploring his mouth. The mouth that used to worship my body. My hands were in his hair while he picked me up, sitting me on the rock, and he was reminding me just how good we were. His hands ran up my thighs, pushing my dress up around my waist.

The word *crazy* ran through my mind again. But it didn't stop me from halting him, from exploring my body like I was still his.

His lips broke from mine. "Come home with me." His forehead was leaning against mine, my breathing rapid. "Come home with me.

Let me remind you how fucking great we are together."

My eyes widened. Kissing was one thing, but sex... he couldn't be serious.

"What about Kayla?" I don't know why that one concern came out and not the others, like how come morning, he would be kicking me out of his bed and going back to her.

"I don't care. I want to fuck you. No" — he took a sharp breath in, "I need to make love to you. I'm dying here without you, and I can't last much longer." His words waved in desire. "Let me have you again."

And just like that, I snapped the fuck out of it. Those five words: let me have you again.

I pushed his hands off me and climbed down from the rock. I had made a promise to myself, and I was remembering it right now. "You nearly had me fooled," I muttered and shook my head. "You put me through hell. You know that? No. Let me rephrase that. You are putting me through hell." Every single fucking day I was suffering because of him. I looked him in the eye. "You told me I was nothing without you."

He may be saying now that he misses me, he may be basically looking at me like I was his world, but I knew better, because he had fooled me before.

"You cut me up and left me to bleed!" That was putting what he did to me nicely. I kept staring at him. If he had a reason—one reason, for doing what he did to me now was the time to tell me. I shook my head when he remained silent. "I loved you, you know that? When you told me that night in that ocean that I was your forever, I fucking believed you!"

Maybe this was the reason I hadn't got over Kyle. We hadn't had a confrontation. I had never told him how much he hurt me. Sure, he confronted me. But I never confronted him about what he did.

He took a step closer to me, looking panicked. "I love you, you hear me, Sophia? I fucking love you and I didn't..." He groaned. "I don't have a choice! But I am still yours forever, you just..." he trailed off and sighed, his eyes locked with mine. "You just need to have faith in me."

Faith in him? He couldn't be fucking serious right now? But then I frowned. He said he didn't have a choice? "Is there another reason you ended things with us?"

I watched his face tighten.

"Kyle? Was Kayla the reason or not?" I couldn't stop myself from stepping towards him as my hopes went up. Maybe he wasn't as madly in love with my ex-best friend as he led on. "Now is the time to tell me. If you really want me to have faith in you, give me a reason to."

Just give me a reason, Kyle. Just one reason. I hoped. I saw the expression on his face; something was boiling in his eyes, and just as I saw it, he hid it.

"No," he said and shattered my hopes.

It was bitter. It was sour. It twisted my stomach. Finally, I nodded my head. I needed to get out of there.

I didn't need to say a word. I just backed away from him. I was done. I was done with him. Done hoping his actions would make sense. I turned my back to him; it was about time I walked away from him. "Soph?" I paused.

"I'm sorry." His voice broke, and if I just took in the sound of his voice, I would think it was breaking his heart watching me walk away from him. If I didn't consider his actions. If I just wiped what he had done and ignored the fact that he had a new girlfriend, I would think his world was shattering.

I didn't turn back. I didn't turn around and tell him we could be friends. I didn't want to smooth the pain out of voice. Sure, it hurt me to hear it in his voice, and it hurt me knowing he was hurt right now. But instead, I just started to walk away from him, officially marking the night I was letting him go.

* * *

I hadn't driven to the beach. Adam had driven us. And because I was at Kyle's it was one easy pick up. Seeing as Kayla, Kyle, and I were all at the same spot. Pity I didn't give much thought into how I would be getting home, considering I knew Adam wouldn't be remaining sober, and would most likely go home with someone.

I kept walking up the foot path. Walking away from Kyle, it was like a huge weight was lifted off my shoulders. I didn't even know there was something weighing me down, but there had been and now it was gone.

I think it was hope—hope that Kyle and I would get back together. Now I knew it wasn't going to happen. Ever. I had been holding onto our relationship. I had been living, mourning a loss, but at the same time I wasn't letting my relationship with Kyle die completely.

I sighed and kept heading towards the house. I was still at least a good half an hour away.

A thought ran through my mind again. The same thought that kept coming back to me as I walked in the dead of the night.

How was Josh?

I hadn't spoken to him since the weekend, since our moment. I chewed my bottom lip and paused, unlocking my phone.

I knew I shouldn't, but at the same time he was my friend. So, I could ring him and ask him how he was, couldn't I?

TWENTY-ONE

Josh

Becoming the Vice President brought on a lot of responsibilities. I knew that when I took on the role. But when I did take it on, I thought I'd be doing that role from prison, at least for the next few years. Then I got released.

Wolf left me in charge of shit. At first, I was in over my head, going in fucking blind. Wolf was expecting me to be able to make decisions like him, even though I didn't have nearly as much experience as him. But when I mentioned that to him, he said I had something a lot of other blokes didn't yet, life experience and a cold heart.

He then gave me a lecture about how only a man who had a hardened heart could do this job. He said it took him nearly half his life for his heart to get to the point where he could be president. He said I was an inspiration and was going to be a success story.

I shrugged it off. But to be honest, that just put more pressure on me. Sure, I didn't give a fuck what people thought, and never let anyone stop me from doing what I want. I took a cold fist to every problem that came my way.

I lit up a cigarette, my eyes on the source of my current headache. I glanced at Bax. He was here because he was meant to be handling this shit — a petty who said what.

Honestly, they were grown men, but here I was being forced to play a parent role.

"Already start spitting shit and tell me why I'm here." I took my eyes off Bax and on to the Grave Robber. "Maybe you could explain where you were last week?" The fact he was meant to be in town as of last week hadn't slipped my notice. "You should have come to us the day you rolled into our town."

The Grave Robber had a reputation, and not a good one. I didn't trust him. The only reason we had to deal with him was because Damon, his cousin, had traded positions with him. Damon was our supplier for the ingredients we needed to cook crystal meth.

They gave us the supplies for our cook houses. I trusted Damon, but the Grave Robber… I didn't. He got his name for going back on deals, doing whatever it took to make his cousin more money. He didn't have standards or loyalty. He lived up to his nick name because he would steal from the dead.

Ryan was his real name, and he would do anything to make sure that his cousin came out on top. He didn't give a fuck if that meant things got dirty. He would burn bridges if it meant more money in their operation.

But right now, Bax and Ryan had a disagreement that had to be sorted. Bax had been one of the bridges Ryan burned when he was last in town.

I looked between the two.

"I said spit it out!" I yelled at them, pulling rank. "Why the fuck am I here!" I was being short with them—shorter than I should be. I was in more of a foul mood than normal since Soph left. It really bugged me she hadn't been home since.

I was on the verge of telling her everything about me, about the club, everything, but she disappeared that night.

"He screwed a chick I was screwing," Bax finally snapped, telling me the purpose of their disagreement. "And he knew I was with her. He is a fucking low life."

Ryan scoffed. "Can you even remember this girl's name, Bax?" I looked at Bax, seeing if this girl had been special to him or not. My phone started buzzing in my pocket and I pulled it out.

"What does that matter?" Bax called for my attention to go back to the situation, but my eyes were on the Soph's name, which was flashing across my screen. She was calling me. "For fuck's sake, Vice! You aren't listening!"

With regret, I looked back at Bax, not answering the call. The sooner I wrapped this up, the sooner I could call Soph back.

"Well, it's been years, right? Surely you two can move on." I attempted to approach this subject with common sense. Now I just wanted to hurry this up so I could call Soph back.

Bax was back at to glaring at Ryan. I wanted to groan. He was going to be childish. Fucking Bax wasting my bloody time.

"Fine then! Bax, pull your fucking head in. Club comes first." I wanted this over. It was childish. "Women come and go. Shit, Bax, why are you even worried about some old fling."

Last time I checked, he was one lucky bastard that had my Soph talking to him. I couldn't bring myself to say she was having sex with him because it didn't bring out the best side of me. The sooner I was honest with Soph, the sooner I could get her away from bloody Bax.

Even if she didn't want to be with me, I could at least get her away from men like Bax. It was a bitter taste in my mouth thinking about it, but I would prefer Soph back with Kyle than with Bax.

Ryan opened his mouth, and I knew my hope of wrapping this up wasn't going to happen. But we were saved from his rant by his ringing phone. Saved me from hearing Ryan throwing insults back at Bax.

But him answering the phone put off me trying to end this petty fight to begin with. I didn't know Ryan very well, but the fact he was taking a call in a business conversation clearly wasn't normal by the way Bax looked at him.

"Well, if it isn't my number one girl." Ryan's voice was friendly and I sure as fuck never heard him speak like that to a girl. Then again, I didn't know him very well. Wasn't even in the club last time he was in town.

Ryan laughed, whatever the girl said had caused the Grave Robber to laugh. Who knew that was possible? "Where are you?" he asked, and his voice dipped in concern.

Bax glanced at me, arching an eyebrow.

"Clearly he is over whatever chick you are bitching about," I muttered to Bax and lit up a cigarette. Bloody hell, I was becoming a chain smoker. I was a heavy smoker in prison because it was the only fucking thing to do.

Ryan said he would see whoever it was soon, and when he hung up, I went back to trying to get this resolved.

"Still lying to women, Ryan?" Bax scoffed, clearly not thinking Ryan had been serious when he said he would see that woman soon.

"Nope, we are done now, aren't we?" Ryan went to get up.

"What, you just backing down?" Bax made that sound like that wasn't something Ryan would ever do.

"I'll drop it if you do?" Ryan looked back at Bax. "I want to keep it business, keep personal aside. Though I didn't realize I screwed the woman of your dreams or something."

His voice had a bit of disbelief in it.

I glanced at Bax to see his expression, which was tight, and then a smile bloomed across his face.

"That chick was just a hang around. The woman I'm with now, well, she is the woman of my dreams." Bax pointed a finger at him. "Go near her and I will fucking kill you."

Ryan started laughing. "Well, what do you know? Bax, the man with an endless appetite for woman, has settled for one."

Bax's huge grin fell slightly. "Nah, as much as I want to lock her down, she's against it."

Now that's my Soph. I kept the smile to myself. At least between the time I had last seen her and now she hadn't let Bax put a label on her. My chances weren't completely fucked yet.

"Seems like a smart girl," Ryan said playfully. "When do you want to pick this back up?" It seemed he wanted this to end.

I took the cigarette from my mouth. "Friday night. Before the club party. Guessing you would be attending anyway, yeah?"

Ryan frowned, seeming to hesitate to agree.

"Don't tell us, this chick has you working around her?" Bax's voice was fully amused and he whacked me on the arm. "And you thought I was pussy whipped!"

Ryan rolled his eyes. "I'll be here Friday." He picked up his jacket from off the back of the seat and threw down the rest of his drink. "Call me if things change in between now and then."

I nodded my head and was already getting my phone out. I heard the club door shut, but I was more focused trying to come to a decision on whether to call or message.

"Well, seeing as my night just cleared, I'm calling the missus." Bax's words caught my attention.

"Thought you hadn't locked her down?" I wanted to see if I had heard him wrong or not.

Bax winked at me. "I will if I work my magic tonight." He got up, giving me a grin. "I've heard my charm is irresistible. Night, Vice."

I already had the phone to my ear, but I would admit I was clenching it tighter because of what Bax just said. I had to get to Soph before he did. My grip on the phone got even tighter when she didn't pick up.

Bax had only just pulled out his phone and was leaving, so there was a chance I'd get to her before him. So, I kept ringing her.

* * *

I slammed the front door shut. Didn't give a fuck if I woke everyone up. For the last hour, I'd been calling her and not once did she bloody well pick up. I knew by the missing car she wasn't here.

I walked into the lounge room and then my eyes landed on Kyle. We hadn't really spoken since I got out. He was always the golden child, and it seemed even though I had been away for a few years that fact hadn't changed.

I watched him bring the glass to his lips, throwing down what looked like Dad's good liquor. I knew he most likely didn't want to speak to me, but something had him drinking hard.

"You alright, Bro?" I asked, walking towards him. I was speaking to him with a level of respect in my voice. As if I was talking to one of my club brothers. I knew blood brothers should have a stronger bond, but Kyle and I didn't have it. We went separate directions in life and our father liked to play us against one another.

There were a lot of reasons why we weren't close. Little reasons and big reasons, all adding to why we didn't get along. But right now, I was going to put that aside.

He glanced at me and I knew as soon as I looked into his eyes he had been drinking for a while.

He remained silent as his eyes went back to his glass.

I couldn't force him to talk to me. I had to admit I don't think I've seen him without his girlfriend not on him.

"Where is that woman who loves to cling to you?" I crossed my arms, not giving up on him answering me.

Kyle sat up from his slumped position. "Ever fucked something really good up?" He reached for the bottle. "Like a life defining type of thing?" He was speaking but his eyes were on the glass which he was filling up with Dad's top the shelf.

I had fucked up. "Do I have to remind you the years I spent locked up?"

"I'd pick prison over this," he muttered and had filled the glass to the brim.

"You trying to save on refills?" I stood in front of the coffee table, my eyes on him and his full glass.

"Saves me filling it up every couple of minutes." Kyle shrugged and his eyes dropped to the glass. "I thought I had a shot tonight."

I had no idea what he was going on about. But I had been around my club brothers long enough to know when a man just needed to get something off his chest.

"She left. Just turned her back on me and left." He leaned forward, placing his glass down. "I had been hoping I'd do something tonight, you know, prove to her that I love her." He ran his hands through his hair and then dropped his head to his hands. "But she fucking just walked away." His words were muffled by his hands.

"I'm sure Kayla knows you love her. You don't have to prove that to her." I didn't know much about his relationship with her, but it seemed like she lived for him.

Kyle took his head from his hands looking at me confused. "I'm not talking about Kayla."

His words slowly sunk in. At first, I was confused, and then I realized. "You're talking about Soph?" My voice hardened. His words that she turned and left ran through my head. "What did you do to her tonight?"

TWENTY-TWO

Soph

There were two sides to this town, and I wasn't going to lie and say that my parents and Kyle's parents had bought on the wealthy side of the town. My parents had expensive taste, not that they rubbed it in to anyone. But it did make sense why Ryan's house was still on the wealthy side of the town.

So, while I was now heading in the opposite direction to Kyle's, it was still a respectable suburb. When the car slowed down, I didn't think anything of it until it started to slow down to a crawl. I glanced at it. I didn't know the car. It was a classic muscle car with heavily tinted windows.

I turned the corner and picked up my pace. Then my heart raced as it picked up and turned the corner as well. Shit. Who do I call?

Police?

Josh?

Ryan?

Josh hadn't answered earlier, but he did call me back. Maybe I should try him? I got my phone out just when I heard the window of the car slid down.

Shit.

I heard the driver turn down the music.

Shit. Shit. Shit.

"Walking around in a bikini like that, someone might call you jailbait." I paused. That voice.

I turned around to look at the car, lowering to the level of the window.

"Since when did you own a car like this?" I looked at my brother. I should have picked up that it was him by the music.

Ryan leaned across the car closer to me, a huge grin on his face. "Borrowing it. Now you going to get your jailbait ass in the car or wanna keep walking the street in your underwear?"

"I'll have you know; this is a designer bikini and I have a cover on." I looked back at him smugly.

"Hate to break it to you, little sis, but it's fucking see-through. Get in."

I rolled my eyes and cracked the door open. "So, who did you get this ride off?" I asked and then glanced in the back seat. "Holy shit, Ryan! You got enough alcohol?"

I had never seen so many bottles of spirits and slabs.

He started pulling us away from the curb.

"That, my little sister, is for us."

I scoffed. "It's the start of the week, Ryan. A school week. I can't get off my face with you."

"Yeah, you are."

"Why?"

"Because we are going to get that bloke you are upset about out of your system." Ryan was lighting up a cigarette, letting the car stir itself. Then, once he had the cigarette lit, one hand went back to the steering wheel.

I was just staring at him. I hadn't told him anything about a guy. Nothing. So how the hell did he know?

"Stop looking so shocked, Soph. I am your brother after all." He rolled his eyes at me. "Now you up for getting him out of your system?"

I was positive I had just got Kyle out of my system. "I'm done with him. I don't need to drink myself to alcohol poisoning to let him go."

"There are stages of breaking up. You clearly are at the stage where you need to drink to let him go completely." He glanced at me. "Trust me, I've had to get an ex out of my system, too."

I sighed. It wouldn't kill me to get Kyle completely off my chest. I had let him go, but maybe I needed a drink to make it official?

"Okay, one drink." I somewhat agreed to his plan. Then I saw his expression.

"Sis, we are going on a bender. And once it is over, you'll be thanking me." Ryan gave me his all-knowing grin, and I knew then he had plans for us, and it wasn't just for tonight.

Kyle

"Josh, I'm fucking telling you again, she isn't here!" I yelled back at my brother who was on the phone. "She didn't come back to school at all last week and now it's the middle of another week, and she hasn't come home or shown up at school!"

"Well isn't it funny she disappears as soon as you speak to her," Josh's voice hissed back at me. "Wanna tell me again what happened last week?"

I groaned. "I didn't fucking make her run away. She has my number blocked, so can you call her again?"

I can't believe I had to rely on my brother to call Soph. I don't know whether he was lying or not. But he said she wasn't picking up.

"Come on, Josh, don't be a jerk, just call her again, please?" I hated asking anyone for a favour. But asking Josh for it was like having my eyes scratched out.

I glanced into my English classroom, which I was skipping because I couldn't fucking think straight, knowing Soph was off the grid and it could be my fault. I heard the hallway door open, and I glanced at it automatically. Then I did a double take.

"She just showed up," I said into the phone at Josh and then hung up, heading up the hallway. She better have a fucking good reason!

She was on her phone.

"So, you decided to show your face?" I snapped at her while approaching her as fast as I could. "Just disappear and don't fucking tell anyone!"

Soph's head snapped up, and she looked at me, startled.

"Why are you looking so fucking shocked? You disappeared!" I yelled at her.

"Um, I don't know what you mean?" Her eyes went back to the phone and then looked back at me. "Sorry for worrying you? I guess. Your parents know where I've been. Didn't realize they hadn't told you."

My parents knew? Why the hell hadn't they told me they knew where she was?

"Were you at the biker's house or something?" I wasn't letting her go. "Why you so late today? School started hours ago."

"Oh, I'm just handing this in." She raised a piece of paper. "Oh hi, Kayla."

You have to be fucking kidding me. I turned to see my bitch of a fake girlfriend step out of class.

"Hi, Soph. You haven't been around." Kayla was actually speaking nicely to Soph. Considering she was trying to ruin Soph's life at the moment, it gave me insight into just how low of a person Kayla was.

"Yeah, um, sick." Soph flashed Kayla a smile. "It was good to see you two. I need to hand this into the office."

She went to step around me, and I blocked her. "You in a rush or something? Do your parents know you are just blowing school off? Moved out of our house?" I crossed my arms, not letting her go.

"Um, yeah, I'm in a hurry. Someone's waiting for me." She put her phone away and gave me a smile. "I'll see you guys around, and Kyle, my parents know where I am."

"Staying with some biker!" I couldn't stop the scoff at the end. As if her parents would let her near a biker, let alone let her stay with him.

Soph's smile just got bigger. "Geez, Kyle, calm down. I'm fine and my parents know who I'm with." She looked between me and Kayla, still smiling. "I'll see you two around, okay?"

Soph was giving us a real smile. A real fucking smile.

Kayla said a goodbye to Soph as she walked past us. I couldn't fucking believe it. Soph was blowing me off. I turned around, seeing her body slightly sway as she walked away from me. Never in my life had I wanted to go after her more.

Soph was acting like there was nothing between us. She just acted like she was fine seeing me. Every time she looked at me since we broke up, I saw pain but also love in her eyes. This time she looked at me like I was nothing. Like she was completely over me.

Fuck, it was even worse. It was like she accepted that she and I were over.

I dialed my brother's number.

"Did she tell you to fuck off, because that's what I'm about to tell you." Josh was ruder than normal to me. To be honest, he had been a dick since I told him about me speaking to Soph. Didn't help she disappeared after that.

"You are connected with bikers, right? Being one of the lowlifes?"

"Why?"

"Cause Soph is shacked up with one." I pushed open the hallway door, going down the steps and spotting Soph getting into a muscle car. "And you are going to threaten him and get him to back off."

I heard Josh scoff in the phone and then he hung up. I knew my brother could be a dick. But he did like Soph. I was hoping he liked her enough to do something about it.

TWENTY-THREE

Soph

I hadn't really been eating solid meals. Ryan wasn't exactly a cook, but we had been binging out on music, games, and alcohol and, in Ryan's case, drugs as well. I got a certificate easily from our family doctor for the week. Plus, he back dated it, which is like a huge no-no when it comes to medical certificates.

I came back to Kyle's. I just wanted a change of clothes, then I was heading back to Ryan's. Though he said he had something he had to do later tonight. I was planning on heading to Bax's when he went to whichever girl's house it was. I assumed it was a girl who had her hooks in him.

His phone was always going off, though he was rude to whoever was calling.

Anyway, I was planning on getting clothes and heading out of here. But I ran into Louise, and suddenly I was roped into a family dinner.

I looked down at the food. I wasn't sure it was a good thing that just the look of food was making me sick, let alone eating it.

"So, Sophia, where have you been?"

My eyes went off the home cook meal and onto Jed. Great, here comes twenty questions.

JOSH

I'm going to kill him. He is going to be fucking lucky if my hands don't end up around his throat tonight. I swear, if he doesn't show tonight, I'm tracking him fucking down and finding out the reason why he kept blowing us off. The only reason he was in this town was business with us, and he seemed to be ignoring that.

Instead, Ryan, the bloody Grave Robber, was always blowing us off. Every meeting he cancelled.

If he didn't show up to the party tonight, well more for the confrontation I was going to have with him before it, he would be lucky to have a beer after I was through with him.

I closed the front door. I needed a new top. Seeing as I was living at the club, I couldn't show up in this one. I was still on a man hunt for Soph. But every time I questioned Bax about who he was seeing, he would shut up or change the subject, not even giving me a hint about what was going on.

Any day I was expecting her to rock up at the club, considering she had moved in with him, basically. Fucking pissed me off to no end. What was worse was I couldn't even get her to answer the bloody phone!

I had never hated hearing a voice message as much as hers. First, it reminded me how sweet her voice was, and that sexy luring swirl to her voice. Second, it reminded me how fucking much I missed her, and I hated she was with Bax.

Had she listened to one word I said about her doing better? I was so close to opening up to her, telling her everything, and she disappeared from the face of the earth. The only thing that reassured me that she was okay was overhearing her parents tell my Dad she was with a friend.

"So, Sophia, where have you been?"

I froze at the bottom of the steps, hearing my father's voice from the other room. No fucking way she was here.

"With family friends." I heard her reply just as I walked into the room.

"Josh, darling, what are you doing here?" Mum was the first one to spot me. Typical.

Kyle threw me a glare; we weren't really on speaking terms at the moment. I ignored his request to scare off the biker that Soph was with. Little did he know I was doing everything possible to get her away from Bax.

Dad turned in his chair, glancing back at me.

But it was Soph's reaction I wanted to see. Her eyes went off Dad and onto me, a smile spreading across her face, like seeing me had made her night.

"Do you want something to eat?" Mom asked, already up and heading for the kitchen.

Still, I couldn't look away from Soph. Did she have any idea how crazy she was driving me? I was taking my temper out on my club brothers. Small things got a huge reaction out of me. I knew I was doing it. I knew why I was doing it. I also knew I wouldn't be able to stop doing it until I heard or saw Soph.

"Here, take a seat, Josh." Kyle's voice was a threatening hiss as he pushed out the chair next to him, making a point to take the seat where it was and not move it next to Soph.

I guess I couldn't just sit next to her, for all I knew, it was me she was avoiding, and I was the reason she had basically moved out.

"So, Sophia, you were saying… family friends?" Dad's attention was back on Soph.

Soph's eyes went off me and onto my dad. "Yeah, more like family, to be honest."

"Oh, any family I'd know? Last time I checked, I know all of your relatives."

Soph took her eyes off him and reached for her water. "Nope, you wouldn't know them, not close. They are only in town for a short period."

"We should have them around for dinner. You can introduce us." Kyle leaned forward, he wasn't hiding his glare, which was locked on her. "Unless you're lying?"

I saw Kayla roll her eyes. Kyle should really redirect his attention to who he is currently sleeping with and off Soph. As far as I was concerned, Kyle was her past, and if I could make it happen, I was her future.

Soph didn't even answer him, her eyes reverting back to her untouched plate.

Was she still not eating?

"Kyle, don't be rude," Dad told him off, cause Kyle wasn't using the manners that Dad had instilled in him. Kyle was basically the robot Dad programmed.

"What? We are all thinking it! We all know Soph's family. So, who could this new relative be that just appeared?" Kyle looked around the table, and then his eyes were back on Soph. "Let's face it Sophia, your family was going to be my family. So, you still want to spin that lie to us that we don't know whoever is in town?"

"Kyle, enough!" Mum told him off, placing a plate of food in front of me. "Sophia's parents reassured us that she was with family. Now who that family is doesn't matter." Mum took her seat again, and even though she said that, you could hear in her tone she wanted an explanation as well.

Soph sighed and dropped the knife and fork she wasn't even using to eat to begin with. Her eyes did a round of the table and then she locked eyes with Kyle.

"It's Uncle Kane." Her eyes went off Kyle and did a round of the table again. "So, like I said, not family, you all know."

"You've been staying with the country's worst drunk?" Kyle scoffed. "No wonder you wouldn't share who you were with. That man is never sober!"

"You've never met him, so you have no right to judge him." Soph's eyes narrowed on him.

"No, but we have all heard your dad's opinion of him." Kyle glanced at his dad.

"Even Dad's heard the stories!"

"That's all they are, stories." Soph had gone into pit bull mode almost, like Kyle speaking badly of her uncle was a personal attack. I didn't know much about her family.

"The world's worst drunk." Kyle wasn't dropping the subject, his eyes still on Soph. "Why don't you admit it, you are lying! You haven't been with your Uncle! Cause he wouldn't be sober enough to hold a sentence!"

I saw it immediately. What Kyle just said hurt Soph, no, beyond that, it looked like he had just taken a knife to heart. I didn't know who or what type of relationship she had with her uncle, but by her expression right now, I knew she cared a hell of a lot for him.

"Soph, can I talk to you?" I got up. "In private?" I watched the tears swelling in her eyes. "Soph?"

I had never seen her so hurt. And any second those tears were going to fall. Just as I thought maybe she hadn't heard me at all, she pushed herself away from the table. I shot Kyle a glare and put my hand on Soph's back as I walked us into the lounge room.

"You okay?" I asked softly.

She didn't stop in the lounge, she kept walking. I wasn't sure where she was heading. But I stopped her when we got into the foyer. My hands dropped to her shoulders and I turned her around.

"Soph?" I sighed, and my hands went her face, my thumbs running under her eyes, wiping away the tears. "You've got to stop letting Kyle upset you."

She nodded her head, but the tears were still falling.

"I need to go." She got out and went to brush my hands off her. "You, um… don't have to comfort me. I'll be fine."

"Where are you going?" I asked and kept my hands cupping her face. I wasn't sure if I should say anything, but at the same time I knew better. "You are lying about your uncle, aren't you? Or at least partly."

I didn't want to completely pull apart her story.

"Uncle Kane is in town." Her tear-filled eyes locked with mine. "But I haven't been with him."

At least she was honest with me. "You have to go out?" I asked.

Confusion ran through her eyes. "Aren't you heading out? I'm guessing you weren't planning on staying home on a Friday night?"

"I'll cancel. Trust me, the guy I had plans with tonight deserves to be cancelled on." I would love to cancel on Ryan. "He's a dick and deserves to be stood up. So, how about you and I spend the night together?"

She was hesitating and then bit her bottom lip. "What about your plans? I don't want you standing anyone up."

"Trust me, I'd pick you over him any day." I smiled. Now, if I could only get her to crack a grin.

Her hands went to mine. "And what do you suggest we do?"

Hell, my mind went wild immediately and all my visions had a common theme—they all involved her in my bed.

I took her hands, linking them with mine. "How about we test out my electric blanket? Last time I checked, we haven't used it together."

Would I get that lucky?

"You really want to stay in with me?" She stepped in closer to me. "Your friend won't mind?"

"Trust me, he isn't a friend." Ryan was anything but a friend. He wasn't even a club member. "Is the *Young Ones* on? Cause we can watch that." I saw her frown. "Unless you have plans you can't get out of?" I had a feeling someone was expecting her tonight.

Then she shook her head. "No. Um, he has plans tonight."

That pissed me off, because I knew she was talking about Bax. And yeah, he did have plans tonight. A meeting with Ryan and me, which I was about to back out of.

"So, you're mine tonight?" I pulled her in closer until she was firmly against me. My hand going onto her back.

"Yeah, I'm all yours." She smiled and then went up on her toes. "Plus, I really want to test out the electric blanket."

And just like that, I had scored one night with her. Now I had to see if tonight was the right time to open up to her and tell her the truth about my life.

I had to admit my life would be easier if I told her the truth. For one thing, I would be able to ride my bike here and wear colors, that is, once the news of being Vice President dropped. And I had a feeling that wasn't going to be far away.

So, I needed a chance to tell her about me before she ended up at the club, or worse, Bax made the connection.

Yeah, she needed to hear it from me. But I wasn't sure if tonight, my first night getting her back, was the right time to tell her.

TWENTY-FOUR

Soph

I don't know why, but as soon as I ended it with Kyle, my taste in men changed. I went from wanting the good guy to wanting the bad boy; the smoker, the drinker, the guy who would throw a right hook without thinking or caring.

Yep, my taste in men had changed.

Josh and I had a total of ten minutes together, then he got a phone call. He said to stay and wait for him. But once it ticked past two in the morning, I decided he wasn't coming back, so I went to my room and spent the night tossing and turning all night.

Which is why now, as I entered the gym hall, my last class, I really couldn't be bothered. I headed for the group of girls, literally dragging my feet. Then the group parted just slightly, and my eyes locked with Kayla's. Kayla's eyes were coated in anger as soon as she looked at me. I knew that look; it was the look she gave her prey before she went for the kill.

"Hi, Soph." She pushed past her so-called friends. "How was your night?"

I frowned. She didn't stay at the house last night, so she couldn't possibly know I spent most of the night in Josh's room. So, I didn't say anything in case she was fishing.

"Well, I hear you were with Josh?"

I rolled my eyes. Here I was thinking she hadn't spent the night with Kyle. I put my hands on my hips. "Why is where I sleep any of your business?"

"I was just wondering." She took a step closer to me, but I heard how her voice raise. "Are you going to get knocked up with his child as well? I wonder how Kyle would take the news, knowing you weren't going to have his child but are now having his brothers?"

Had she really just said that? The crowd around us gasped and then whispered. I looked at Kayla. I didn't know what to do. I was just staring wide eyed at her. She couldn't have done that…

But the whispering got louder, and then the stares—who was I kidding, they were glares—became more intense. Kayla had just made it so I could never show my face again.

It was when the word slut started to get thrown at me. I turned, starting to walk away, hearing them call me a child killer to my back.

The tears started to fall before I even made it out the gym door.

*** * ***

I didn't know where to go. In fact, I hadn't even planned on going to him until I pulled into his driveway. I guess when it came down to it, he was the only one that wouldn't judge me. I couldn't believe that Kayla had shared that with everyone.

I was a mess. I was crying so much I could barely see while driving. It was lucky that I got here without writing-off my car. I was physically shaking, tears running down, and I burst through his front door.

"Ryan?"

I slammed the door after me. "Ryan!"

I was storming through the house. I had never been this upset. Not even when Kyle broke my heart.

"Ryan, I fucked up. I—"

As I walked into his lounge and my words stopped. My eyes went from Josh to Bax and then to Ryan.

"Shit, Soph, are you okay?" Ryan was up and heading for me.

"Why… why are you all here?" I staggered out. How did three men in my life come together? How the hell did they all know each other?

"Soph, what the hell is going on? Why the fuck are you so upset?" Bax was up now and his eyes went to Ryan. "Wait, did you say you were here for Ryan?"

My mouth dropped open, but it was when my eyes locked with Josh's I started to back away. I couldn't face this. I couldn't face all three of them before one of them reached me, I turned and ran. Seemed like today was a day for running and I had to move quicker when Ryan started catching up to me. But when I reached the car, it was Josh who was right behind me.

His firm grip missing my arm by an inch.

I managed to close the car door and lock it, then threw the car into reverse. It seemed today was the day for all my worlds to collide.

My brother.

My fuck buddy.

My crush.

And my past.

All my worlds collided and as I fled from Ryan's house. How the hell could all my worlds be connected like that?

I scoffed, shaking my head at my bad luck.

I had no idea where I was going, or what to do.

* * *

I wasn't a coward, or at least that's what I told myself when I pulled into Kyle's driveway. I knew by now the word would have got to him and now was my chance to explain myself before he really did think the worst of me.

I walked in the door and could hear his voice. He was shouting into the phone. I felt pity for whoever was on the receiving end of that because I knew I was about to be, too.

He turned around, his eyes landing on me. He just hung up. Didn't say bye, just hung up. His heated eyes were on me.

"So, you fucking drop a bomb like that and disappear?" His voice was venomous and sent a shiver through me. The fact he was a lot larger than me occurred to me.

I paused, not sure what to say. I had spent an hour parked near the highway, wanting so badly to disappear. But I knew I couldn't do that to Ryan or my parents, and mainly I couldn't leave Josh with questions.

"So, you gonna start fucking explaining yourself!" Kyle shouted at me, this time causing my body to go stiff. Okay, I was now terrified of him.

"I, um…" The words just dried up in my throat.

"You umm?" he snapped at me immediately. "Fucking pregnant, Sophia! And you didn't fucking tell me? You killed my child! What gave you the right to kill my child?" he roared at me.

"Kyle, just let me explain."

His voice got sharper with each word. "Like fuck I will! What line are you going to give me? You weren't ready? We were too young?"

"Kyle, please hear me when I say—"

"When did it happen? When did you decide to kill my child?"

"Kyle—"

"And now you are fucking pregnant with Josh's kid?"

Oh my god. Why wouldn't he let me get a word in! "Kyle, I'm—"

"A slut, that's what you are." His words whipped across my body. He had never directly insulted me. It was always Kayla. But he was the one to just call me slut. "A useless, coward of a whore. That's what you are, Sophia." He was pointing his finger at me now. "Your shit is at the door. Take it and get the fuck out of my life. As for Josh's baby, I'm sure you are planning on killing that too."

The tears swelled and then started falling as he insulted me and my character. He had never said one hurtful word to me, and now he was calling me a murdering whore?

"Stop fucking crying and get the fuck out!" he roared when I didn't move. "Now!" I stumbled back as he approached me.

"I'm so fucking happy I broke up with you the way I did." His words were lower, nastier as he approached me. "If I could do it again, I'd call you for what you are. A cheap whore who might as well sell it at the corner. By the way, I phoned your parents about it."

My eyes widened. "You didn't."

He grinned. "I didn't think you would have told them. So what do you know? Their perfect little daughter, the slut. Now pick up the bags and get the fuck out!"

I wiped the tears off my cheeks quickly. This situation had gone from bad to fucking serious. If my parents thought for a second, I was pregnant, they would be back on the next flight. They were needed over there. They weren't needed here.

I was picking up the black garbage bags. I could only carry two, so I left the others.

I was about to open the front door when it swung open.

"Why the fuck did you hang up on me?" Josh came in shouting louder than his brother. His eyes flickered to me. "Fuck, Soph, I've been looking everywhere for you."

Kyle scoffed. "Mate, she won't keep it. She's a murderous slut. No better than a corner whore."

Josh's eyes snapped to his brother. "What did you just say?" Josh's words were clipped short and so deadly low. A hell of a lot scarier than Kyle's shouting.

Kyle laughed. "Seriously, you want to fight for that? She's a slut, Josh. A no good one at that. Hope you had more fun with her than me."

Josh's fist was connecting with Kyle's jaw, over and over, and a distinct breaking noise followed.

"Want to say that again?" Josh's voice was still low, like a snake about to bite, as he held Kyle against the wall, his feet dangling in the air.

"She's pregnant!" Kyle shouted in Josh's face. Josh's grip on Kyle was gone, and he turned to look at me. The tears were still falling,

"It's yours, too." Kyle wiped the blood off his lip and smirked at his brother. "Have fun bringing up the town slut's child."

I couldn't take another word. I turned and ran out the front door, dropping the bags on the way. I had never been so hurt. I thought Kyle breaking up with me was painful, but what he just did it was…

"Soph!"

A hand wrapped around my arm, pulling me to a stop. Josh's worried eyes were on me.

"Is that what's wrong? Is that why you were so upset?" Josh was being calm, so calm.

Maybe because he knew there was no chance of me being pregnant and it being his. Yeah. That had to be the reason. "Look, Ryan isn't that bad of a guy, neither is Bax.

If it is one of theirs, they'll step up, Soph." He took a step towards me, his eyes holding mine. "If they don't, then fuck them, I'll be there. Every step, I promise."

His words caused more tears. How could he be so amazing? How could he be willingly offering to be there for another man's child?

"I'm not pregnant." I finally got out what I wanted to say all bloody night. But it didn't ease the tears. I was falling apart now. My eyes ran over him and I started to walk backwards.

Josh was frowning at me like he couldn't understand any of his brother's ranting now.

I reached the car, opening the door, and I think I had confused him so much. He was frozen for a few moments. Enough time for me to get to my car door.

"Nice vest, Josh." My lips twitched up just slightly and then I was in the car. My words had snapped him out of the confusion, and he was shouting at me to come back as I reversed out of the driveway.

But I didn't listen. I wasn't his problem. I wasn't anyone's. And I knew where I was going now. I was going to the airport. My passport was in the glove box.

My parents always wanted me to volunteer, and I was going to do it. Though how I was going to get in contact with them before they flew back here, I wasn't sure. How did Kyle even get in contact with them? They didn't have phones, so it would have to be by email.

I pulled out my phone. Emails were the main way my parents reached out to everyone. I was creating a new email typing in urgent, typing in I'll get a blood test to prove I'm not, but as I was writing the details of the email, I heard a loud horn coming at me.

TWENTY-FIVE

Josh

"Chain smoking, darling, isn't the answer."

My eyes went to my mother. "If you don't want me to kill your golden boy, you'll give up trying to make me quit smoking." It was taking all my willpower not to attack Kyle as he sat in one of the armchairs, not giving a fuck about the shit storm he had caused. "You proud of yourself?" I couldn't stop myself from snapping at him.

He just shrugged his shoulders.

"She's not even pregnant!" I added. Kyle was a fucking idiot.

"You mean you aren't sure if it's yours." Kyle smirked at me.

That's it, I'm killing him.

"Josh, stop it!" Mom went in between us. "Boys, please don't fight!"

My fists were clenching at my side. "Move, Mom." If I didn't get this anger out, I was sure blood vessels would burst. Plus, Kyle deserved to have his head caved in.

"Come on now, Josh, is that any way to talk to your child's uncle?"

If my mother wasn't standing in front of him, he'd be dead. "Mom, move before you get hurt."

"Yeah, Mom, move. I'm not afraid of Josh. Plus, he's really just panicking that he will have to change diapers."

Then I heard it. The tiniest flaw in his voice giving it away—he was jealous. He was so fucking jealous, and now I knew how to hurt him without physically touching him.

"You clearly let her down, Kyle." I suppressed the smirk and the pleasure I was going to get out of doing this to him. "Mom, you can go. I won't touch him." I wasn't going to hurt Kyle, physically that is. "Go call Dad again, see if he has had any luck chasing down her uncle."

Mom frowned and then nodded her head. She didn't need me to say I wouldn't hurt Kyle. I always kept my word; she knew that.

"What do you mean by that?" Kyle asked as Mom left the room.

"About sex with her." I wanted to make him suffer. "Trust me, there is nothing wrong with her."

His eyes narrowed at me, and I knew I had his attention.

"The way she takes top, I swear I've never seen a more beautiful woman. The way she takes all of me and the slight moan that comes out when she does." The truth was, Soph and I hadn't had sex. But that didn't mean I hadn't pictured what it would be like. "Then those sweet noises she makes when I flip her over and go in deeper." I leaned in closer to Kyle to serve my final punch. "And the best bit? Doing all that without protection."

And then it was Kyle who wanted to get physical, his hands going for my throat.

"Boys, stop it!" Mom was back, but it was her tone that caused me to look at her, and I think it was the same reason Kyle let go.

"Mom, what's wrong?"

"It's Sophia. She's been in an incident."

Those few words were like a cold slap across my face, and it was the most fucking painful thing I had ever felt.

* * *

"They won't release details." Dad walked into the waiting room. "They said it was a breach that I was told she was even in an accident."

"Fuck it. I'll tell them I'm married to her." I was sick of waiting. I wanted answers. I wanted to know if she was alive or not. I wanted to know how serious. Then there was that fucking question in the back of my mind: was she telling the truth when she said she wasn't pregnant?

"They know her, Josh. That isn't going to work." Dad's voice had a frustrated snap to it.

Fuck it. I'll punch answers out of someone.

"You agreed not to wear that vest around us."

I turned back to look at Dad. He couldn't be serious. He was complaining about me wearing my vest? I had forgotten I was even wearing it until Soph commented on it.

"Sorry, Dad, in between looking for Soph and then dealing with your son's crap, I didn't think about changing my clothes." My glare went from Dad to Kyle. "You know it's your fault she's in here." And that was what was boiling inside me. This whole thing was Kyle's fault. Another reason I wanted to kill him.

His eyes narrowed on me. "How do we not know that she didn't do it on purpose?"

"How dare you say such a thing, Kyle!" Mum was the first to jump on him for saying that. And for once her voice wasn't sweet when she spoke to him. "That is a horrible thing to say! She is family, Kyle!"

He rolled his eyes. "You wouldn't be saying that if you knew. In fact, all of you wouldn't be defending her."

"What is it that she's done that is so bad?" I was trying my best not to push Dad out of the way and get in Kyle's face. "Come on, Kyle, spit it out."

"She was pregnant." He looked around us. "With my child and she had an abortion. Didn't even fucking tell me."

"So?" I was the first one to speak.

"That's it?"

"That's it! She killed my child!"

I scoffed. "Look how you treated her, Kyle! Look at what you did to her. What you put her through. She's eighteen, her parents are never around, and she would have had to do it all herself!" Was I the only one that could see that Soph had made the right decision?

I glanced at Mom and Dad and they were nodding their heads.

"Josh is right, Kyle, it isn't your place to have an input after what you did to her." Mum's words were gentle but firm. "But if she is pregnant now, we will support her. Just like we would have if she was carrying your child."

Kyle scoffed, shaking his head. "You are just saying that because it's Josh's child. If it was my mine, you'd be going on about how stupid I am for letting it happen."

"Why are you so angry about this?" I couldn't stop myself from asking. "Soph made the right decision and even if she didn't, you should be supporting her, not fucking yelling at her and insulting her."

"Don't you get it? Are you all that stupid? It's another thing taking her away from me! It's killing me watching her live a life without me! If she has your child, or whoever's child, it won't be mine." Kyle was tearing up. "And I'll really lose her completely." His voice broke, his emotions clear for everyone to see.

I looked between Mom and Dad. Was Kyle for real? He lost her and every right to be in her life when he broke up with her. And I was about to remind him of those facts when Kayla burst in.

"Is she okay, is there any news?" Kayla was rushed and I was surprised she had even showed up. Wasn't like she got on with Soph anymore.

"We don't know." Kyle answered her and his eyes went to me. "Josh is worrying about his child."

"What are you going on about?" Kayla snapped at him.

Kyle pulled his head out of his hands. "You said she was pregnant?" He looked at her like she was stupid.

You've got to be kidding me? She was the source of whether Soph was pregnant or not? Kayla wouldn't fucking know one detail about Soph's life right now. I knew that.

Kayla looked guilty and I knew why. So, I was waiting for her to cough it up.

"Kyle, we will talk about that later."

Kayla's words got Kyle's full attention, his eyes widening. "You lied about her being pregnant?"

I stepped away from Kayla, glad someone could get into her.

"Yeah. I did." Kayla crossed her arms, narrowing her eyes at Kyle. "You better stop there, Kyle, otherwise this conversation might lead in another direction."

Kyle scoffed. "Fuck it." He looked at Dad. "Kayla has a picture of me doing drugs. She blackmailed me with it. So there goes your chance at running." He looked back at Kayla. "Was Soph pregnant with my child, or not?"

Kayla went silent. Her lips tight. I grabbed her by the shoulder and turned her around.

"Fucking answer the question? Was she pregnant or not?" I was more direct than Kyle.

"No." She finally spat out. She looked at Kyle. "She had a scare, but it was nothing."

Kyle's expression was blank. He was slowly coming to terms with the fact that he had been lied to, and he believed it.

"Fuck off." Kyle staggered out. "Now. Someone get her out of my sight before I kill her."

Mom was quick to guide her out of the waiting room, which caused my eyes to follow them, and I spotted Ryan at the nurse's desk.

You've got to be fucking kidding me. Ryan had some guts showing up here. When I heard Soph was in an accident, no… before that, when I first saw her in the bathroom after all those years. I knew then that I loved the woman she had grown up to be.

And that love for her grew until now. I wasn't letting any other guy have her. It was about time I showed Ryan and Bax why I was the Vice President.

TWENTY-SIX

Josh

"Leave now before I fuck you up." I gripped Ryan by the shoulder, forcing him to look at me. "Mother fucker, I don't give a fuck, I'll take you down, now leave." If he had any idea how frustrated and furious I was, he would take my warning and leave. He and Soph might have had a fling, but it was over because she was mine.

And I was done with letting her be with other men.

Ryan whacked my arm away. "Fuck off, Vice. I'm not here on club business."

"Yeah, I know. You somehow found out Soph was here and I'm telling you to piss off."

I had already told Bax he was a dead man if he showed up here.

Ryan opened his mouth, but the doctor rounded the corner at the same time. "Ryan, are you ready to see her?"

My eyes widened. How the hell did he manage to get in to see her?

"He isn't her fiancé and she sure as fuck isn't married to him." I informed the doctor rather abruptly. I wasn't letting Ryan near her. Her relationship with him was over too. In fact, her relationship with every man was over.

I was so stupid to let it go on as long as it did. I knew I had feelings for her. Yet, I let her do what she wanted. I should have told her how I felt. Then at least there would have been a small chance that the baby was mine.

"He isn't the father either. I am," I added quickly, just in case he knew she could be pregnant.

The doctor frowned, his eyes going to Ryan. "You are family correct? Ryan Butcher?"

"Family!" I scoffed. Ha, that was a good line to use. "He isn't related to her."

The doctor looked down at her notes. "You're listed as her brother?" His eyes went from Ryan to me.

Wait, he was listed? Now I was confused.

"Yeah, because I *am* her brother." Ryan threw me a dirty look. "Our parents can't fly out. They informed you of this?"

"Yes." The doctor nodded her head. "Come through, Ryan, you can see her, and we can explain her condition."

Ryan nodded his head, and the doctor turned, walking up the ward. His eyes went to me. "If she is pregnant and it's yours, I'll fucking kill you." And with that threat said, he walked off, following the doctor.

I didn't know what to say. How the hell didn't I know about this, and why was I finding it hard to believe that it was true? Not once had anyone in Soph's family mention Ryan Butcher. Not once.

Which was making me think that maybe he was lying? That somehow, he had got his hands on her information and put himself down.

I walked back into the waiting room. If there was one person who might know the answer, it was my dipshit of a brother.

"Kyle, does Soph have a brother?"

Kyle looked up at me from the chair he was sitting in, looking guilty and sick to his stomach.

"Yeah, she does." Kyle sighed. "But he disappeared as soon as he turned eighteen. He was her adopted brother. Doesn't like to talk about him." Kyle ran his hand through his hair. "We should call her uncle. Kane might be a drunk, but when it comes to Soph, he cares and sobers up for her. And I have a feeling, that's the only way we are going to get any information."

So it was true. Ryan was Soph's brother. It sent a wave of relief followed by nausea. It meant she wasn't sleeping with him, but he could be dragging her into his dirty drug business.

"No need," I said as I watched Kyle get his phone out. "Her brother is here."

And just like that, I had the attention of the room.

* * *

Waiting wasn't my favourite thing to do, but I was good at it. I could wait for an enemy to break. If you ask me, it's the waiting that is the most painful of any experience. And I was getting a good dose of it now.

Hours turned into days and I still hadn't left. Unlike Kyle, I didn't answer to my parents. He had to piss off to rest. I stayed. I was craving a smoke, but I knew there was a chance if I went for one, I could miss my chance to see her. So, I stayed.

Didn't realize how much I depended on my cigarettes until now.

I didn't know if she was okay. I didn't even fucking know if she was breathing. For all I knew, Ryan was planning her funeral or had discharged her and taken her back to his place.

These facts were getting louder in my head just when the waiting room door swung open and my eyes landed on Ryan.

"Didn't know you had one, Vice."

I frowned. "What?"

"A heart."

I really wanted to get my hands around his throat. Yeah. I had showed my cards. I was known for being careless. Well, I was anything but careless when it came to Soph.

"How is she?" That's what I wanted to know. He could throw as many lines at me, taking down my character later. "She okay?"

"You know I never put two and two together." Ryan walked towards me. "You and her, never made the connection."

"Yeah, well that goes both ways," I gritted out. Why couldn't he answer my fucking question?

"The Vice I know I can't stand, and I don't want anywhere near my sister." He crossed his arms, looking at me determined. "But the Josh that Soph would gush on about… well, that guy I wouldn't mind getting to know."

I frowned. Soph had mentioned me? To her brother?

"She's fine, by the way. Though, when I mentioned you were still in the waiting room, she was threatening to have me killed." He sighed. "Her room is number twenty-six. I need a smoke, anyway."

He reminded me of my need for a cigarette, but my need to see Soph was stronger.

I got up and was heading for the door when I stopped, turning to look back at Ryan.

"So, it's Bax's baby then?" I hadn't really given it much more thought. But now the answer was obvious.

"Does that change how you feel about her?"

Did it matter if she was carrying Bax's baby? Would my love change for her? I loved her, didn't I? Ryan was waiting for an answer.

"No, it doesn't." I don't know why it took me so long to answer him. Fuck, why did I even have to think about it? "As far as I'm concerned, the baby is mine. And that's that." I was going to make sure Bax wasn't in the picture.

Soph needed a man that would stand by her, not a man that would fuck anything that walked while she was at home caring for his child. But at the end of the day, it didn't matter if Bax was going to be the best dad ever. He still wouldn't get the chance because Soph was mine. And that baby was mine as well.

"Well, Vice, you surprise me again." He looked at me rather impressed. "Soph may have been more right about your character than I was."

I wanted to know so badly what Soph thought of me, what she had told Ryan about me, but from what I could understand, whatever she said had Ryan questioning me and who I was completely.

I turned and left, heading up the ward.

Finally, I was going to see her. I don't think I'll take an easy breath until I see her. I was getting more nervous as I looked at the room numbers going up and then I was at her door.

What if she didn't want to see me? That was possible after what Kyle had done. *Okay, time to man up.* I pushed the door open. Worse case scenario, she threw something at me, or yelled at me for what Kyle said to her.

"Josh?"

My head snapped up, I had been a coward and was looking at the ground, before getting the guts to look at her, now my eyes were locked with hers.

"Fuck, Soph." My voice cracked seeing the bruises across her face, the swollen lip, and deep dark eye that looked like she had taken a right punch.

"It isn't that bad. Just some bruises." She brushed it off like she wasn't looking like a victim of family violence. "Have you really been here since I came in?"

I didn't know what to say. How can she just be brushing off what she went through? I managed to nod my head when she kept staring at me for an answer.

She huffed. "Bloody Ryan being a dick. I swear he can be so selfish sometimes."

"He knew who I was, so I don't blame him."

Her eyes narrowed on me. "No. I know who you are. He knows the front you put up."

I cracked a small smile and walked towards her. "Who said it was a front?"

She started to move over on the bed, and I didn't know what she was doing it for, then I realized she was making space for me. God, she was so bloody sweet.

I gingerly sat down and then took her hand carefully because it had an IV in it.

"You scared me, Soph." My eyes were on her hand, that was bruised and the needle in it, giving her body fluids. Then I felt her other hand on my cheek, causing me to look at her—into those beautiful eyes. She was making me speechless.

What would someone like her, so beautiful, so flawless, see in me?

"Josh?"

I couldn't pull my eyes from hers. Then she moved closer to me. Her hand still on my cheek. "Umm?" I managed to get out, while watching her get closer—those plumb red lips getting closer. Fuck, she needed to stop because I barely had the will power to not kiss her.

"I just wanted to say, what you said out in front of your house—"

"Don't." I cut her off. "Don't say thank you, Soph. I meant it. I'll be the father to your child. I don't care if Bax is the father. He is out of your life now, Soph." I put my other hand over hers, which was on my cheek. Now was the time to tell her. "I love—"

"Don't, Josh. I'm not pregnant, so you don't have to pretend you love me." She took a staggered breath in. "I don't need you to be with me out of pity. I'm not pregnant. So…" She sighed. "You can stop."

Before she could say another word, or before I did, I kissed her. It was soft and short. I needed to make a message clear to her. "No more Bax, you understand?" I was going to ease her into realizing she was mine now. But I wasn't about to tell her that directly, I was going to earn her love.

I knew I loved her, but her love for me. I wasn't sure of that.

Her lips were slightly parted, and she slowly nodded her head. "No more Bax."

"Or any other guy?"

Her lips twitched up slightly. "Well, there is another guy, and he might be hard to get rid of."

I wanted to scoff. A few minutes with my fists and he would be gone. "Name him, I'll personally tell him to piss off."

A full smile spread across her face, and she leaned in, her lips nearly touching mine. "He goes by the name Vice." And then she was the one to kiss me.

✅ ✅✅✅

STAYING CONTACT

Other ways to stay in contact

Follow on Instagram

Join the Facebook Group

Follow on Amazon

Follow on Twitter

Copyright © 2021 by Simone Elise

All rights reserved.

No part of this book may be reproduced in any form or by any electronic or mechanical means, including information storage and retrieval systems, without written permission from the author, except for the use of brief quotations in a book review.

Created with Vellum

Printed in Great Britain
by Amazon